PRAISE FOR STINA LINDENBLATT

I Need You Tonight

"Ms. Lindenblatt has penned another remarkable read for this series. . . . Full of exquisite heat and passion, and the ending brought happy tears to my eyes. . . . I would highly recommend *I Need You Tonight*."—*Book Magic*

"*I Need You Tonight* is one of those books that you go into thinking one thing and end up getting your mind blown because you were not expecting the emotion that this made you feel. Honestly, this had to have been the best book of the series because of that."—*Life of a Crazy Mom*

"[Stina Lindenblatt's] writing shows superb talent and care for both the storyline and her characters. This is not a book you want to pass the chance at reading."—*Ellie Is Uhm . . . A Bookworm*

"There are so many, many things that I loved about this story. . . . I hadn't realized I'd been missing and I was craving the

Pushing Limits boys until this one came along. And it came with a bang!"—*Collectors of Book Boyfriends & Girlfriends*

"Ms. Lindenblatt has penned another remarkable read for this series. . . . Full of exquisite heat and passion, and the ending brought happy tears to my eyes. . . . I would highly recommend *I Need You Tonight*."—*Book Magic*

This One Moment

"A well-written story that kept me entertained from start to finish."—*Harlequin Junkie*

"I loved this book; this is romance at its best, this is that perfect ending we all read romance for, this is an absolutely beautifully told love story."—*Guilty Pleasures Book Reviews*

"Very satisfying . . . Stina Lindenblatt is a new author to me and a very good one I may add. . . . I will sure keep an eye on her in the future. She is really worth it!"—*Collector of Book Boyfriends & Girlfriends*

"The story is amazing and the suspense is thrilling."—*Just One More Chapter*

"Filled with emotion, intensity, a lot of sexual tension and the perfect amount of heat."—*About That Story*

My Song For You

"Romantic angst powers this fast-paced novel, and readers will return to the series to learn more about the enigmatic side characters whose own stories are waiting to be told."
—*Publishers Weekly*

"The author has an amazing and deep connection with her characters. . . . I loved every single page."—*Extreme Damage Blog*

"From the first to the last page—greatness unfolded."—*Ellie Is Uhm . . . A Bookworm*

"Filled with romance, misunderstandings, lies and a whole lot of heat . . . [*My Song for You*] has everything to satisfy the romance itch in all of us."—*Twin Spin*

"Six stars—Stina Lindenblatt has a skill to write heroes with some depth like few can."—*Collectors of Book Boyfriends & Girlfriends*

"Oooh, a secret baby story with a twist . . . and I liked that twist. I also really liked that this was somewhat of a friends-to-lovers story. . . A really good, entertaining read and I enjoyed it a lot. I'd definitely recommend it."—*Smitten with Reading*

ALSO BY STINA LINDENBLATT

Contemporary Romances

Pushing Limits Series

This One Moment

My Song For You

Carson Brothers Series

One More Chance

One More Secret

One More Betrayal

Lost in You Series

Tell Me When

Let Me Know

Romantic Comedy Novels

By The Bay Series

Decidedly Off Limits

Decidedly with Baby

Decidedly with Love

Decidedly with Mistletoe

Decidedly by Chance

Decidedly with Luck

Decidedly with Wishes

Visit stinalindenblattauthor.com for more books

I NEED YOU TONIGHT

STINA LINDENBLATT

To my family,
Thank you for all your love
and support over the years. xox

I NEED YOU TONIGHT

1

──────

MASON

"**I** pronounce you husband and wife," the minister announced as the warm fall breeze tugged at the guests sitting in front of the wooden gazebo. "You may now kiss the bride."

He didn't have to tell Jared twice. Our guitarist's lips were on his new bride's mouth faster than you could say *I want to fuck you now*. And, knowing Jared, that was exactly what he wanted to do. Pushing Limits had been on the road for almost five months—the halfway mark of our tour opening for Endless Motion. With the exception of a brief visit two months earlier, when Callie and their son, Logan, joined us for a few days, Jared hadn't fucked her in a long time. How he was surviving without a bad case of blue balls at this point was beyond me. I couldn't do it.

Nor did I want to. That was one of the perks of being a rock star. I could get laid anytime I wanted. I glanced around at the prospects, sitting on the chairs in front of the gazebo. Unfortunately, the wedding was small, with about forty guests, and only a handful of the females were of legal age. When you factored in how many were here without a boyfriend, that left me with one. Not a bad option either. Pretty, petite, with long black hair. Beckie something. Callie used to work with her at the diner. I'd have gone after her . . . if Kirk, the band's bassist, hadn't already been eyeing her.

So that left me with no possibilities. Which sucked. Royally.

The happy couple unglued their lips from each other and stepped down from the gazebo, where I was standing with the other groomsmen (aka the members of the band). Nolan pulled his girlfriend, Hailey, into his arms and whispered in her ear. She laughed. If I'd been a betting man, I would've wagered those two would be married (or at least engaged) before the band hit the studio again.

At the thought of making a bet, a shiver of excitement rolled through me. I pushed it away. I couldn't go there. Not again. I had destroyed enough people with my past gambling addiction. I was a new man. A new man who wouldn't fall down that rabbit hole again.

My fingers unconsciously went to the tattoo on the inside of my forearm, hidden under the tuxedo: LIVE. LOVE. LAUGH. The words were in Sanskrit. Along with several other tattoos, I'd gotten that one after my stint in rehab several years ago. This one in particular was a motto I lived by every day. I lived and loved the music. And the laugh? Well . . .

I checked out the guests now milling around the backyard and spotted Tomas York, the drummer for the up-and-coming band Burning Wire. Perfect. I grabbed a napkin from the refreshment table. Jared and Callie's names were printed in gold on the cream-colored paper.

"Do you have a pen I can borrow for a second?" I asked the woman next to me. Her short white hair was puffy, and she had one of those oversized purses that contained everything, including two kitchen sinks.

She smiled at me. "I'm sure I have one." She rummaged through her purse and removed a silver pen. Classy. I took it and wrote, *Hi, sexy. Your place or mine?* I handed the pen back to her, thanked her, then made my way over to Tomas.

"Hey, a woman asked me to give you this." I passed him the folded napkin.

He opened it and read the note. His head shot up and his gaze searched the backyard for the note writer. I pressed my lips together to keep from laughing out loud.

His gaze settled on Beckie, who was talking to Jared and Callie. Tomas's eyes lit up with a lusting fire.

"Not her. *Her.*" I pointed at the woman who had loaned me the pen.

The heat in his gaze was instantly extinguished, and his eyes practically popped out of his head. I snickered. I couldn't help it.

Tomas's head swiveled to me and he backhanded my chest. "You jackass."

I burst out laughing. "I might be a jackass, but it was so worth it."

"For you, maybe." He looked back at Beckie. "Do you know who she is?"

I shrugged. "Not really. She used to work with Callie." I didn't get a chance to warn him that Kirk might also be interested in her. Just then Kirk sidled up to her, and it was clear she was as taken by the tall, brooding former hockey player as he was with her. At least one of us would get lucky tonight. Which left Aaron and me as the only members of Pushing Limits who weren't going to have a good fuck tonight.

Maybe he, Tomas, and I should bail on the wedding sooner rather than later and find some action elsewhere, I thought.

And I would have if Jared hadn't been like a brother to me. All the guys in the band were like brothers to me. The only brothers I had left. No, bailing so I could get laid wasn't the cool thing to do.

At the tug on my pant leg, I glanced down to find Logan

grinning up at me. Inwardly I chuckled, knowing what the hopeful expression was for. He was hoping that I'd cuss and contribute to his swear-word jar. With the band touring, he had no one to donate regularly to it. I was the only idiot unable to control his cussing around the four-year-old. It was an expensive habit when the fine was a dollar per swear word. "Hey, buddy."

"Play with me, Uncle Mason." He signed the words as he spoke. Logan was deaf, but his cochlear implant allowed him to hear most things, except for music.

I crouched to his level. "Logan, do you remember my friend Tomas? He's almost as good a drummer as I am." And with the way Tomas's band was gaining interest within the L.A. music scene, maybe one day they would be opening for us.

Tomas laughed. "Actually, I'm even better than your uncle Mason."

He wished.

"You must be good," Logan said, "because Uncle Mason is amazing." What he meant was that the vibrations through the floor when I played the drums were amazing. Logan didn't listen to the band's music. He felt it.

"What do you want to play?" I asked him.

"Soccer!" That came as no big surprise.

"Do you think your parents would mind?" I surveyed the backyard. It wasn't huge, and while under normal circumstances it would be fine, it might be problematic with so many guests milling around.

Logan tugged on my hand. "It's all good."

I somehow doubted it. I scanned the area for Jared and Callie, but they were nowhere to be found. Guess they couldn't wait until nighttime to consummate their marriage. Lucky bastard!

"Why don't we ask your grandmother first, okay?" I signed

the "okay" part. "Don't go anywhere," I told Tomas. "You might get drafted into the soccer match."

"Wouldn't miss it for anything," said Tomas, who was part Latino and had grown up on soccer.

Logan and I walked over to his grandmother, who was talking to a few guests near the refreshment table. "That should be fine," she said after I asked her if it would be okay to play a low-key game of soccer. "Just keep the ball away from the patio, okay?" She said the last part to Logan, then to me she added, "And no kicking it hard. We don't need it landing in the food."

Good point.

Logan hurried off to fetch his soccer ball. A few minutes later he and I, along with the other guys in the band, Tomas, and the cute little flower girl, were kicking the ball around the lawn. Callie cheered on her boys, who were on my team, while Hailey cheered on Nolan, who played on the opposite team.

Kirk kicked the ball past Aaron. I high-fived him. "Nice job, puck boy."

"As if you ever doubted me, drummer boy," he said with a smirk.

The phone in my tux pant pocket vibrated. I ignored it. Everyone who was likely to contact me was at the wedding. So unless my estranged family had a sudden longing to forgive me for the mess I'd dragged them into a few years ago—and I doubted they had forgiven me, or ever would—the call could wait.

Logan kicked the ball past Tomas, who was positioned between two wedding chairs, and scored a goal. He squealed with joy and jumped up and down, as did Emma, the toddler flower girl, who was on the other team. We laughed at their reaction.

Jared hugged Logan, and the memory of my father once doing the same when I was a kid almost knocked me onto my ass. I'd just scored a touchdown. It had been only flag football, but that hadn't mattered to him. He had been proud of me no matter what—as long as I gave it my all and worked hard. As long as I played fair.

I shoved away the memory and the hurt. I had moved on. No point picking at the scab again.

I high-fived Logan and got back into position. Callie tossed the ball onto the grass and the game resumed. Giggling, Emma kicked the ball, and kept on kicking it away from the rigged-up soccer field. Logan chased after her. The rest of us stood on the grass, laughing.

A bird tweeted near the tree house. Without warning, Emma stopped and pointed at where the sound had come from, the soccer game instantly forgotten. Not expecting her to stop, Logan almost careened into her. He took advantage of the distraction and kicked the ball away from her. Emma didn't even notice.

He dribbled the ball back to us but then forgot about the no-kicking rule. And wow, could the kid ever kick. The ball smacked the ass of the woman who had loaned me her pen. We all cringed as it made impact, and cringed even more at the dirty ball print it left on her beige skirt.

She turned around to find Logan staring at her backside, his mouth a perfect circle. She smiled sweetly at him. "Your daddy said you were a good player. He just failed to mention how great a player you are." She ruffled his hair and returned her attention to the elderly couple she had been talking to.

The phone vibrated in my pocket again.

I don't know what compelled me to check it, but a weird feeling warned me it was important. I removed my phone and looked to see who had texted me.

Call me ASAP! Important.

The last I'd heard, Zack was off who-knew-where on a mission for the navy. He'd been gone for a few weeks now.

Striding to the side of the house, away from the noise, I speed-dialed his number. He answered moments later.

"Hey, McCormick, what's so important?" I asked.

"You remember my sister, Nicole?"

"Yes." She was two years younger than Zack and me, and had gone to a different high school. Whenever I had hung out with Zack at his house, she was usually there. Most fifteen-year-old little sisters loved tormenting their older brother. Not so with Nicole. You could tell she worshipped him. He was her world—and it was obvious he adored her just as much, despite how much he teased her.

But who could blame him? She did make the best chocolate chip cookies known to man.

"I've been trying to contact her for the past two days. She isn't returning my texts or messages."

"You think something's happened to her?"

"Who knows? She's a workaholic. Sometimes she gets so focused on what's she doing, she ignores the rest of the world. But if something has happened to her . . ." He couldn't say the final words.

"You want me to go to her place and check if she's okay?"

"Yes, if you can."

"What's her address?"

He told me. "It's in Desert Springs. About two and a half hours southeast of L.A."

"I'm at a wedding, but I can leave in about an hour."

"Thanks, Dell. I owe you big."

Not as much as I owed him. If it hadn't been for Zack, I would have died the night my gambling addiction caused me to hit rock bottom and I attempted suicide.

I owed him my life . . . and so much more.

With my fork, I pushed the linguine around on my plate, searching for the other succulent, this-date-wasn't-a-complete-waste-of-time scallop. There had to be another one—just had to be.

I lifted a forkful of pasta, unearthing the desired prize, and speared the tender morsel, vaguely aware of my date droning on. Before I'd tuned him out and focused on my food, he'd been blabbing nonstop about taxes, the excitement in his voice too over-the-top for his topic of choice.

I popped the scallop in my mouth. "Mmm."

Carl's eyes widened and his gaze dropped to my lips. It was only then that I figured out why. The scallops should've come with a warning: "The restaurant isn't legally responsible for all erotic noises you might make while ingesting the food." *Oops.*

"Heidi said you're a florist." Carl took a bite of his steak.

"Not a florist. That's Heidi." Whom I was personally going to kill for this dud of a date. Yes, Carl was good-looking and he fit my criteria for a future husband—especially the part about him being a professional with a steady job—but none of that made up for him being boring as hell. Correction: even hell would be more interesting than him.

"I'm part owner of Blooming Love with Heidi, but she's the florist. I focus on the business side of things." Thanks to my business degree.

His eyes brightened, and he whipped out a business card from his wallet and handed the nondescript card to me. "Do you have an accountant?"

My business card stayed firmly locked away in my purse. Not that it mattered. He knew where to find me. "I do the book-keeping."

"What about at tax time? Do you use an accountant for that?"

I nodded, fighting back a yawn, and shoved a forkful of linguine in my mouth. I had to just endure dinner, then I could go home and drown my bad-date sorrows in a carton of triple-fudge almond ice cream while watching Bruce Willis save his wife from Alan Rickman. *Die Hard* . . . the perfect end to a lousy night.

I sighed, the sound too soft to be heard over the restaurant chatter, the laughter, and the clinking of cutlery against ceramic. "Did you go anywhere this summer?" Always a safe question in situations like this.

"Yes. I spent a few days in San Francisco for a tax conference. It was a great write-off."

"I bet." In my head, a voice reminded me it didn't matter if he was boring; maybe he might be interested in moving this date to the bedroom, and the evening wouldn't be a total bust. I couldn't remember the last time I'd had sex. The drought had been that long. Heidi blamed it on my workaholic personality. It was hard to get laid when you were always working.

Another sigh slipped from between my lips, and I sipped my wine. Ice cream and *Die Hard* wouldn't be enough to make up for tonight. I might have to add another glass of wine to the mix.

I finished my pasta while Carl explained something earth-shattering (his words, not mine) that had happened at the conference. "What kind of music do you enjoy?" I blurted once he paused long enough to take a breath.

"Classical music and classic rock. What about you?"

"Country music." I also liked some pop music, but mostly listened to country. This further proved that Carl and I were not fated to be together. We didn't even like the same music.

I finished the final bite of my pasta and willed the waitress to return with our bill. Clearly I didn't will hard enough. Several painfully long minutes ticked past before she came back to remove our empty plates.

"Would you like to order dessert?" she asked us.

"No, I'm good," I said, faster than a rabbit being chased by a mountain lion, and counted down the seconds until Bruce Willis, the triple-fudge almond ice cream, and I could hang out together. *Please don't order anything else,* I silently pleaded to Carl.

"Maybe you'd like to share something?" he asked.

I patted my flat stomach, hidden under my sexy black dress. The sexy black dress that Heidi had insisted I wear tonight. "I'm full."

He winced, possibly understanding what I really meant, and asked for the bill. He paid for our food and drove me home, the entire time quizzing me on the store's accounting strategy.

Forget another glass of wine. I needed a bottle of my finest ten-dollar-a-bottle white.

"I had a great time," he said, walking me to my front door.

"Me too." I sneaked a glance at the cloudless dark sky, with stars speckled across it. No lightning bolts appeared. I let out a relieved breath. "Well, it was nice meeting you."

"You too." Before I could take a step back, he leaned in to kiss me. I moved my head at the last second, and his lips missed mine and landed on my cheek. "I'll call you."

I translated that as "Don't expect to hear from me again," or maybe that was just wishful thinking. "Okay."

His footsteps receded down the sidewalk as I unlocked the front door and turned the doorknob. Without looking back to see if he was watching, I pushed the door open. Or tried to. As usual, it refused to budge.

I'd been meaning to fix the problem for the past few months. And I would . . . as soon as I figured out how. In the meantime, I stuck with the proven method for opening the door. With a solid shove of my shoulder against the dark-stained wood, I pushed the door open.

Rubbing my shoulder with my fingers, I slipped inside the house.

After tonight, I didn't care what Heidi said; there would be no more blind dates. Same deal with Cindy's attempts to set me up. Before tonight, the last lame date, with a guy whose name currently eluded me, had been Cindy's contribution to their goal of finding me a boyfriend who fit my criteria of the perfect man. Too bad the perfect man sounded a lot better on paper than he was proving to be in reality.

I flipped on the light switch. Darkness continued to embrace me. Great. The lightbulb had burned out last night, which I'd forgotten about. Fumbling around in the dark, I kicked off the black stilettos Heidi had also suggested I wear tonight.

Fortunately, the light on the stairs was still working. I walked upstairs to my bedroom and grabbed my pajama bottoms with the cute pandas on them, as well as the white tank top with a matching panda on the front. Perfect post-bad-date clothing. In the bathroom I changed out of my dress, washed my face, and pulled my hair back into a messy ponytail.

My phone rang from where I was charging it in my bedroom. I ignored it, figuring it was Heidi wondering how the date had gone. I didn't have the energy to tell her. Instead, I entered the kitchen and headed for the freezer—and my date for the remainder of the night.

The doorbell rang, and for a second I considered ignoring it. But even with the hallway light not working, whoever was outside could tell someone was home. And if it was one of my neighbors, I didn't want to be rude.

I walked down the hallway, the only illumination coming from the kitchen behind me, and yanked the front door open, using my body weight to help me. Beatrice, my sixty-five-year-old neighbor, was standing in the glow of the porch light. She was the same sixty-five-year-old widow who had baked me cookies the day I'd moved into the tiny old house. The same sixty-five-year-old widow who had shared on more than one occasion her dating wisdom. Too bad for me it originated from the 1800s . . . or close enough.

"Hello, my dear," she said. "I saw that your gentleman friend dropped you off, and I wanted to talk to you before you went to bed. Is this a good time?"

I could practically hear the ice cream groan from the freezer. "Sure, it's fine." I stepped away from the door to let her in. "Sorry, the hallway light doesn't work."

She peered up at the porch light, where tiny gray moths were going berserk, fluttering around it. "That's all right. We can talk out here. I won't be long. I just wanted to tell you that my medical appointment in L.A. was moved up to tomorrow, and I was wondering if you could look after Bernie while I'm away." Bernie was her dog. "I'll be back in five days."

"That's fine. I love spending time with him." At least he would be a more enjoyable "date" than the guys I'd gone out with lately. And at the rate I was going, he was the closest thing so far to my goal of a husband, two-point-four kids, a dog, and a cat.

"And he loves spending time with you," she said. "I'm leaving at seven-fifteen tomorrow morning, but I won't have time to take him for his daily walk."

"I'll take him."

"You're such a dear. I don't know what I would do without you. So, tell me . . . how did the date go?" At my grimace, she chuckled and patted my shoulder. "Don't worry, Nicole. You're a sweet and beautiful woman. You'll find your Prince Charming one day soon."

Forget Prince Charming. I just wanted a man who wasn't anything like my father. Hence my list of what I was looking for in a man, the top four traits being that he was a professional with a good steady job, didn't have any bad habits or addictions, was kind, and had a good sense of humor. Heidi had added the requirement that his life not revolve around his job. She'd spoken from experience when it came to her own father.

Beatrice left and I closed the door. As I was heading back to the kitchen, my doorbell rang again. Figuring she'd remembered some instructions she'd forgotten to tell me, I returned to the door and yanked it open . . . then blinked.

Instead of my neighbor, a man who was easily six inches taller than me stood on the porch. Even in the poor lighting, his skin was a gorgeous warm brown. Shaved-short black hair peeked from under a gray beanie, something I could've guaranteed tonight's date from hell wouldn't have been caught dead wearing. Too bad for him. There was a slight chance I had a thing for men in beanies.

Okay, make that a big chance.

The stranger's T-shirt stretched across his defined chest and shoulder muscles and revealed strong, tattooed arms. With his lush, sexy lips and chocolate-brown eyes, he was sex-on-a-stick and then some.

Except sex-on-a-stick looked very familiar.

"Mason?" That was all the Rolodex in my brain could come up with when it came to his name. But that was because I didn't think Zack had ever told me his last name. Mason had hung out at our place from time to time. Not enough so that we became good friends or anything. But enough to know that he was funny and a nice guy.

A nice guy who had a thing for cookies. Whenever I used to bake them, I swear he'd eat at least a dozen in a single sitting.

Mason gave me the once-over in a non-sleazy way, as if evaluating me for signs of injury. Once the appraisal was complete, his lips curled up to one side, possibly due to my panda pajamas. "Cute PJs."

"I think so." I grinned while several questions in my head battled it out—the number one being what Zack's friend was doing here. As far as I knew, he didn't live in Desert Springs. "If you're looking for Zack, he's off on another mission in Europe." Being in the navy, he'd seen a lot more of the world than I had.

"Zack actually sent me to check up on you. He was worried about you. He's been texting you, but you haven't been responding."

"I accidentally dropped my cellphone and apparently it didn't appreciate the sidewalk making nice with it. I didn't have a chance to get it fixed for several days, and only got it back today after work. I haven't had a chance to read the messages yet."

The smirk was back on his face. "That would do it."

"You don't live here now, do you?"

"No. L.A."

"So you drove all this way from L.A. just to see if I was okay?" That sounded like the Mason I remembered. In high school, he had driven across the city to rescue Zack after his truck broke down while on a date.

"That's right."

And because of that, my next words came without a second thought. "I'm about to eat ice cream and watch *Die Hard*. You're more than welcome to join me if you want."

3

MASON

For a second, all I could do was hope Nicole didn't notice the effect she was having on my dick. When Zack had asked me to check on his little sister, I hadn't expected to find that the awkward fifteen-year-old had turned into a sexy woman—her blonde hair in a messy ponytail, her face free of makeup, and wearing pajama bottoms with cartoon pandas on them. I hadn't expected to find her braless, if the way her nipples pressed against the fabric of her tank top were anything to go by.

I also hadn't expected her to invite me in to eat ice cream and watch *Die Hard* with her—because what girl watches *Die Hard*?

But no way in hell was I saying no to that.

"What flavor?" I asked.

"Triple-fudge almond. The good stuff."

One eyebrow jerked up. "What's the special occasion?"

"Does there need to be one?"

I placed my hand on the chipped doorframe above her head. "Let me rephrase that. I have a sister, and the only time she used to eat the good stuff was when she had boy problems. And *Die Hard* isn't exactly your standard chick flick."

She shrugged, her shoulders pale and delicate. But the shrug had a touch of sass—the same sass I remembered from all those years ago. "What can I say? I happen to love the movie. It's filled with action, love, and redemption. And Alan Rickman always played the best evil guys. And did I mention there's lots of action?"

I laughed. "I'll give you that. And I definitely won't argue against the movie. It's one of my favorites. . . . So, you're telling me you're not dealing with boyfriend problems?"

She snorted a laugh. "Does a series of really bad dates count?"

I pulled my hand away from the doorframe. "I'd say that counts. And yes, I'd love to watch the movie with you and eat ice cream."

I entered her house and she locked the door behind me, then I followed her down the dark hallway toward the warm light. We stepped into the small kitchen. Whoever had decorated the place had a thing for avocado green. Green cabinets. Green fridge. Green linoleum floor. Even the yellowing wallpaper had green in it—along with brown—and reminded me of pineapples. Large, hideous pineapples.

"Wow," I said as Nicole picked up her phone from the counter. "The seventies called and they want their kitchen back."

"I know," she said with a grimace, "it's pretty bad. Zack likes to refer to it as the frog-got-caught-in-the-blender room."

"More like a gremlin. The large, ugly kind from the movie."

Nicole laughed and typed something on her phone. "Hey, I love that movie. But yeah, you do have a point."

At those words I pretty much fell in love with her, but who wouldn't when she had such great taste in movies? Luckily, the guys in the band had no idea that I loved *Gremlins*. They would revoke my man card if they knew.

"I bought the house from an old couple who lived here most of their lives," she said. "I'm slowly redecorating it." Very slowly, from the look of things.

Her phone buzzed in her hand. She checked the screen and grinned. "Zack says hi, and told me to play nice with you because you're a good guy."

I laughed, mostly because I appreciated that he felt that way after everything that had happened in the past. If I was a good guy, he was the goddamn pope.

While I appreciated the view of her fine ass, which I didn't remember her having before, she grabbed two bowls from the cupboard, put them on the counter, then took down a wine-glass as well. She glanced over her shoulder at me. "Would you like some wine? I'm having some. It's been one of those days."

"Do you have any beer?"

She shook her head. "Sorry."

"Wine's fine."

She got another glass and retrieved the ice cream from the freezer. She then loaded the bowls with a healthy amount, which let me know just how crappy her series of bad dates had been. After that, she filled our glasses and led me to the small living room. As with the kitchen, it was like stepping back in time, with hideous puke-green shag carpeting and dark wood paneling.

The furniture at least looked to be from this century, although there wasn't much to it—just a love seat, armchair, coffee table, and large-screen TV.

She parked her bowl and glass on the table and loaded the *Die Hard* DVD into the machine.

I sank onto the love seat and waited for her to join me. For a second I thought she was going to take her bad-date sustenance over to the armchair, but she plopped herself down next to me.

And for the first time since arriving at her house, I noticed her sweet yet subtle floral perfume. It was different from the type I was used to with groupies and the women who were interested in nothing more than a quick lay. Their fragrance was always sensual, aimed to seduce. Not so with Nicole's scent . . . yet I was still hyperaware of her sitting next to me.

Lay off, Dell. She's the little sister of your friend, the guy you owe your life to.

The movie began—and I had to say the ice cream girls ate to get over boy problems was definitely the best. This wasn't the cheap crap. This ice cream meant business.

"Christ, this is good," I said, lifting my bowl so Nicole knew what the heck I was talking about.

She gave me an *I know, right?* smile, then shrugged. "I had a feeling I would need it tonight."

Shit, just how bad had her last dates been? Not that I would be much of a judge when it came to determining what made for a good date or not. I couldn't remember the last time I had been on one. I wasn't exactly the dating type—more like the screw-'em-and-leave-'em type. None of the women I'd been with lately had complained about that. I doubted any of them had left the arena in need of ice cream to get over a great fuck. If anything, they had always left looking satisfied.

"Have you ever tried that?" Nicole asked when we got to the part in the movie where Bruce Willis removed his shoes in the bathroom and curled his toes in the carpet. It was supposed to help with jet lag, but in reality it was to leave Bruce vulnerable in a later scene, when he was running around barefooted and one of the bad guys shot out the glass. Bruce's feet were cut to shreds. It was one of the best scenes in the movie.

"No, have you?" I asked.

"I haven't really traveled much. Nothing like Zack. Guess I haven't had the chance."

"Because you're a workaholic?"

She laughed, the sweetest, sexiest sound I'd ever heard. My dick twitched with interest, having missed my earlier reminder that Nicole was off-limits. "Zack told you that, huh?"

"So you're not?" I asked.

"According to my best friend, I am."

"But you disagree?"

She shrugged again, her shoulders tempting me to run my tongue along the soft skin. "I like what I do. And besides, I don't have a choice."

"Why's that?"

She pulled her feet onto the couch and tucked them next to her. The movement shifted her body, so only a couple of inches now separated us. For some reason, I wanted to shorten the distance between us even further. I craved to touch her, taste her, explore her. Everything I wasn't supposed to do to my friend's little sister.

I reached for my glass and took a long sip of wine.

"My best friend and I own a floral boutique," she explained. "But it doesn't run itself. Heidi is brilliant at arranging the flowers, but she's at a loss when it comes to the business side. That means I have to put in the long hours to make sure everything's done."

"Do you enjoy it?"

"Yeah, I do. Plus I'm always working on ways to attract new customers, and that allows me to exercise my creative side." She smiled, and damn if my cock didn't respond once more. The smile was nothing like the deliberately seductive smile of groupies. Like everything else about her, it was sweet and innocent, yet sexy as hell, especially when teamed with her panda pajamas.

Unconsciously, my body leaned toward her, enough so her shoulder brushed against my chest. It was barely a touch, but that didn't stop an electrifying hum from vibrating through my body. I drained my glass.

Nicole did the same with hers, and for a fleeting moment I wondered if her body had reacted to the touch the same way mine had. "Let me get some more wine," she said.

Before I could say anything, she pushed herself off the couch and left the room. She returned with the bottle of white wine and filled our glasses. Then she sat next to me again, her body practically cuddling against me, and for a goddamn second I hungered for her to do just that.

I pushed the urge away and continued watching the movie.

Bruce Willis killed a bad guy and sat him on a chair in the elevator with a message scrawled on the guy's T-shirt. This angered the dead man's brother, who now thirsted for revenge . . . and nothing would stand in the way of his getting it.

I tried not to think about what Zack would do if he knew how much I craved to sink inside his sister. He wouldn't try to kill me, right? Not after he'd gone through all that trouble to save my sorry ass last time.

"Do you have any siblings other than your sister?" Nicole asked, her words tearing me away from thoughts of what else I'd like to do with her that Zack would frown on. I guess during all those times I'd seen her in the past, the topic of my family had never come up.

"A brother. We aren't close like you and Zack." Epic understatement of the century.

I hadn't seen either of them in three years, after they made it clear I was no longer welcome in the family and I finally moved on.

They hadn't left me much choice.

Nicole slid me a quick glance, and I had to look away before the sadness in her eyes gutted me. "That's too bad. I don't know what I would've done without my brother."

I expected her to explain, but she returned her attention to the movie and sipped her wine.

"Oh, I love this part," she said a short time later as Bruce

Willis crawled under a conference room table to get away from a bad guy who was walking on top of it, machine gun in hand.

The man arrived at the end of the table and aimed the gun at where he assumed Bruce was located. "Next time you have a chance to kill someone, don't hesitate."

Before the bad guy could fire a round of bullets into the table, Bruce shot up through the wood, killing the man, and then thanked him for the advice.

Nicole laughed. "That's what I love about this movie. Everyone is trying to kill Bruce Willis and he can still be funny."

I had to admit that was one of the reasons I loved it too. The explosions and the feds looking like a bunch of dumbasses didn't hurt either.

We finally got to the part where Bruce was in the bathroom, talking on the walkie-talkie to Al the cop, who was outside the building with the FBI and police. Bruce's feet had been cut beyond belief and he had a bad feeling things weren't going to end well. "She's the best thing that ever happened to a punk like me," he said in obvious pain—pain from the wound and pain from suspecting he would never see his wife again. It reminded me how my family had seen me as nothing more than a dumbass punk who had done nothing but screw up. But unlike with Bruce's wife, I couldn't see them ever forgiving me. The worst Bruce had done was put his career before hers.

Nicole hung on his every word, and I could see clearly in her eyes what she was thinking as Bruce told Al what he wanted him to tell Bruce's wife when everything was over. Nicole thought it was super romantic how he admitted that he should've been more supportive of her career. I could almost hear her sigh. But it wasn't until the end of the movie that she teared up. It was the scene where Bruce was meeting Al for the first time.

She brushed the tears from her face and gave a small chuckle. "You probably think I'm lame for crying."

"No, not lame at all," I said, voice low. Tears glistened on her eyelashes and in her eyes, but humor was also there, challenging me to say something.

And that wasn't the only thing there. Lust and need flirted at the edges. My gaze dropped to her lips, and a sudden urge to kiss her took over.

I shook it off and practically leapt off the couch. "Well, I should be getting back to L.A."

"I have a spare room. You're welcome to stay there tonight. It's nothing much, but it will save you from having to drive all that way in the dark." She looked so earnest—and completely uninterested in me in the way that my body was interested in her.

"Are you sure?"

She pushed herself off the couch. "Of course. And you know if Zack was here, he would insist on it too."

That was probably true, but for different reasons.

Nicole led me upstairs to a small room that didn't look much different from the rest of the house when it came to the era it had originated in—except this room had obviously belonged to a teenage girl. The carpet was Pepto-Bismol pink, with matching floral wallpaper on one wall. Strips of paper had been torn away—the work of Zack, no doubt. Like me, there was no way he would've fit on the couch downstairs. Which meant he had stayed in this room.

Going insane.

"It's very . . . um . . . ," I started to say.

"Pink?" Nicole laughed. "Yep, that's the exact same face Zack makes every time he stays here. I'm almost considering leaving it as is, just because he loves it so much."

"I'm sure he'd appreciate that." Like he would appreciate a lobotomy . . . without anesthesia.

Nicole laughed harder. "Anyway, the bathroom is across the hallway. If you need anything, just let me know."

Before I could thank her, she was out the door—leaving me to wonder how I'd gone from a wedding with no possibility of getting laid to spending the night in Pepto-Bismol land.

4

MASON

The next morning I opened my eyes to find myself in a bedroom that wasn't mine, with morning wood that rivaled any I'd ever had. Light sneaked through the blinds, creating a striped pattern on the floral bedding—which, thank God, wasn't the same nauseating pink as on the wall and floor.

Memories of Zack's sister looking as hot as hell in her panda pajamas sneaked into my head, as did the memory of wanting to kiss her—neither of which offered any relief from my current below-the-waist situation.

I climbed out from under the covers, quickly dressed, and went downstairs. In the living room I retrieved my phone and checked my messages. Kirk had texted me to ask where I'd bailed to last night, since I'd said goodbye to Aaron and Tomas but no one else. Kirk had been busy with Beckie when I left, Nolan had been preoccupied with Hailey . . . and I could hazard a guess where Jared and Callie had disappeared to.

Not wanting to explain about last night, I simply replied:

Me: Visiting a friend.

Zack had also sent me a text.

> Zack: Thanks for checking on Nicole.

> Me: You're welcome

I shoved my phone in my back pocket and headed for Nicole's kitchen.

Suddenly in the mood to cook, something I didn't get to do enough of while touring, I rummaged through her fridge. Normally I wouldn't make breakfast for a one-night stand. I was more like the screw-'em-and-bail type. But since Nicole and I hadn't fucked, I was pretty sure she wouldn't have an issue with me making us breakfast.

Besides, my stomach was doing its impression of a starving grizzly bear, and I had no idea how long Nicole would sleep.

I removed cheddar cheese, eggs, asparagus, mushrooms, and red peppers from the fridge and placed them on the counter. Then I started the coffeemaker and began chopping the vegetables for the omelet. My phone pinged. Kirk had responded to my text.

> Kirk: You'll be back in time for the tour, right?

> Me: Of course.

For the past several years I'd been busy with the band, touring, recording our first two albums, then promoting them. There hadn't been enough time to recover before the cycle started again. I needed a brief break from being a "rock star." I needed a brief break from the groupies and tabloids and L.A.

Even if it was just for one day, I needed to be a regular person—something I hadn't been in what felt like a lifetime.

I poured myself a cup of coffee and got to work on the omelet. The water from the tap drip-drip-dripped in the sink.

While I ate my breakfast, I whipped up an omelet for Nicole, then hunted around for tools to fix the sink.

5

———

NICOLE

I woke with a start . . . from a very erotic dream. Damn it. Why couldn't I have at least stayed asleep for five more minutes? I'd just been getting to the good part—with Mason. My brother's friend. Who by now was driving back to L.A.

I groaned, although that might've had more to do with the wine-induced pounding in my head than with how I'd been dreaming about screwing someone I shouldn't.

But I guess what my brother didn't know . . .

In desperate need of caffeine before walking Bernie, I scooted out of bed. At least I could start the coffee, then have a shower while I waited for my caffeine fix to perk.

When I got downstairs I was greeted by the happy scent of coffee and something that smelled delicious. Exactly what my stomach had requested.

That wasn't the only thing that greeted me when I entered the kitchen. A pair of jean-clad legs were sticking out from under my sink. The open door obscured the body, but the bare brown feet gave the owner away.

I walked over to Mason and peered down at him. He had a

wrench in his hand and was tightening or loosening something.

I crouched beside him to get a better look. "Is there a reason why you're under my sink?"

"Your tap was dripping."

"So you thought you'd fix it?"

"Sure, why not?"

"Are you a plumber?"

"No, but it really wasn't all that hard."

For him, maybe.

"I made you an omelet," the man still under my sink said. "It's on the table."

"Wow, you made me breakfast *and* fixed my sink. Mason, how is it you're still single?" I laughed. Then a thought leaked in. "Are you single? Or do you have a girlfriend waiting for you to get back home?" *Waiting for him to make her breakfast in bed.*

We'd been so busy watching the movie last night, we hadn't bothered to talk about our lives—other than my bad luck when it came to dating.

"Yes, I'm single. I like my freedom too much to settle down." He pushed himself out of the enclosed space, somehow managing to avoid hitting his head. "There you go. The sink's fixed."

I wondered if it would be too much to throw my arms around him and hug him. The dripping had been driving me nuts. But other than paying a lot of money to hire a plumber, I'd had no idea how to fix it.

Instead of hugging him, I settled on saying thanks, then walked to the table and removed the plate covering the omelet. The food looked as delicious as it smelled, with the sautéed vegetables spilling out, along with a healthy dose of cheese oozing from the edges.

"You really made this?" *No, dummy! A bunch of elves whipped it up during the night while we were sleeping.* I took a bite and almost died on the spot. "Mmm," I said around a mouthful. I swallowed it down. "This is amazing."

"Thanks!" He turned the hot water on and washed his hands. "I was just thinking how I don't have to rush back to L.A. just yet, and there are a few things around here I could fix before I go. Like the hallway light, for one."

I stood there stunned for a moment. "You don't have to do that, Mason," I finally managed.

A smile danced across his lips. "I know, but I really don't mind. I kind of like fixing things. I'm handy that way."

"Sure, if you really want to." Who was I to stop a guy who wanted to make my life a little easier?

I finished the omelet and loaded the plate into the dishwasher. "My neighbor had to go to L.A. for a couple of days, and I promised her I'd walk her dog. I won't be long."

A lazy smile grew on Mason's face. "I'll help. I've always wanted a dog, but can't have one because I'm on the road a lot."

"All right." I hoped Bernie wasn't too upset because Beatrice was gone. The last time she'd gone away, he'd destroyed one of her sofa cushions. "I'll just have a quick shower first."

I hurried upstairs. A few minutes later I was showered, dressed, and ready to walk Bernie.

"Do you guys have a mall or something down here?" Mason asked, coming downstairs after finishing with his own shower. "I wouldn't mind picking up a couple of T-shirts. I don't usually get much of a chance to shop."

"There's a small shopping center near here that will probably have what you're looking for."

The temperature was warm enough for me to wear my favorite white lacy dress, the hem brushing several inches above my knees. I added my short cowboy boots and a light denim jacket. My hair lay loose around my shoulders. If I could've dressed like this for my date last night, I would've at least been happy. More so than I had been in the black dress and stilettos.

I grabbed Beatrice's key from the kitchen counter, and Mason and I headed over to her house. "Bernie comes off as scarier than he really is," I said, unlocking the front door. "He's nothing more than an overgrown baby. The only danger is of being drooled on." I opened the door and entered, Mason right behind me.

"Hey, Bernie," I called out. "It's Nicole. Your mommy wanted me to take you for a walk." A deep woof came from the direction of the living room. A moment later, the giant English mastiff lumbered into the hallway. His short fur was golden, his black face a mass of wrinkles. Drool dangled from one side of his mouth.

"Holy shit," Mason said. "What the hell is that?"

Bernie didn't take offense at Mason's language. He leaned against me, waiting for me to fuss over him like I always did. He really was a big baby.

"Bernie, this is my friend Mason."

That was met by another woof.

"We're gonna walk you," I told him.

"Or ride him," Mason suggested, his expression a cross between shock and amusement as he eyed the massive dog.

"He's just kidding," I told the dog as I rubbed my hand along his body. He leaned more into me, coming close to knocking me over. I glanced up at Mason. "I'm guessing this isn't the type of dog you wanted."

"I would love to have a big dog—just not this big. I was thinking more like Lab-sized, not monster-sized." The shock on his face had given way to a smirk.

I crouched in front of Bernie and hugged his thick neck. "You're not a monster, are you?"

The answering woof almost deafened me.

I retrieved his leash from the hall closet and attached it to his collar. Then the three of us walked down the street at Bernie's slow pace.

Giant palm trees reached toward the clear blue sky on either side of the residential street. Ahead of us, the low desert mountain range stretched for as far as I could see, beckoning me to be more adventurous, calling me to explore it.

And I would've been adventurous if I wasn't so busy. My big adventure in life was the boutique—not quite what I had envisioned back in college. Then I had planned to travel the world after graduation, to visit the countries my mother had always longed to see.

"So you know what I do for a living," I said as a car drove past. "What do you do back in L.A.?"

"This and that."

"So you're unemployed?"

"Not exactly. I'm a musician."

So, basically, unemployed. "Oh. What instrument do you play?"

Bernie let out a thundering bark, preventing Mason from answering my question. Heading toward us was one of Bernie's friends, a cocker spaniel named Elis. The teenager who was walking him stared at Mason, eyes wide. That didn't surprise me. The man was incredibly hot, after all. What girl wouldn't be staring?

Bernie stopped to sniff his friend's butt.

"Hi, Amy," I said to Elis's owner.

She was too busy gaping at Mason to answer. *Way to be obvious, Amy.*

"Amy, this is Mason," I said. Only then did she finally notice me, her gaze flicking in my direction.

"I didn't know you were dating Mason Dell," she said to me. Then her gaze switched back to Mason.

Okay, that was weird.

"We're not dating. He's a friend of my brother's," I clarified, then looked quizzically up at Mason, waiting for him to explain why the sixteen-year-old thought she knew him.

"Do you know the rest of the guys in the band or just Mason?" she asked me.

"Band?"

"You know, Pushing Limits? One of the best rock bands around. All the guys are super hot, but Nolan Kincaid, their lead singer, is engaged, and Jared Leigh just got married, so they're no longer available." She didn't take a single breath during that, her words coming faster than a cougar chasing down his dinner.

"Technically, Nolan isn't engaged," Mason said, "but he and Hailey are serious, so he's still unavailable."

My head spun around to him so fast, I was surprised I didn't get whiplash. "You . . . you mean you're really *that* Mason Dell?"

Amy grunted, as if to say, *Of course he is. Who did you think he was?* I ignored her.

Mason nodded.

"How could you not know he's the drummer for Pushing Limits?" Amy asked, her tone indicating that she thought I was an oblivious idiot. I was beginning to feel like one.

"I don't listen to rock music. I prefer country." And my brother had never mentioned it.

That got another noise out of her, which I chose not to translate.

Deciding the walk was over for the day, Bernie lay down on the sidewalk. I was surprised the ground didn't tremble as he flopped down. He had to easily outweigh even Mason. Elis barked at his friend, maybe to tell him that he was a lazy goof.

"Can I have your autograph?" Amy asked Mason, ignoring the two dogs.

He nodded. "Sure. You have anything to write on?"

It wasn't like she had a purse on her. She looked at me.

"Sorry, I don't have anything." Other than the empty doggy poop bags, and I didn't think that would help her.

"Do you know where Nicole lives?" he asked.

She did because she had occasionally walked past my house with Elis. Although after today, I wouldn't have been surprised if she walked past my house on a daily basis, just to see if Mason and the rest of the band were there—especially after Mason told her to swing by in an hour with something for him to sign. In truth, it was the only way to get rid of her. I had a feeling she would have otherwise joined us on the walk, and that was the last thing I wanted. Not when I had questions for Mason—the first of which being why he hadn't told me from the start who he was.

Because what difference does it make if he's the drummer of a famous rock band, when all we were doing was eating ice cream and watching a movie last night?

After Amy and Elis trotted off, I tugged on Bernie's leash, hinting that we should get moving again. It took him a few seconds, but he eventually heaved himself onto all fours.

"So when were you going to tell me you're a rock star?" I asked Mason as we started walking.

"I did tell you."

Right. I gave him a look that said as much. "You told me you're a musician. Being a musician doesn't mean you're a rock star."

"Exactly. And I wouldn't say I'm a rock star. Jon Bon Jovi? He's a rock star. Our band has two albums out."

"That was enough for Amy to know who you are. Did they go to number one or something?"

"Well, no. But the first two songs off the second album hit the top twenty on the U.S. charts."

"So you *are* a rock star, then." With the jeans, T-shirt, military-style boots, and tattoos, he looked the part.

"I like to think of us as currently popular. But we're still an opening-act band—hardly rock star material."

"Who are you opening for?"

"Endless Motion."

Now, *them* I had heard of. Heidi talked about them all the time. She had a mega-crush on their lead singer, which meant she probably knew who Pushing Limits was. Now that I thought about it, the name did sound vaguely familiar. Maybe she had mentioned them a few times, but because they weren't country music, I hadn't paid a whole lot of attention to what she'd told me.

"So you're not on tour right now?" I asked, remembering how he had said he couldn't get a dog because his job involved a lot of traveling.

"We have a week off, and Jared, our guitarist, got married yesterday afternoon."

"And that's why you were able to check on me after my brother called you?"

He nodded.

"And that's why you can spend the day in Desert Springs?"

Again he nodded. "Maybe even tomorrow too. I figured I could use a minivacation before we get back to touring, and this place seems as good as any."

Made sense.

"Do you enjoy it?" I asked. "The touring?"

Bernie stopped, almost yanking my arm out of my shoulder because I wasn't paying attention to him. He lowered his head, nose to the ground, sniffing.

"I do," Mason said as we waited for Bernie to start moving again. "It's a great way to meet the fans. The industry is crazy, but the music and the fans are the real thing. They make everything worth it."

I'd have to take his word for that.

"Is that your favorite part about what you do?"

He didn't even have to think a moment before answering. "Well, that and being with my brothers—more specifically, my bandmates. They mean everything to me. They're my family."

Bernie finished sniffing and lumbered onward, his pace that of an elderly woman with a walker.

No, correction—the woman would have moved faster.

6

MASON

Bernie might have been the size of a horse, but he didn't move as fast as one. Not even one headed for the glue factory.

His sluggishness as we walked along the sidewalk reminded me why I was staying in Desert Springs for a day or two. And it wasn't just Bernie. The street was the opposite of what I was used to in L.A. Here it was quiet, with the occasional car driving past. I'd seen more cyclists and pedestrians than cars in the last few minutes, and none seemed to be rushing to their next destination. They were appreciating the slow pace of living in a small town.

The last few months had been hectic, and it was nice for once to take it easy. Until now I hadn't realized how crazy everything had been. After our last tour, we had originally been scheduled to have several months off to recover and write songs for our second album. Too bad Ronald Remar, the president of the record label, hadn't bothered to check the memo—he'd pushed up the recording date for that album so we could work with a famous producer. No sooner had we finished with our final date in L.A. than we were forced to spend three intensive weeks writing new material for the next album.

After that came the preparation for the next tour, promoting the new album, and then opening for Endless Motion during their ten-month tour. But at least I was getting to live the dream. Thousands of musicians would kill to be where I was.

"Do you like living here?" I asked.

"I do. I originally grew up in Vegas, then my mother moved to L.A. when I was eleven. I was used to the crazy city life. At first, when Heidi suggested I join her here, I thought she was nuts. But the town grows on you."

"Would you ever move back to L.A.?"

She shook her head. "No. This is my home now. Plus I've got the boutique, where I'm practically my own boss. Heidi trusts me to do what's best for our store."

"When do I get to see it?"

She eyed me like I was as crazy as the L.A. city life. "You really want to see the place?"

"Sure, why not?"

"All right, I'll take you there this afternoon. I have to pick up some paperwork from there anyway."

"You're working even though it's the weekend? I thought the benefit of living in a small town was the more relaxed lifestyle."

"Welcome to the realities of owning your own business. And like you're one to talk. I bet you don't get weekends off while touring."

She had a point.

Bernie stopped walking and took a dump on the grass alongside the sidewalk. If I thought he was massive, that was nothing compared to his pile of crap. You know the scene in *Jurassic Park* when Laura Dern's character shoves her hand into the mountain of triceratops poop? Well, that dinosaur had nothing on Bernie. "Holy shit."

Nicole screwed up her nose and untied a blue baggie from the leash. Better her than me. "And this is why I want a smaller breed," she muttered.

"You want a dog?"

She nodded as she scooped up the shit. Bernie oversaw her work, and I could've sworn he looked proud of his accomplishment, head held high.

"I want a dog one day, and a cat," Nicole said. "But I also want the husband, the two-point-four kids, and the white picket fence." She shrugged. "So far the closest I've come to any of that is walking Bernie the few times Beatrice has been away."

She finished picking up after the giant dog. "What about you?" she asked as we continued walking. "Are you looking to one day settle down and have a family, or are you going to be a rock star forever, always on the road?"

Now it was my turn to shrug. "Can't say settling down is on my agenda for anytime soon. Maybe one day. But my career's associated with a high divorce rate." Mostly because musicians have a hard time keeping their dicks in their own pants while on tour. And while Nolan and Jared weren't the type to cheat on the women they loved, they were a rarity.

"I guess that's true," she said. "It's the same with actors, especially when they're married to other actors. Someone is always away on location. Must make for a lonely life." And a lot of cheating, if what I'd heard about the Hollywood scene was anything to go by.

Nicole glanced at me, as if to determine whether or not my life was lonely. I guess that depended on how you defined *lonely*.

Not wanting her to come to her own conclusions, I picked up the pace, to poor Bernie's dismay. Nicole tugged on his leash as she tried to keep up with me.

We finished our walk, which was a lot shorter than I'd expected . . . but I doubted Bernie would have agreed with me.

He looked ready to take a good long nap. We said goodbye to him, with the promise to walk him again in a few hours, and left his house.

At Nicole's home, she unlocked the front door, then threw her body against it as she turned the handle. The door remained stuck for a second, then gave way. She stumbled through the doorway with an unfazed expression.

And I mentally added "fix front door" to my to-do list.

7

NICOLE

I parked at the far end of the strip mall parking lot. The hem of my dress was halfway up my bare thighs, and for a second Mason's eyes were focused on them before he glanced away. Just the thought of his lips against my skin was enough to cause an ache between my legs, and I sighed dreamily.

You're not having sex with Mason. So get your head out of the gutter.

Easier said than done, especially since I wasn't getting sex on a regular basis.

"You sure you want to come inside?" I asked. The only time guys ever entered the store willingly was to pick up flowers to impress a date or a significant other.

"You know all about my job. Now I want to see where you work."

I laughed. "This is hardly the same thing. It's not like I was on tour with you."

We got out of the car, and Mason and I headed to the store.

I opened the door and stepped inside. A blast of air-conditioning greeted me, along with the classical music playing softly in the background. Cindy was at the register, taking a customer's order, and glanced up. She smiled at me, and her gaze darted momentarily to Mason before returning to the customer.

Mason scanned the store, which hadn't changed since Heidi and I had taken over the boutique. Other than the brick wall behind the register, the walls were light gray. The shelves and counters were brown and fully stocked with tubs of various types of flowers. A sweet floral scent filled the air. The smell was one of my favorite parts about working here—it soothed the soul and calmed even the crankiest of customers.

"Eventually I plan to have a section of gift glassware," I explained to him. "I've been working on my own designs to etch on them."

Well, it was more like I'd been playing around with ideas for the theme surrounding the designs. So far I hadn't come up with anything meaningful. All I'd figured out was that I wanted to avoid anything to do with flowers, which seemed too clichéd.

"Did you make those?" Mason pointed to the floral arrangements filling one counter.

"No, that was all Heidi. She's a natural. I tried to do it a few times. The outcome wasn't pretty." Which was like saying it was slightly cool in Antarctica. "That's why I stick to the business side of things and dealing with the customers. I even created our website." A few small businesses in town had asked me if I could design theirs too. Heidi didn't know about that—she complained enough as it was about how much I was working. "We're even on Instagram and Facebook, and I blog a few times a month about special events Heidi's been hired for, which lets me showcase her creations."

Cindy finished up with the customer and came over as I was explaining the different flowers to Mason.

"Oh my God," Cindy said, her eyes as round as daisies. "You

look exactly like the drummer of Pushing Limits." Her gaze shot back to me with an unspoken question.

"I get that all the time," Mason said, his expression serious—other than the glint of mischief in his warm brown eyes. "Except I'm better-looking than him."

I snorted a laugh.

Mason turned to me, eyebrow raised. "What, you don't think I'm better-looking?"

"Oh, I don't know. I bet the real deal has amazing abs." I had no idea if that was true or not, but based on what I could tell, I'd have bet I wasn't far off.

He yanked up his T-shirt, revealing some very lickable abs. Cindy was practically drooling at the sight of them.

"Not bad," I said, doing my best not to laugh.

Mason crossed his arms, chin raised, one side of his mouth tilted up. "Damn straight they're not bad."

"But I bet the real deal is a better kisser." The words tumbled out of my mouth before I could stop them.

"Only one way to find out," he shot back. "Kiss me."

I'd been ready to tell Cindy the truth, but his eyes possessed a challenge I couldn't ignore, so I reached up on my toes and planted a quick kiss on his lips. The action was innocent—the unexpected electrifying hum through my body not so much.

As if hit by a bolt of lightning, I jerked away from Mason, my gaze going everywhere but to him.

"Looks like fake Mason kisses better than the real one," Cindy said mischievously. Mason opened his mouth to protest, but Cindy just giggled and waved her hand. "I know you're the real Mason Dell. Your voice gave it away."

Just then the bell over the door jingled, followed a second later by "Oh my God! You're . . . you're . . ."

Cindy laughed as I turned to find Heidi staring at Mason as if she was either going to faint or start screaming like a fangirl.

"Yes, he's Mason Dell," Cindy said.

"Mason," I said, "this is Heidi."

The tattooed rocker held his hand out to her. "Nice to meet you."

"Nice to meet you too," Heidi replied, shaking his hand. She threw me a questioning look.

"He's Zack's friend," I said in an attempt to explain everything. "As you know, my phone died when I accidentally dropped it, and because I was so busy, it took several days before I could take it in to be fixed. Zack freaked out and figured something bad had happened to me. And the next thing I know, Mason was at my front door, making sure I was still alive."

Heidi rolled her eyes. "When will your brother realize you're a big girl?"

I snorted. "Never."

"That sounds about right."

"I think it's great that he's so protective," Mason said. The slightly defensive edge to his tone made me wonder if I was missing something.

"I dropped by to pick up some paperwork I need to finish before Monday," I told Heidi, ignoring Mason's comment.

"It's the weekend, Nicole. Do you even know what that means?"

"Sure. It's the two days between Friday and Monday."

"God, what am I going to do with you?"

"Says the woman who just came into the store today."

"Because I have a big order for tomorrow and I need to get started on it."

"You know I can help, right?"

The answering smirk said it all. Then she changed the subject. "So what happened with your big date last night?"

"Let's just say there won't be any more with him."

"Why not?" She briefly glanced at Mason, as if he had

crashed the date and caused Carl the accountant to run for the hills.

"We had nothing in common."

"You knew this from one date?"

"And there was no chemistry between us," I added. "Let's just face it. You're dating the only guy in Desert Springs who's worth dating."

She flashed me the same dreamy look she always wore when it came to her boyfriend, which I took to mean she agreed with me. "So what are you gonna do?"

"Become some crazy cat lady."

"You can't do that!"

"Can I become a crazy cat lady?" I asked Mason. Before he had a chance to respond, I said to Heidi, "See? He agrees. Crazy cat lady it is."

Mason chuckled. Heidi didn't.

"Is that why you two kissed?" Cindy asked from the counter. I hadn't realized she was listening to our conversation.

"It was a joke," I explained.

Cindy laughed. "Didn't look like a joke from where I was standing."

"Seriously? If you call that kissing," I said, barely bothering to stifle a snort, "then you're doing it all wrong."

"We could do it again to prove it was a joke," Mason added. I threw him a you're-not-helping-me-here look. "Just a thought," he said, grinning.

"No, that's okay," I choked out, heat rising to my cheeks.

If that was what happened when our lips barely touched, what would've happened if we had *really* kissed?

Kaboom, my girlie parts not-so-helpfully pointed out.

Unfortunately for them, they would never find out if that was true or not.

His smile widened, perfect white teeth contrasting against beautiful brown skin and dark stubble. "You sure?"

I was so busy staring at those full lips, I only vaguely heard what he said. It took a second for it to sink in. I blinked and turned away from his mesmerizing smile before it pulled me in deeper.

"Yes, I'm sure." I decided to walk toward my office. Surprisingly, my legs complied.

I could hear Heidi following me as I approached my desk, cluttered with floral design catalogs, sketches of wildlife I'd drawn, and educational journals for small business owners. I gathered the papers together in a small pile, waiting for her to say whatever it was she felt she needed to say to me. The soft sound of the door clicking shut seemed louder than normal.

"So what's really going on between you and Mason?" she finally asked. It wasn't concern that I heard in her words, just curiosity.

"I already told you." I located the documents I needed and turned to face her. "Zack sent him down to check on me. He's going to spend a day or two here to relax before he and his band return to touring." And I would go back to dating boring men while searching for Mr. Right.

"But you're interested in him."

It wasn't a question, but no way was I letting her in on the truth. "Right. Because he's everything not on my list," I said with what I hoped was enough sarcasm to distract her from the real answer. Plus it wasn't like that between Mason and me. It was just my body that was reacting to him. It didn't go both ways. "And have you not seen his tattoos?" The tattoos that elevated his hotness factor.

"Just how many tattoos does he have?"

My first mistake? Ignoring the alarms in my head at her deceptively casual tone. The second was blurting out, "Four."

Her eyebrow jerked up, followed by the corner of her mouth. "Four? Because with his T-shirt on you can only see three. So you want to explain why you've seen one more than I just counted?"

"Because before you arrived, he flashed his abs for Cindy. He has one on his rib cage. Honestly, Heidi, you're reading way too much into this."

She opened her mouth to say more but never had a chance. The office door opened and Mason popped his head in.

"Are you ladies finished talking yet, or should I wait a little longer before Nicole and I go shopping?"

"No, we're good," I said, brushing past him as I walked out of the office—saving me from accidentally blurting out something to Heidi that I shouldn't.

That something involving thoughts about Mason that would make a virgin nun blush.

8

MASON

"I was thinking we could hit the hardware store next," I said, after paying for my purchases in the clothing store Nicole had taken me to, "so I can get moving on some projects around the house while I'm here."

"You don't need to do that. You're supposed to be taking a few days off to relax, not work."

To hell with relaxing. I did more than my share of that while stuck on the tour bus for all those long hours. There wasn't much else you could do while traveling between gigs, unless you were planning to write the next great American novel.

"I don't mind," I said. "I used to help my old man around the house as a kid. My talents go beyond being a drummer extraordinaire." I winked at her, doing my best not to think about how her lips had felt against mine not that long ago.

Doing my best not to think about how she would taste if she kissed me again—only this time deeper, longer, harder.

"I feel bad letting you help me with house-related projects," she said.

I pulled open the store door and waited for Nicole to exit,

then followed after her. "Like I said, I don't mind at all. And after the hardware store, how 'bout we get some ice cream?" You could never have too much ice cream.

The supermarket-sized hardware store wasn't too far away. "What are you looking for?" she asked as we wandered down an aisle, with me pushing the shopping cart I'd insisted we would need. Various styles of sliding bolts and locks adorned a section of the wall.

"You need a new latch for your back gate." The other one was missing. All that was left were the holes from where the screws had originally dug into the wood.

"I don't need a new latch."

"Do you know where the old one is?"

She considered it for a second. "There wasn't one when I moved in."

"Well, there will be by the time I'm finished. It won't keep anyone out, but if you ever have kids, you'll thank me."

She laughed, and God, I couldn't get enough of the sweet sound. "I'll be sure to send you a thank-you card once they arrive."

"You do that," I said with a snicker. I surveyed the assortment of iron sliding bolts and selected the hardiest one. By the time I'd finished hunting for everything, the shopping cart was filled with an odd assortment of home improvement supplies—everything from lightbulbs to tools to a new showerhead, which she'd insisted she didn't need. I'd used her shower this morning, so I had to disagree with her there.

"How attached are you to the wallpaper in your kitchen and hallway?" I asked as we strolled down the paint aisle.

"Why?"

"I was thinking of removing it." I would leave Zack the pleasure of removing it from the guest room.

Nicole folded her arms, head tilted to the side. "Do you

have something against my wallpaper?" She tried to sound offended, but the humor in her eyes said otherwise.

"You mean beyond the part where it's goddamn ugly?"

"It's not ugly." She laughed at my expression, which clearly said, *You've got to be freaking kidding me.* "Okay, it's ugly. I'll give you that. But won't it be hard to remove?"

I had no idea, so I Googled the instructions for it on my phone. "It says it's not hard, just time-consuming. But from the looks of things, we could finish it in a day. Then we'd just have to paint the walls afterward."

"Are you sure? It's not really necessary."

I snorted. "I've seen your walls, Nicole. It's necessary." It just meant staying in Desert Springs one day longer than I had originally planned. No big deal.

"I don't know...."

"It'll be fun." All right, *fun* might be a stretch, but it would give me something to do while waiting to get back on the road again with the band. I needed to do something physical, and you couldn't get any more physical than this—if you didn't count sex.

Nicole deliberated for a moment before finally agreeing to it. A short time later we had all the tools we needed, as well as cans of gray-blue paint, similar to what she had used in her bedroom.

"You shouldn't be paying for this," she said when I produced my credit card and handed it to the cashier before she had a chance to do the same. "It's my house and my responsibility."

"But you're putting up with me for a day or two." And what could I say? Helping Nicole around the house made me feel needed—something I hadn't felt since those days when I'd helped the old man around the house. It gave me an odd sense of accomplishment I hadn't experienced in a few years. A feeling of satisfaction different from what I got from being in the band.

"I'm hardly putting up with you. You're fun to have around. Plus you're helping me remove the wallpaper. I should be paying *you* for hanging out at my house."

"Well, I'm insisting, and because I'm your brother's friend, you can't argue." Weak logic, but it was the best I could come up with.

I really didn't mind. I had the money, thanks to the band's recent success. And I figured this was just part of paying Zack back for everything he had done for me. If my family wanted nothing to do with me, the least I could do was this.

"I'm buying the ice cream." Her eyes had a glint in them, warning me that if I thought otherwise, there would be hell to pay.

I pushed the shopping cart to her car and we loaded the supplies into the trunk, then she drove us to what looked like a small barn with windows. Inside, the sweet smell of freshly made waffle cones instantly greeted us, and my thoughts drifted to the last time I had been in an ice cream store . . . with my father. He had insisted that nothing tasted better than ice cream in a waffle cone. Had to agree with him there.

Along one wall, country-themed giftware sat on decorative wrought-iron shelves. On the other side of the room, a glass-topped counter displaying tubs of ice cream took up almost the entire length of the store. On the wall behind it, the ice cream flavors were listed on a chalkboard. I couldn't remember the last time I'd seen so many flavors of ice cream, frozen yogurt, and sorbet. Jared's son would love this place.

And judging from the line stretching to the door, the store was popular—which was just as well. It gave me time to study the menu and narrow down my choices.

I wasn't the only one captivated by the board. And because of that, everyone was too busy to notice me—other than a toddler with wild black hair perched in her mother's arms. Head tilted to the side, she was studying me like I was someone from her favorite kids' show.

I smiled at her and she grinned back, then hid her face in her mom's neck. A pang of regret bit me in the ass at how much she reminded me of my sister when she was younger.

I turned back to Nicole to find her still studying the chalkboard. "What are you getting?" I asked.

"I haven't decided what I'm in the mood for yet."

"Not the triple-fudge?"

She lightly pressed her lips together—the look of deliberation. "I'm leaning more toward something fruity. Or maybe maple walnut."

Good news for me. Since she'd ruled out the heavy hitters, it meant she didn't view our time together as the equivalent of a bad date.

"What about you?" she asked.

"Cappuccino fudge sounds good. And I think I'll also have maple walnut. And vanilla bean."

"Three?"

"Hey, I'm a growing boy."

The toddler next to us giggled. Her father was tickling her and she was squirming in her mother's arms.

"She's cute," Nicole whispered, also watching the happy family. Judging from her expression, I wouldn't be surprised if her ovaries were getting excited over the prospect of one day having her own toddler in her arms. A toddler who was giggling because her father was tickling her.

"She is," I said. Without realizing what I was doing, I brushed my thumb up and down Nicole's bare arm, as if to reassure her that one day it would be her. She would experience the life she dreamed of, with the husband and kids and pets.

With a soft smile, she returned her attention to the menu.

"Whatever flavor I get, I'm going to have it in a waffle cone. They make the best ones I've ever tasted."

A waffle cone was a given for me. It was impossible to have three scoops of ice cream in a regular cone, since the law of gravity was not in your favor.

The main door opened and a group of teenage girls entered, talking and giggling. None were paying attention to anything beyond their conversation . . . at least not until one of them looked in my direction. She came to an abrupt halt. The girl behind her slammed into her, not expecting her to stop so suddenly.

By now the other girls had realized something was up, and they were peering in the direction of her gaze. They all stared at me for a heartbeat, as if their own eyes were deceiving them. Then, in unison, they screamed in the way girls do when they see their favorite musicians and actors. One or two of them looked like they might faint.

Even without checking over my shoulder, I could sense the puzzled glances behind me, wondering what the heck was going on.

"Does this usually happen?" Nicole asked under her breath.

"Not all the time, but definitely more often when I'm not in L.A. People there aren't so fazed by seeing celebrities." Or at least the non-tourists weren't so fazed.

"Oh my God," a tall blonde shrieked, "aren't you Mason Dell from Pushing Limits?"

"Of course he is," her short brunette friend said, sounding mildly irritated at what she perceived to be a dumb question. She glanced around the store, possibly checking to see if the rest of the band was here.

Finally getting over the shock of seeing me, they joined the end of the line, where Nicole and I were standing.

"Aren't you supposed to be on tour?" the brunette asked.

"We have a few days off, so I came to visit a friend." No point giving the full reason for why I was here.

"And then you're back on tour?"

I nodded.

"Wow, it must be so cool being famous," the blonde said, this time in a calmer voice.

"I wouldn't know about that. I'm not exactly famous."

All five girls looked at me like I was insane. I guess if being featured from time to time in tabloids made me famous, then yes, I was. But as the band's drummer, I wasn't as well known as Nolan and Jared. Whenever we were at fan events, their names were the ones most frequently yelled out.

"Well, that doesn't matter," the brunette said. "You're still my favorite drummer when it comes to rock music. I just wish I was half as good as you."

"You play?" I asked.

"Yup. I've been playing percussion in the school band since middle school, but I've only started playing on the drum kit like yours."

I thought for a moment. "Is there a music store in town that has drums?"

"Sure, on the corner of Robertson Boulevard and Twenty-third Street."

"Good. If it isn't an issue for them, maybe I can show you a few things on their kit. I didn't exactly bring mine down with me."

Her eyes widened, and it looked like she could barely stop herself from jumping up and down, like a little kid on Christmas morning. "You'd be willing to do that?"

"Sure, why not?" That was how I'd gotten my start too. A guy at the music store showed me a few things on the drums and I was hooked. The least I could do was pay it forward. Plus it might not be a bad idea to appease the karma gods, because payback from all the pranks I'd pulled over the years was going to smart like a bitch. "Can you meet me there in, say"—I looked at the time on my phone—"an hour?"

"Okay," she squeaked.

"Can we come too?" her friend asked.

"I don't see why not."

"Next," the girl behind the counter called out. Nicole and I stepped up to it and placed our order.

"No maple walnut?" I asked Nicole after she'd finished ordering hers. She had gone for mango and strawberry.

"I was hoping for a lick of yours instead." She winked at me, and my dick twitched at the sudden thought of where else I'd like her to lick.

Down, boy. "I think that can be arranged."

Once Nicole had paid for our ice creams, we went outside to the playground nearby and sat on the grassy embankment under a tree. Several little kids were running around playing tag, their giggles and screams filling the warm air. Seeing them brought forth questions I'd been able to ignore until now. Ever since my family had locked me out of their life, I had managed to avoid thinking about them. But the kids made me wonder if I had nephews or nieces I didn't know about. Were they as oblivious to my existence as I was to theirs?

That possibility was like a rusty nail in my gut. Just because I was too busy with my career to have kids didn't mean I didn't want any in my life. I loved spending time with Jared's son. But since my family had turned their backs on me, the only kids I would have in my life were those of my bandmates.

"This is really good ice cream," I said, pulling my thoughts away from the nieces and nephews I'd never get to meet and focusing instead on what I could enjoy now. "Is that where you got last night's ice cream from?"

"Only the best will do when dealing with crappy-date blues. I bet if the owners expanded outside of Desert Springs, they'd be rich from all the broken hearts they could heal." She ran the tip of her tongue across her mango ice cream.

And the urge to run the tip of my tongue along those sweet, glossy lips poked me in the ribs, edging me on. "So your heart is broken from those bad dates?"

She laughed. "I wouldn't go that far."

"Have you ever had your heart broken?"

"In a way, I guess. But in my case it wasn't a boyfriend who broke my heart. It was my father. He used to be a gambler. He almost destroyed my family." A familiar sadness rolled over her, one I had witnessed with my family in the beginning, when I first struggled with my addiction.

That rusty nail in my gut felt like it had been upgraded to a blunt knife stabbing me repeatedly. I didn't say anything, though. And I did my best to keep off my face any emotion that would betray the truth.

"I'm sorry. I didn't know. Zack never told me." But it did explain why he had been so adamant about helping me when my gambling addiction pulled me down and almost killed me. "What happened?"

"We were living in Vegas at the time. And as far as we knew, he was just gambling occasionally, nothing more than that. Then one day Zack and I overheard our parents arguing. My father had gambled away the money they had saved for Zack's and my college education. Not only that, they didn't have the money to pay the mortgage that month. My mom borrowed some from my grandparents, and my father promised that he was done with gambling and wouldn't screw up again."

"But he did?" I asked, knowing the answer.

"That's right. The lure was too strong. My mom begged him to get help. At first he agreed to do it. Later she discovered he never called Gamblers Anonymous. That was just another of his lies. She discovered how deeply in debt we were because of his addiction, and that because they were married she was legally responsible for his debts. She divorced him soon afterward and moved to L.A., where my grandparents live.

"She worked hard to give Zack and me the life she felt we deserved. She wanted to make up for everything. She worked long hours, making sure we had a roof over our heads, clothing, and food. She refused to date—she didn't have time, and after what my father did to her, she didn't trust men. She was afraid of ending up with another man like him. She kept telling Zack and me that we meant everything to her. That we were all she needed to be happy.

"She died of cancer several years ago, but before she died, she apologized for all the pain she had caused me and Zack because she hadn't walked away from my father sooner."

Each of her words twisted the knife a little more. Her father had been a lot like me.

"And that's why you're only interested in marrying a professional?" I asked.

"That's right. My father was a mechanic. He never earned enough from his job to pay the bills, so he was easily lured into the gambling lifestyle."

"There are plenty of professionals who get caught up in that lifestyle too. It has nothing to do with income." I should know. I'd met plenty of them as they were dragged down into the same fiery pits of hell I'd eventually found myself in. Income, race, gender—none of it mattered. Gambling was an equal-opportunity addiction.

Her lips curved down at this revelation, and the itch to kiss her was too strong to ignore. I leaned closer and brushed my mouth against hers. Her sweet taste encouraged me to lightly run the tip of my tongue against the seam of her mouth. Her lips immediately parted and I plunged my tongue into her warmth.

I craved to make her forget everything her father had done

to her. And maybe part of me just longed to forget everything I had done to my family.

Our kiss lasted no longer than a minute, during which I came to the conclusion that I couldn't tell her the truth about my past. In the last few hours I'd had more fun with her than I'd had in . . . well, I couldn't remember. I didn't want the man I used to be to tarnish our limited time together.

"Our ice cream's melting," Nicole said, smiling once more. She licked hers. "By the way, your maple walnut tastes delicious."

I barked a laugh. "Sorry, my brain just went into the gutter." And it was thoroughly appreciating the view there.

A light blush swept across her cheeks, and damn, did it look hot on her. I chuckled at her reaction. "So what else is on your list of qualifications for this so-called perfect guy?"

"Other than being a professional, he has to have a steady job, no bad habits. You know, like gambling. His life can't revolve around his job. I don't want to be an afterthought. He has to be kind, sweet, have a good sense of humor, be honest." Her gaze dropped to my forearm. "And he can't have any tattoos or piercings." She mumbled the last part, as if embarrassed to say it.

"So we can safely say I'm not on your list of perfect guys." I playfully nudged her shoulder with mine.

She nudged me back. "I guess not. I mean, other than the part about being sweet and kind and honest and having a good sense of humor. And I have no idea if you have any bad habits." She paused, as if considering this for a moment. "Do you have any I should know about?"

"Nope. None at all." And that lie just erased the honesty vote.

The heat of the day made it necessary to stop talking for a few minutes while we finished our ice cream before it melted.

What I really wanted to do was go back to kissing her. With just that one, I had already become addicted to her kisses.

But unlike with my previous addictions, there was no rehab center that could help me kick this habit. I'd have to go cold turkey—starting now.

"If you have something you need to do," I said after popping the last piece of waffle cone in my mouth, "you can just drop me off at the music store. I'll find my way back to your place afterward."

"No, I don't mind. I would love to watch you in action." She bit into her cone.

"Well, technically, you won't be seeing me in action. For that, you'd have to watch me in all my glory during a concert."

"I guess until that day happens, seeing you give some tips to a sixteen-year-old will have to do."

A small warmth tickled me down to my bones that she wanted to watch me share a drumming pointer or two with the girl. Nicole could be doing something else, but she chose to hang around and watch me instead.

Once it was time to head to the music store, I pushed myself to my feet and held out my hand to help Nicole up. I must have pulled her arm with more strength and enthusiasm than I'd expected, because she took a staggering step forward and her body crashed into mine. My arms automatically went around her waist.

And Christ, did she feel good wrapped in my arms—like she belonged there.

9

NICOLE

Mason and I stepped into the music store, and instantly his expression reminded me of a kid in a toy store during Christmas season. His eyes were filled with hopes, dreams, and possibilities, and I fought the desire to reach up and kiss his cheek. But with five teenage girls, all with cellphones, standing next to a drum set on the far side of the store, I didn't want to risk ending up on the Internet, with everyone speculating on Mason's new mystery woman.

And kissing him on the mouth was a definite no-no—even if the one earlier today had been the best kiss I'd had in, well, who knew how long.

Before heading over to the girls, Mason approached the sales counter near the door, where a man with long gray hair pulled back in a ponytail and a neatly trimmed gray beard stood. A well-worn Rolling Stones T-shirt skimmed his lanky body. His gaze was locked on Mason, his eyes slightly wide from shock. It would seem Mason had that effect on people wherever he went.

"Hey, man," Mason said. "If it's cool with you, can I show those girls over there a few things about drumming? One plays percussion in her school band, but she'd like some pointers. We'll only be a few minutes."

The man gave him a brief nod. "That's fine. Go ahead. I'm Andrew, by the way." He held out his hand and Mason shook it. "Let me know if you need anything."

"Will do. Thanks, man."

We joined the girls, and Mason climbed behind the drum kit and adjusted the seat. He then spent the next thirty minutes teaching Kylie various rhythms and techniques. All the girls looked on with awe, but Kylie's expression seemed to have less to do with *who* was teaching her than with *what* he was teaching her. Gone was the fangirl. Now she was in serious musician mode, asking lots of questions and listening intently to Mason's every word.

My cellphone pinged with a text from Zack.

> Zack: Just checking you haven't broken your phone again. :) Are you able to chat for a second?

I grinned and texted back.

> Me: Ha ha. Since when do you use smiley faces in your texts? :) :) And yes call me!!! As you can tell, my phone is still happy and in one piece.

When my phone rang, I stepped away from Mason and the girls so that I could hear Zack over the noise from the drums.

"Because I've been told girls like getting smiley faces in texts," Zack said.

I laughed. "True. So what's up?"

"Nothing much. Some of the crew and I are about to head out for a pint or two. But I just wanted to make sure everything's good with you first."

"Awww, aren't you sweet? No wonder you're my favorite brother."

He chuckled, my favorite sound. During the darkest times with our father's addiction, Zack's laugh had been a rarity. "I'm not sure that means a lot, given that I'm your *only* brother. So, is Mason still around, or did he already head back to L.A.?"

"No, he's still here. He decided to spend the day in Desert Springs." Mason picked that moment to generate an impressive riff. "Hear that?" I held my phone up for a couple of seconds so that Zack could hear him. "We're currently at the music store, where he's teaching some teens how to play drums. Hey, you know how you love the wallpaper in my house?"

Zack snorted. "That's one way to put it."

"Mason has the same level of respect for it as you. We're giving it a decent burial tomorrow."

"Tell him I owe him. I was ready to slit my wrists if I had to look at it one more time."

"My soon-to-be-ex-wallpaper loves you too." I didn't have the heart to tell him we were just doing the wallpaper in the kitchen and hallway. That would take long enough as it was—we wouldn't have time to do the guest room too.

Zack and I talked for a few more minutes while Mason continued his lesson, and then we said goodbye.

"That's really good," Mason told Kylie after she had finished playing the rhythm he'd just taught her. "You have a good ear."

The smile on her face was brighter than if she had been six years old and received a gold star on her artwork. "Thanks."

After the girls had left—though not before Mason had signed their Pushing Limits albums—I told him, "You were really good at that."

"What, at signing my name?" The corner of his mouth twitched; clearly he was fighting off the urge to smirk.

I rolled my eyes. "No, teaching. Have you done that before?"

"Not really. I went to a few drumming seminars in L.A.

when I was first learning to play. Guess I might've picked up a few teaching tricks from those."

His gaze briefly darted to a room near us where electronic keyboards and other instruments were kept. "Do you mind if we go in there?"

"Not at all."

He headed to a keyboard and turned it on. Before I had a chance to ask him if he knew how to play the piano, he placed his fingers on the keys. The simple yet beautiful melody he played had me swallowing the question.

"Is that a Pushing Limits song?" I asked, then realized how that must have sounded. My face heated up even though he knew I didn't listen to their music. If I did, I would have known that he wasn't just Zack's friend Mason when he first showed up at my house.

He shook his head and kept playing. Something about the ballad warmed me from the inside, which was crazy. I had no idea what the lyrics were. For all I knew, it was a sorrowful song about heartbreak.

The final notes drifted away and Mason glanced up at me. My breath paused in my lungs at the vulnerability in his eyes. But it wasn't because I had heard him play and he was nervous about what I thought of the song. There was something else. Something deeper.

Without thinking what I was doing, I stroked my fingers against his cheek, and the vulnerability eased slightly. "I loved it. What is it?"

"It's just a song I wrote."

"Will it be on the band's next album?"

He turned away and I let my fingers slide from his face. "Probably not."

"Why not?"

"I'm not the one who writes the songs for our albums. I'm just the drummer. Which is fine with me." He tried to shrug it off, but would have done a better job convincing me Santa really did exist . . . and spent his summers in Hawaii.

"So who writes them?"

"Nolan and Jared. Both are talented songwriters. I've just been messing around with stuff while we aren't touring."

I blinked. "Are you telling me they haven't heard this song yet? You seriously need to play it for them."

He laughed—and my girlie parts clenched at the deep, sexy sound. Every time he laughed, it sent a delicious shiver skipping across my skin. *Every. Single. Time.* "You only heard me play the music. You might not be so impressed if you heard the lyrics."

"Why? Are they obscene?"

He shook his head, laughing again.

"Well, I can tell from what you've played that it's a great song."

He smiled, but the smile was nothing like the one Kylie had given him after his compliment about her playing. It came up short by several miles.

Disappointment at his reaction sat down hard in my gut. I had no idea why it should have bothered me, but it did. "So the band has never heard you play the song? Ever?" I asked.

Mason stood up from the bench and started toward the door. "They don't even know I play piano."

I hurried after him. "Why don't they know you play? I would've thought it would come up at some point during your time together as a band."

"You've obviously never heard Aaron play."

"Is he in the band?"

Mason waved at Andrew, who had looked up from helping a customer. "Thanks, man."

"My pleasure," Andrew called out.

"So who's Aaron?" I asked again as we stepped out of the store into the bright afternoon sun. I didn't want to be a pain about the song, but I really didn't understand why I got to hear it while none of his bandmates did.

"He's the band's keyboardist. He was Juilliard bound, but then changed his mind and joined the band instead. Next to him, I sound pretty lame."

"But I still don't get why you can't play the song for them. I mean, it's not like I'm suggesting they kick Aaron out of the band and you switch to playing the keyboards."

"Because it's nothing like what Jared and Nolan write," Mason said as we walked toward my car in the parking lot. "Besides, like I said, I'm the band's drummer. I love drumming and I'm good at it. That's why I switched from piano to drums when I was a teenager." He smirked. "Of course, it also didn't hurt that it's easier to get laid if you're a drummer in a rock band than if you're a pianist playing in some dinner club."

The corners of my mouth twitched. "You probably have a point there."

We returned to my house. After checking on Bernie and taking him for a brief walk so he could do his doggy business, I went into my bedroom and got started on the paperwork I'd picked up at the store. Once I'd finished, I went to see what Mason was up to. I found him with screwdriver in hand, fixing the sticky front door.

"I've almost got it." His arm muscles bunched as he turned the screwdriver, twisting the screw into the doorframe. He closed the front door, then opened it. Unlike before, it opened smoothly.

I had to fight back the urge to throw my arms around him and kiss him. Escaping my bad dates had become that much easier, thanks to him.

But kissing him was definitely a bad idea—because if I had another one, I'd never be able to stop. I'd only want more.

"Wow, thanks. I can't believe you actually managed to fix it."

As soon as I said it I realized how bad it sounded, so I hurriedly added, "I mean, I didn't think it could be fixed."

"You're welcome." He stepped into the house and flipped on the hallway light . . . and it worked. "And your back gate won't keep opening and banging shut when it's windy. I fixed that too."

"I'm definitely gonna miss you when you're gone." And it wasn't just the fixing up around the house that I would miss. I'd been having fun hanging out with him. He was funny, as well as incredibly giving—which was the last thing I would've ever expected from a rock star. I'd always thought they were just into drugs and alcohol and sex, but none of that described the down-to-earth guy standing in my hallway.

"I'll fix the toilet and shower now," Mason said, stepping out of the house and grabbing his new toolbox off the porch.

I laughed under my breath. "Well, have fun with that. I'm going to make dinner." Momentarily forgetting my earlier resolution, I gave him a quick kiss on the cheek, then headed for the kitchen.

But that didn't count as a real kiss, right? It wasn't on the mouth.

Dinner was just about ready when Mason emerged from the bathroom, freshly showered. In the background, the latest Pushing Limits album was playing through the Bluetooth speakers. Yes, I might've been a tiny bit curious and downloaded it onto my iPhone. I'd heard a couple of their songs a few times with Heidi, but back then I hadn't really paid much attention to them because the band wasn't country. Now I had a reason to listen to them.

"So what do you think?" He did the chin-nod thing I'd seen him do a few times.

"You guys are really good. I especially like your drumming." Not that I was knowledgeable about that aspect of the music, but it did sound good to me.

"Enough that you're a new fan?"

I pretended to consider it for a second. "Yes, I think I could definitely be a new fan."

He grabbed hold of my hips with both hands and pulled me against him. "And it has nothing to do with me fixing your front door?"

With the erotic sensation of his stubbled jaw against the skin of my cheek and the sound of his I-want-to-have-sex-with-you-now voice—even though he didn't actually want to have sex with me—I almost had an orgasm right there. "Among other things."

Clearly unconcerned about having left me in an aroused state, Mason pulled back and sniffed the air. "Hmm, that smells good. Are those your world-famous chocolate chip cookies?" His face brightened.

I smiled back. "Possibly."

He glanced at the stove next to us and the covered skillet. "What's in there?"

"Beef stroganoff." I turned to the stove and lifted the skillet lid. With a spoon, I scooped up a small amount of the creamy sauce and raised it to his lips.

He sampled the liquid. "Mmm. It tastes as good as it smells."

The food wasn't the only thing that smelled delicious. "Do you know you smell fruity?" I giggled.

He glared at me, or at least attempted to. It was hard to be convincing when he had mischief gleaming in his eyes. "I didn't have much choice. You need a soap that's more manly."

"Just how often do you think I have men staying over?" I pretended to be indignant, which wasn't easy when all I craved was to sample the man in front of me, fruity-smelling or not. "Besides, I happen to think you smell sexy." Kudos to my acting abilities, since I managed to say it without giggling again.

Mason stepped closer, our bodies a hair's width from touching. "You do, do you?"

I swallowed hard. "I do."

His gaze dropped to my lips. "We probably shouldn't kiss, should we?"

I shook my head, the movement negligible. "No, we probably shouldn't." That might be what my brain was saying, but my body definitely wasn't agreeing with it.

In the background, a ballad played, the lyrics speaking about taking things slow and how it would be worth it in the end. The song was beautiful and I loved the melody, but it was nothing like the song Mason had played for me earlier. Even without the lyrics, that song had touched me deep in my soul.

Mason moved back a step. "Do you need any help?"

My body already missed his closeness. "Sure. You want to chop the carrots? Then I can cook them."

"Chopping carrots happens to be my specialty."

I laughed. "I thought drumming was your specialty."

"No, that's just my day job. By night I'm a super carrot cutter." He winked at me.

"Ooh, does the job come with a cool superhero cape?"

"Normally, yes. But I had to leave it at the dry cleaner after my last carrot-chopping mission. You would've liked it. It's red."

"So, like Superman's cape?" I tossed over my shoulder as I walked to the fridge and removed the two-pound bag of carrots.

"Much cooler than Superman's cape."

I giggled again. I couldn't remember the last time I'd laughed so much in one day. "Now I'm really sorry I missed out on that." I set the carrots on the counter next to him and fished through the utility drawer for the vegetable peeler. "Do you want a glass of wine?"

"Sounds good."

Mason peeled the carrots while we joked around and he told me about the guys in the band. The last time I'd felt this comfortable around a man was . . . well, a long time ago. Maybe knowing that what we had between us wasn't going anywhere in the end made it easier. There were no expectations. We were two people who had become friends.

After dinner we washed the dishes, I popped popcorn in the hot-air popper, and we retired to the couch to watch another movie.

"I think I'm in love with you," Mason said, removing a DVD case from my collection. He held it up for me to see: *Die Hard 2*.

I laughed. "Glad to see you appreciate me for my *Die Hard* movies."

"I might have to kiss you due to your brilliant collection." A smirk appeared on his face. Stupid, panty-dropping, sexy smirk. "Except we already agreed, no more kisses."

"I don't think one more would really hurt." The words slipped from my mouth before I could stop them—before I was even aware I'd been thinking them deep down. "I mean, it's really just once. Nothing more than that." Nothing that would signify what we had between us was anything beyond friendship.

He didn't say anything, but the smirk remained in place. He put the disc into the machine and joined me on the couch. He then removed the bowl of popcorn from my lap and set it on the coffee table. Before I could say anything, his lips were against mine.

There was nothing tender about the kiss. It was a kiss heavy with promises: promises to melt me to the core if we didn't stop soon, promises to leave me wanting if we did stop. If I was to rate it on a scale from one to ten, it was a definite twelve.

My tongue glided against his, and once again I felt the electrifying hum that I'd experienced when we'd kissed at Blooming Love and then again after going to the ice cream shop. It also caused the ache between my legs to become more demanding.

How was I planning to survive once he left for L.A.? No other man would ever come close to being as great a kisser as he was. He had spoiled me for all other guys—nobody else would ever stand a chance.

Somewhere in the back of my head, a rational, slightly irritating voice reminded me of the list of traits I was looking for in the perfect man. Mason might be perfect when it came to the kissing (which wasn't even on my list—silly me!), but he didn't have the traits that counted the most.

Just try telling that to my body.

It took a few moments to realize the previews were over. Mason moved away, grabbed the remote control, and started the movie. And instantly my body and lips wanted more of him.

It was official. I was going to need some sort of substitute while I recovered from my newfound Mason addiction—only I didn't think there was a gum or patch that could help in a situation like this.

10

MASON

"Are you ready?" I asked.

"Ready," Nicole replied.

"Okay. On the count of three."

We were standing in her kitchen late Monday afternoon, ready for Operation Wallpaper Removal. Bernie had been recently walked, so we were good to go for a few hours. Following the directions I'd Googled yesterday, we had already prepared the kitchen with plastic and towels to protect the floor and floorboards from the water needed to strip the walls bare.

"One . . . two . . . three," I said from the stepladder. With the putty knife, I loosened the wallpaper near the ceiling and peeled it downward. Nicole was on the other side of the room, dealing with the paper between the countertops and the overhead cabinets.

I managed to pull a foot of paper free from the wall before it ripped, the rest still clinging to the wall like its life depended on it. *Fuck*. And based on the grunt from Nicole, she hadn't had much luck either.

"I was really hoping the article had lied about old wallpaper," she said. According to it, the longer the paper had been up, the tougher it would be to remove. And given that this paper had to be from the 1970s . . .

"Me too," I said as I pried another strip of paper from the wall with the putty knife.

Over an hour later, we were still battling with the reluctant-to-be-freed wallpaper. Various-sized bits of it lay scattered over the floor and counters.

"Wallpaper should be permanently banned from the planet," Nicole said, shoving back a wayward strand of hair that had fallen from her ponytail. Between the hair, short shorts, and tank top, she was easily the sexiest woman I'd ever seen. My arms were about to fall off from the effort of removing the wallpaper, but the sight of her like this made the pain worth it.

"Obviously whoever created it never had to remove it," I said. Or maybe he did and that was what had killed him.

I ripped off the last remaining piece from the section of wall I'd been working on and turned around . . . to find Nicole staring at where my ass had been.

"See anything you like?" I asked. Her face turned red, and I laughed. "That would be a yes?" I joined her by the counter and plucked out a few tiny shreds of paper lodged in her hair. I knew I was pushing the boundaries of the easygoing friendship that had developed between us—well, the easygoing friendship that involved a few hot kisses—but that didn't stop me. "You know, you look adorable with wallpaper in your hair. It's a great look for you."

She snickered. "You really do know how to charm the panties off girls, don't you?"

"Is it working?"

Her smile shifted to one side and she glanced down at her shorts. "Nope, still there."

"Oh, really?"

Even though I knew I probably shouldn't, I took a step toward her. She backed away, her ass banging squarely into the counter behind her. I parked my hands on either side of her, caging her in. "Guess I must be losing my touch."

The smile that grew on her lips was neither a sweet smile nor a smile aimed to seduce. It was a smile meant to disarm a man, to play his game—and to win.

She placed her hands on my chest and gave me a small shove. I didn't budge. "Guess that must be so. So since you've lost your panty-dropping touch, let's get back to the wallpaper. It's not getting any more in style."

Disagreeing with her assessment, I leaned in to kiss her. But as I was making my descent toward her luscious lips, the fucking doorbell rang. Whoever it was, I thought, had better have a damn good reason for interrupting us—like the house was on fire. Nicole gave a quick what-can-you-do shrug and left the room to answer the door.

While she was gone, I resumed the task of removing the final bits of wallpaper on the wall where she'd been working.

Footsteps approached the kitchen. Turning to the door, I said, "What do you say—" But I bit off the final words when I saw Amy, the teen we'd met while walking Bernie yesterday, enter the room, along with a little girl Logan's age.

"Hi," the little girl said. "My sister likes you."

"Bree!" Amy's tone was sharp, but she looked as though she wished the floor would conveniently open up and swallow her whole.

I walked over to them and crouched in front of the little girl. "Hi, I'm Mason."

"I'm Brianna, but my sister says you're famous, so you can call me Bree."

Amy groaned. "Just ignore her. Her goal in life is to humiliate me."

I laughed shortly. "I think the goal of most kids is to humiliate their older brother or sister. It's in their genes."

Bree's gaze dropped to my legs and she studied them, a

slight furrow between her eyebrows. "What's in the jeans? Can I see it?"

Deciding this was a pointless conversation to have with a four-year-old, I switched topics. "Did you guys come to help us remove the wallpaper?" I gestured to the torn paper scattered around the room.

"No, my sister—" Bree began, but she didn't get very far, as Amy's hand shot out and covered her mouth. The little girl wriggled free and glared at her, lower lip sticking out. "Daddy told you not to do that."

"Well, stop embarrassing me," Amy said through clenched teeth.

Still pouting, Bree crossed her arms over her chest. "You're so bossy."

I placed my hand next to my mouth and stage-whispered, "Big sisters are supposed to be bossy. Just like you're supposed to embarrass her." I winked at Bree, and her pout transformed into a huge grin.

I pushed myself up to a standing position. "So, what can we do you for?" I asked Amy, knowing that she was the reason they were here.

"Er . . . I came to see if you would sign this picture for me." She held up an interview with the band in a recent issue of *Rolling Stone*. She had already been around yesterday, when I signed her Pushing Limits concert T-shirt.

With a smile, I took the pen from her and walked over to the kitchen table to sign the article.

"Nice picture," Nicole said, examining it. "Who's that?" She pointed at the guy with wavy light brown hair.

"Nolan, our lead singer." Then I indicated the dark-haired guy next to him. "That's Jared, our guitarist." My finger shifted to the other dark-haired guy. We were all tall, but Kirk towered over the rest of us by a good two inches. Handy when you were playing hockey, I guess. "And this is Kirk, our bassist."

"So this must be Aaron," she said, pointing at the blond man at the edge of the group.

"That's right," I said, impressed she'd remembered his name from our conversation earlier.

Amy must have had a thing for him as well, because she let out a dreamy sigh.

Bree peered up at her and giggled. "She loves him," she singsonged. "She told her friend she wants to have his babies."

Amy's eyes bulged as if she had downed a bottle of hot sauce, and I choked back a laugh. She wasn't the first girl to announce that she planned to have one of the guys' babies, but she was definitely the youngest I'd heard it from. Given that none of us were into jailbait, the chance of her becoming pregnant with Aaron's baby was a big fat zero.

"Okay," Amy said, drawing out the word. "It's time for your nap." She tugged on her sister's hand, attempting to pull her toward the door.

"I'm a big girl," the little girl huffed. "Big girls don't nap."

"They do now," Amy muttered under her breath.

"Bye," I called out, doing my best not to laugh at the pair as Amy led the reluctant Bree from the kitchen. But at least now Nicole and I could get back to work.

While Nicole was escorting the girls to the front door, the need for some fun bubbled up inside me, like a Jacuzzi turned on full speed after you dumped in too much bubble bath. Tearing ancient wallpaper off the wall didn't exactly make it onto any ten-fun-things-to-do-this-weekend lists. At least not without a little help.

Some girls would get prissy at what I was about to do. But if there was one thing I'd learned about Nicole in the last two days, it was that underneath the workaholic exterior was a girl who loved to have fun as much as I did.

I grabbed the empty water mister I'd seen under the sink and filled it with water. I hid it in the corner where Nicole wouldn't see it, then got to work, filling the bucket with hot water.

Nicole entered the room as I was turning off the tap. I set the bucket on the floor near where she was working and filled the second one. We wetted the walls with sponges and carefully scraped the wallpaper paste off the walls. In the background, her favorite country singer sang about falling in love with his best friend. Much like what had happened with Nolan when it came to Hailey.

Nicole's hips swayed back and forth as she sang softly to the lyrics, focused intently on the wall while removing a patch of glue that still remained. She had a sweet voice and for a second I watched her, mesmerized, before I slowly backed up to where I'd hidden the water mister. I picked it up, set it to stream, then squirted her from behind, soaking the back of her tank top.

She shrieked and spun around. "Oh, you think so, do you?" Laughing, she hurled her wet sponge at me.

I ducked out of the way, but not fast or far enough to avoid water splashing me. The sponge hit the wall near me with a splat and fell to the floor.

Nicole lunged for it but wasn't fast enough. As I reached down to snatch it up, she wrapped her arms around my waist and tried to pull me away from the sponge. For someone so small compared to me, she was surprisingly strong. She tugged me back a step. But my foot slipped on the water that had spilled at some point, and I went down—pulling Nicole with me.

I landed on my ass. "Oof!"

She ended up sprawled on top of me, her legs tangled with mine. She then shifted to straddle my hips. "I win!"

No, I would say I was definitely the winner here, with her sex pressed against my cock. Granted, there were two layers of denim between us.

I thought Nicole would climb off me and put some space

between us, to try to reduce the sexual tension between us, which had shot off the scale. That might have been the wiser thing to do.

But apparently wise didn't count when it came to us.

Her gaze searched mine for a moment. Whatever she found there she must have agreed with, because the next thing I knew her lips crashed into mine and we were kissing.

Kissing like there was no tomorrow.

Or kissing because we knew that come tomorrow, I'd be heading back to L.A.

11

NICOLE

The world wasn't just black and white. It also contained various shades of gray. And right now, with my lips attached to Mason's, we were smack-dab in the middle of the gray zone.

What did I know? That Mason was my brother's friend and I shouldn't be kissing him. He was leaving tomorrow, which was another reason for not kissing him. But I also knew he wasn't the dating type, so as long as there were no expectations between us after tonight, there was no harm in this kiss. And judging from the way he was kissing me back, he was fully on board with the plan.

The kiss alternated between slow and delicious, then fast and hot. It was everything you could possibly want in a kiss—except for one thing.

At the sound of my stomach, which put the rumble of a thunderstorm to shame, Mason chuckled. "How about I make us dinner?"

"You sure?" I liked to cook, but from what I'd tasted of Mason's food, I liked his cooking even more.

"Positive. Why don't you walk Bernie and I'll get started after a quick shower?"

"Sounds good to me," I said, lifting myself off Mason.

Over an hour later, after I'd walked Bernie and soaked my weary body in the shower, we sat down at the kitchen table for the best spaghetti and meatballs I'd ever tasted.

"So, *Die Hard with a Vengeance* tonight?" Mason asked.

"Naturally." I popped a meatball into my mouth and closed my eyes as I chewed it. "Mmm. Oh God. This is so amazing." That was the third time I'd said it, but it was the first time I sounded like I was racing toward an orgasm.

I opened my eyes to find Mason watching me with smoldering eyes. Heat and wetness flooded my core, and I squirmed under the intensity of his gaze.

"Glad you're enjoying it," he said, that goddamn sexy smirk of his back to tease me.

"Definitely enjoying it." I returned my attention to my food. One more night and then he'd be gone, and I would be back to . . .

To what? To more mindless dates while waiting for Mr. Right to show up? *Go me.*

After we finished our meal and cleaned up the dishes, we retired to the living room for the last *Die Hard* movie we'd get to watch together.

The movie started out well—other than the part where I couldn't focus on it. All I could notice was the man sitting next to me, the way he smelled, the way he filled out his jeans and T-shirt, the way he laughed.

The way my body felt alive when I was around him.

As if unconsciously sensing my dilemma, Mason leaned closer to me. His warm breath brushed against my ear. I turned to him, and before I could say anything, his mouth was on mine. And because I had already proven I had no willpower when it came to Mason's kisses, my lips immediately parted for him.

Our kisses were rough, hungry, impatient. Sublime. His stubble brushed against my face and I moaned at the delicious sensation of it. He deepened the kiss.

My body took over, not interested in my brain having any say as to what would happen next. Shifting my leg, I straddled his hips, our mouths remaining locked together. If they could have stayed that way for the rest of my life, I would've been more than okay with that.

Again, my body ignored what my brain was telling it, and I ground my core against Mason's hardening length. Good—I wasn't the only one dealing with a lust-heightened body.

Mason's lips moved from mine, but before I could tell him not to stop kissing me, his mouth moved to my jaw and the stubble on his face brushed against my skin again. And that made the ache between my legs beg breathlessly for relief.

His mouth continued forward, his warm breath caressing my ear. "Christ, I want to touch you. All of you." If I burned any hotter at his words, fire trucks would be the only things capable of extinguishing the flames.

I made a sound that was closer to a squeak than a moan. Up until this point, Mason's hands had been on my hips. Now one trailed along my side, skimming my tank top until it reached my breast. He lightly scraped a thumb against my nipple, and I sucked in a hard breath.

I expected his mouth to return to mine. Instead, his fingers, which had been resting on my hip, slipped under the fabric of my top and slowly slid it up, up, up, revealing my stomach . . . and then my breasts. A moment later, my bra was open, Mason having easily clicked open the front clasp.

At Mason's hungry scrutiny, his eyes dark with desire, my panties grew even wetter. Reverently he circled a fingertip around one nipple. The bud tightened greedily with need. "So perfect," he uttered. "So goddamn perfect."

He leaned down and his tongue replaced his finger. Then he sucked my nipple into his mouth and teased it further. And for a second, I wondered what else his talented tongue could do.

While he was entertaining himself with my breasts, I ran my hands up his solid arms. He worked out, that much I could tell. Every inch of him was taut, pure male muscle. Eager to see his abs again and to finally touch them, I moved my hands to the bottom of his T-shirt and pulled the fabric up, caressing the ridges and valleys of his ripped abs with my fingertips.

Mason paused his teasing of my nipple and released it from his mouth. It pouted at being abandoned, not quite finished with what he'd been doing to it. He grabbed the collar of his T-shirt, yanked the fabric over his head, and tossed the shirt aside. It landed somewhere on the floor near the love seat.

My gaze shifted to the tattoo on the right side of his ribs. I couldn't be sure, but it looked like a foreign language, using an alphabet I didn't recognize. I ran my fingers down the length of it. "What is it?"

"Sanskrit."

"It's pretty. What does it say?"

He cringed at my reference that his tattoo was pretty. "Without music life shall be a mistake."

My mouth tugged up into a full smile. "I like that. It's very poetic. What about this one?" I traced my fingertip along a similar design around his left biceps, except this one was a lot shorter.

"I am a fighter."

My eyebrows rose. "You're a fighter? You mean like in MMA or martial arts?" Which would explain why he was in such great shape.

"You watch MMA?" If there'd been a contest as to which of us was more surprised, he would've won the prize.

I shook my head. "No. It's just I've read a few romance novels in which the heroes trained for it."

He smirked. "Romances, huh? What other kinds of romances have you read?"

"Not *Fifty Shades of Grey*, if that's what you're thinking."

He feigned an innocent expression. "I wasn't thinking that at all."

I laughed. "Sure you weren't. And in case you're wondering, I'm not into BDSM."

"Good to know." The smirk was back on his face. "And you're telling me this because . . . ?"

"Because if we're headed where I believe we're headed"—and I hoped I wasn't out to lunch on that—"then I want to make sure our expectations are the same." God, I sounded like an idiot.

"Don't worry. When it comes to BDSM, I'm pretty sure we're on the same page."

"Good. And just so you know, I realize this is more like a one-night stand. I won't be expecting you to call me after tonight." Tomorrow morning he would go back to his life in L.A., and I would go back to mine here . . . which hopefully didn't include any more bad dates.

Or better yet, no more blind dates, period.

"And I won't expect you to give me your number," I added. "It's just one night of fun between two consenting adults. I mean, if you want to call me as a friend, that would be cool too. But no expectations beyond tonight."

"Sounds good."

With that awkwardness out of the way, I asked, "So when you say you're a fighter, you mean . . . ?"

"It means I don't give up, no matter how difficult something seems at the time."

I gave him a soft smile. "I like that. So, what does this one mean?" I ran my finger over the three short patterns on the inside of his right arm.

"Live. Love. Laugh." He pointed at each word in turn.

"Good advice. What about this one?" I caressed the Sanskrit words on his right pec. I had never been into tattoos before, which was part of the reason my future husband would be tattoo free, but there was something extremely sexy about Mason's.

"Each breath is a gift."

My mother had believed the same, especially while she had been battling her cancer. Unfortunately, her gift had come with an expiration date.

I gently pressed my lips against the tattoo, as though I was kissing her cheek once more.

"Do you have any tattoos I should know about?" he asked.

"Nope, only virgin skin on me."

That got a raised eyebrow.

"No, I'm not a virgin, if that's what you're thinking. I've had sex before," I babbled, my mouth now a runaway train, picking up speed. "Just not in a long time."

Amusement glinted in his eyes. "And why's that?"

"Do you not remember the part about my recent dating history?"

"What does that have to do with sex?"

"Well, most of the guys I've gone out with lately have been boring during the date. I just figured that didn't bode well for them—or me—when it came to the bedroom."

Mason barked a laugh. "I guess not. But it just means you've been dating the wrong guys."

I shot him a look that said, *You think?* Or at least that was the expression I was aiming for.

That only made him laugh harder.

I glared at him. "Glad you find it so funny."

The laughter died away, and he ran his thumb against my lower lip. The skin tingled at his touch. "So, what do you say we end your dry spell, if that's what you still want?"

"That's what I still want," I whispered. "And I have condoms in my bedroom. They should still be good. And I'm on the pill." Not that it had been necessary for the past many months.

His mouth returned to mine and he teased me once more with a brief kiss. "How about we take this to your room?"

"Okay." I led him upstairs and switched on my bedroom light. Two of the three bulbs in the light fixture had burned out, resulting in the fixture casting nothing more than a soft glow.

Unsure what to do next, I just stood there. I'd never had a one-night stand before—which was what Mason technically was, even if we had spent the last few days together hanging out. The last time I'd had sex was with my boyfriend back in college—so, almost two years ago.

Mason's arms encircled me from behind, and he pulled me against his hard body. "Relax," he murmured against my ear. His deep, rich voice did all kinds of crazy things to my legs. Good thing he was holding on to me. This was further confirmed when he nibbled the shell of my ear. I moaned, positive I would be a melted mess before we even got to the main event.

"That's better." He turned me around and his mouth was back to devouring mine. I was doomed. After this, after the incredible way he kissed, no other guys could compare. Not even close.

His hands knotted in my hair. At some point he started walking me backward until the backs of my legs hit the mattress. I lost my balance, taking Mason down with me.

"Patience is a virtue, you know," he said with a wink.

I laughed. "I'll keep that in mind for next time." I'd said it casually, without thinking much about it, so it took a second for me to realize how it might've sounded. *Oh God*. The last thing I wanted was for him to think that I was expecting a next time with him—even though I had made it clear I had no expectations after tonight.

Before I could clarify what I'd meant, he pushed my tank top up again and went back to teasing my nipples with his tongue. Clearly not wishing to miss out on the action, his fingers drifted down my stomach and disappeared under the waistband of my denim skirt. They continued south, over the top of my underwear, until he found what he was looking for.

My body jerked at his touch.

His head moved away from entertaining my breasts and he looked up at me. "Like that, huh?"

"Very much." *Wow, did my voice just sound bedroom sexy?*

A wicked grin slid onto his face. "I wonder what else you like."

He didn't give me a chance to answer—not that I had an answer. He peeled the waistband of my skirt over my hips and down my legs. It ended up on the floor somewhere. My non-sexy white cotton underwear got the same fate, as did my tank top.

"I think I'm at a disadvantage here," I said, fighting the urge to cover myself with my hands.

"How so?"

"I'm naked and you're not." I pushed myself to sit and reached for the waistband of his jeans, then yanked him closer. I slipped the button out of the hole and slid the zipper down, purposefully rubbing my hand against his hard length.

"I'm liking where you're going with this," he said.

I rolled my eyes. As if he didn't already know where this was headed.

I tugged down on his jeans, revealing his black boxer briefs and a cock straining to be freed. "Someone's happy to see me," I said, feeling a little smug that I was having this effect on him.

Mason practically ripped his jeans off the rest of the way,

and they joined the clothes on the floor. Then, before I could say or do anything, he hooked his hands between my legs and spread them wide, my feet dangling above the floor. "I think it's about time I taste you, Nicole. Lean back."

At his demand, wetness flooded between my legs. I did as he requested, propping myself on my elbows so I could watch him. Somehow I couldn't imagine Mr. Boring Accountant from the other day being this way in the bedroom. Not that I wanted to imagine him right now. Or ever.

My last boyfriend had never gone down on me, but I had read about it in the romance novels I'd enjoyed. That didn't come close to preparing me for how it felt when Mason's tongue lashed against my core. Heaven of all things holy. As much as I tried to stay still, I writhed on the bed. I grabbed a fistful of the sheets, although I had no idea why I believed it would make a difference.

And just when I thought I could handle it, Mason proved me wrong. He slipped a finger inside me and then another. He alternated between plunging them inside me and pressing against my heat. The sensation was too much. "I'm going to come," I warned, figuring if he aimed to be inside me, he'd better do that now, before it was too late.

"Good. I want to feel you come against my face. I want to taste you as you fall apart."

Those words and the husky way he said them were enough to send me over the edge. I cried out as a powerful orgasm detonated low in my belly and spread through me, like a volcano erupting after being dormant for hundreds of years. I couldn't remember the last time it had been like this. Clearly I had been missing out.

It took me a few seconds to regain awareness, my body still floating around the heavens.

Mason stood over me, a smug expression on his face. "I take it you approved?"

I eyed him from under half-lowered eyelids. "You're not one of those guys who lets his ability to make a woman come hard go to his ego, are you?"

He laughed. "So I made you come hard, did I?"

The corner of my mouth quirked up. "As if you didn't know." I pushed myself to sit and reached for his boxer briefs.

"You said you have condoms?" he asked.

"Yes, in my bedside drawer." I reached over and pulled out the sealed box. A quick check of the expiration date told me they were good to go . . . except for one thing. "I think these are for regular-sized penises." I glanced at his cock. "And I have a feeling you aren't exactly regular size. I wouldn't want to cut off your circulation. Your penis might fall off." Okay, maybe that was an exaggeration, but I had no idea what would happen. I just figured it wouldn't be a good thing.

Mason burst out laughing. "You're the first person who's actually made me laugh during sex."

"And you're the first person who I've made laugh during sex. Go me."

Still laughing, he removed his wallet from the nightstand. "Don't worry about the condoms. I have a couple here that will fit."

He handed me a foil square.

I traced my finger around the tip, spreading the pre-cum, then wrapped my fingers around his length. Mason groaned, but his eyes remained on me, trusting me, challenging me. I cupped his balls with my other hand. Another groan.

I moved my hand up and down his length a few more times, then reached for the foil package and opened it. "I've never put one on a guy before," I said, my face heating at the confession.

"There's a first for everything."

"You mean other than making you laugh during sex?"

He snickered. "You're on a roll with the firsts tonight, aren't you?"

Concentrating as if I were doing brain surgery, I repeated what I'd seen my last boyfriend do when he had put on a condom. It went on more easily than I'd expected. Once finished, I scooted back on the bed.

Mason climbed onto it, positioned himself between my legs, and slowly pushed inside me. "You okay?" he asked, his voice low and soothing and doing all kinds of amazing things to my body just from the sound of it.

"Yes," I breathed while my body begged for more of him.

He continued his slow plunge forward, allowing my soft heat to stretch and pull him further in. I moaned, unable to hold back how incredible it felt with him inside me.

"Christ, Nicole. You're so fucking hot and tight." Based on his erotic groan, I took this to be a good thing.

Once he was fully seated in me, he asked me one more time if I was okay, and then he began thrusting in and out . . . until another orgasm crashed over me.

"Oh God," I cried out, a little louder than last time. Mason joined me a moment later in happy land, with a guttural grunt. He half collapsed on me, kissed me long and hard one final time, then pulled out of me.

He climbed off the bed and disposed of the condom. Then he returned and snuggled under the covers with me, pulling me against him so my back was pressed against his torso.

"So I was thinking," Mason said a minute later, "that maybe I could stick around one more day and paint the walls. You're busy with the flower shop, and who knows how long it will be before you can get around to doing it yourself."

I shifted around to face him. "You really don't have to do that, Mason. You were only expected to check on me, not help me renovate the house. Not that I don't appreciate it." I gave him a soft, brief kiss, my girlie parts already excited again to have more of him. "You have a life waiting for you back in L.A.

A more exciting life compared to spending your days here removing wallpaper, painting walls, and fixing faulty doors."

Although after what we just did, it wouldn't be that big a sacrifice on my part to have him stay another day . . . or ten. I could get my fill of sex before returning to drought status again.

"I really don't mind. It's been fun. Plus then I can replace those lightbulbs." He pointed to the ceiling light.

"It *has* been fun." My fingers drifted up his inner thigh, toward one very happy part of him. "Okay. If you want to stick around one more day, I'm definitely not going to argue against that."

And then I showed him just how much I wasn't going to argue against him sticking around for another day—until he was left groaning out my name.

12

MASON

Two days later

I was dreaming. That much I knew because in reality I wasn't married . . . and definitely not to Nicole. Nor did I have any kids.

Yet here I was walking down the street with Bernie on a leash and some little dude strapped to my chest in a baby carrier, fast asleep.

Somewhere in the distance a cellphone rang. And then to further confirm I was dreaming, the warm body in my arms stirred and pulled away from me. I opened my eyes to find Nicole reaching for her phone on the nightstand. The alarm clock numbers glowed red, as if in warning. It was 2:06 a.m.—seven hours before I was planning to drive back to L.A.

What the fuck?

"Hello?" she said in a drowsy voice that was this side of sexy. My cock sat up and took notice, despite the fact that no one called at this hour unless they had misdialed the number or something was wrong.

Nicole's body stiffened as she listened to the person on the other end, then she scrambled out of bed, naked. "I'm on my way." She ended the call.

"What's going on?" I asked, sitting up, as she disappeared into her closet.

"The store's on fire." Her voice cracked, and I was instantly out of bed, snatching my clothes from the floor.

She emerged fully dressed as I was pulling on my jeans.

"I'm coming with you," I told her.

"You don't have to do that, Mason," she said, walking toward her bedroom door. "You're hitting the road soon. You won't be able to drive if you're too tired."

"You don't have to do that" was a phrase I'd heard quite a few times since arriving at her house four days ago. That's right. Four days. All those "Heck, what's one more day?" added up. Zack knew that I was still here. But he had no idea I'd been fucking his sister. It had been Nicole's idea not say anything to him—and considering that I valued my life, I completely agreed with her.

I grabbed her arm, stopping her. I could see the panic in her eyes. "Yes, I do. You can't go there on your own. And no way am I returning to L.A. until I know everything is okay."

"I won't be alone. The firefighters will be there, as will Heidi."

I released her arm. "That's not what I meant."

My words weren't enough. She ran out the door. I raced after her, still shirtless. She flew down the stairs and snatched her keys from the hallway table next to the front door.

I parked myself in front of the door and held out my hand. "Let me drive."

"I can drive."

"I'm driving, Nicole." My tone didn't leave room for argument. She was barely holding things together as it was. I couldn't risk her getting behind the wheel.

"Fine." She handed me her keys. After we put on our shoes,

I opened the door and followed her outside, pausing long enough to lock the door behind us.

Two fire trucks were parked in front of the strip mall when we arrived, as was a police car. No flames were visible, but a heavy smell of smoke hung in the air. I took the lack of flames to be a good thing. If the sprinklers had done their job, Nicole and Heidi would be facing just smoke and water damage instead of something more serious.

Heidi was standing to the side, face pale, tears staining her cheeks. Her arms were wrapped around herself, as were the arms of a man who I could only guess was her boyfriend. It didn't look like he was trying to comfort her as much as hold her back from rushing into the building.

"What happened?" Nicole asked, her face equally pale. She hugged her friend.

"I don't know. I got a call from the building manager saying the building was on fire." Heidi glanced over at an older woman a few yards from us, standing next to a gray-haired man. Both were wearing light jackets.

"How bad is it?" Nicole asked, staring at the row of stores. The night was cool and she had nothing more on than a short skirt and tank top. Goosebumps covered her arms.

"I have no idea. No one is telling us anything." Heidi flashed me a grateful smile. It wasn't a huge smile, but it was enough to thank me for being there for Nicole. "Mason, this is my boyfriend, Chris."

"Good to meet you, man," he said. "I don't know if you've heard, but Heidi's a huge fan of the band and of you. So much so that I'd be jealous if I didn't know how much she loves me."

I had a feeling he was just saying that to temporarily distract Heidi and Nicole from the fire.

And it worked. Heidi elbowed him in the stomach—gently, but enough to give him a hard time for his comment. "Of course, if you were shirtless right now like Mason, I'd love you even more." She gave him a faint smile to show that she was trying to stay calm.

Chris chuckled. "Sorry, but the T-shirt stays on."

We watched in silence as the firefighters worked. A few more people, who I soon figured out owned the other businesses in the strip mall, showed up and asked us questions, but quickly realized we didn't have any more in the way of answers than they did. They moved to the side, lost in their own uncertainty.

Nicole shivered. I pulled her against me and wrapped her in my arms. She leaned back, exhausted but unable to leave.

A sudden need to do whatever I could to protect her rushed through me, and I kissed the top of her head. She sighed and sank deeper against me.

The early signs of dawn were stretching across the sky when a firefighter approached the man and the woman Heidi had indicated earlier. Without saying anything to us, Heidi walked over to the small group. Chris, Nicole, and I joined them.

"Fortunately, the sprinklers were working and the fire was quickly extinguished," the fire chief said. "Only the store at the end suffered some structural damage due to the flames. Unfortunately, the smoke and water damage is extensive, and the premises won't be usable in their current state."

"When can we go inside and check the damage?" Nicole asked.

"I'd say not for a few more hours. Go home and get some sleep. Call your insurance company. We have to finish our investigation first, and then we'll let you back inside to remove whatever you need."

"Do you have any idea what caused it?" Chris asked.

"Not yet. It started in the pet store, but for now we don't know the cause."

The group asked him a few more questions, but for the

most part there was nothing more he could tell us. Heidi and Nicole made plans to return later in the morning, and I drove Nicole home.

It was six-fifteen by the time we entered her house. She traipsed to the kitchen, which like the hallway was now a gray-blue, and removed the single key from the counter. "I need to walk Bernie," she told me, palming the key for his owner's house. Her words were slurred from exhaustion.

"No, what you need is sleep, Nicole. Go to bed and I'll let him out to do his business. We can walk him before we go back to the shop later."

She opened her mouth to argue. I placed my finger against her lips. "Either you go willingly to bed or I'll hoist you over my shoulder and carry you upstairs."

"Mason, it really isn't necessary. I'll be fine. Plus you're supposed to return to L.A. today, since you're hitting the road in three days."

"Hey, as long as I'm back there by Friday afternoon, I'll be okay. Which means I can stick around until then and help you and Heidi out. So unless you're planning to kick me out on my ass, you're stuck with me." Besides, if Zack were here, he would've done the same. I was merely filling in for him while he was away.

You just keep telling yourself that, said an annoying voice in my head, almost as if rolling its eyes.

It took a few seconds, but she eventually nodded. Her eyes drifted shut for a heartbeat and she swayed on her feet.

"C'mon, I'll help you." I was prepared to scoop her up and follow through with my original threat of carrying her upstairs, but she started toward them before I had a chance.

I parked my hand on her lower back and assisted her up to her room. Once I had her settled back in bed, I left to deal with the oversized beast next door.

A car drove past, likely on its Wednesday morning

commute to work, as I walked next door. I opened the front door and called out, "Morning, Bernie."

A deep woof answered, and a beat later the monster of a dog lumbered into the hallway from the living room and barked again. He leaned against me, the same way he usually did with Nicole whenever we had walked him during the past four days.

"Hey, dude," I said, rubbing his side the way he liked it. "Nicole's still sleeping, so you've got me for a few minutes. But I'm only taking you out to do your business, okay? We'll be back later to take you for a walk."

At the word "walk," Bernie let out a rumbling bark. I guessed I shouldn't have used that term. Now he had expectations that I wasn't planning to meet.

I retrieved his leash from the hall closet, along with his poop bags. "All right, let's get outta here," I said, snapping the leash onto his collar.

Bernie was obviously eager to do his doggy business. He dragged me out the door as soon as I opened it. If Nicole had been the one holding his leash, I wouldn't have been surprised if he'd dragged her along on the ground behind him. Determination was his middle name.

We walked a few yards before Bernie dropped the biggest dump known to dogkind. With a groan, I crouched down and scooped it up with the blue bag. Thank God Kirk couldn't see me now—he might've given me a hard time, claiming I must be in love with Nicole because I was picking up the monster's shit so she could sleep.

"C'mon, boy." I tugged on his leash, hinting I wanted to return to his house. Bernie yanked me forward instead. Evidently he wanted to sniff out a squirrel or two.

"Look, I get you're a bachelor and you don't understand. After all, I'm a bachelor too. But unlike you, I love sex and right now there's a warm, sexy woman waiting for me. And yes, I know that she and I won't be having sex once I'm in bed with her. That's okay. But what I would like to do is hold her while I still can—because in three days I'm hitting the road again, and it's back to mindless one-night stands with groupies. So give me a break and let's go home."

I stumbled as what I had said about the one-night stands being mindless hit me. What the hell was wrong with me? Since when did I consider them mindless?

Bernie woofed and resumed heading in the direction I didn't want to go. I huffed a long breath. So much for our man-to-man talk.

"Okay, you win." I had a feeling I wouldn't enjoy what would happen to me if I tried to get my own way. He looked like the kind of dog you didn't want to piss off if you could help it.

Luckily, he was also the kind of dog who didn't like to go for long walks. After traveling two blocks, he decided that walking was overrated and turned around. So I was happy when I opened the door to his house and he went inside without complaint. I washed my hands thoroughly and jogged the short distance back to Nicole's home.

In her room, I slipped out of my clothes and carefully climbed under the covers, doing my best not to disturb the sleeping blonde next to me. I watched her for a few minutes before sleep crept into my brain and body. The last thing I remembered was thinking how much I would miss her once I returned to my regular life.

13

NICOLE

I stood in the doorway of Blooming Love, unable to take another step inside as I surveyed the disaster. Tears blurred my vision.

Heidi was standing in the middle of the mess, Chris next to her. She turned around, taking it all in. The crushed flowers on the floor. The smoke-covered walls. The shattered vases. The upturned metal containers that had once held flowers. The dirty tile floor beneath a layer of water.

I stepped forward. Glass crunched under my sneaker. I opened my mouth to say something, but the words couldn't squeeze past the tightening in my throat.

"It's all ruined," Heidi whispered, voice strained with unshed tears.

I moved closer to her, another round of crunching glass accompanying me. "We'll start anew. We can redesign it. Finally make it the place we've dreamed of." We'd never had the money to do that before. But thanks to the insurance money we'd be getting, it was going to be possible.

She surveyed the destroyed store again. "You're right," she finally said.

I nodded, wishing it was as simple as that. Sure, the store would be better than before and the insurance would pay for it, and it would also cover the lost income while we waited for the place to be renovated. But that was as far as our insurance coverage went. So if it took awhile for our business income to get back up to what it had been before the fire, we'd be hurting.

I kept that to myself. Heidi didn't need to worry about it yet.

"Oh God!" Her hand flew to her mouth. "I've got the Walsh-Philips wedding next weekend."

"Not a problem. You can make everything at my house. And you can use it as a work space for the other events that have already been booked. Everything's going to be all right."

She nodded, still in a daze. "You're right," she said as she surveyed the mess. "And that vacation you've been putting off for forever? Now you can finally take it."

"True." Not that I could afford to go anywhere.

"Maybe the beach," she said, her voice faint and distracted. "You wanted ideas for your glassware designs. That would be a perfect spot for it." She glanced at me, her eyes glossy with tears.

"True again." The smile I gave her was small, but enough to convince her I was on board with her idea.

I left Heidi with Chris and Mason as they searched through the wreckage for anything salvageable, and entered my office. The computer was unusable, thanks to water damage, but luckily I had my laptop at home and could use it in the meantime.

I sorted through the desk drawers. Some of the papers had been ruined by the water that had leaked in, but the rest were fine, though they reeked of smoke.

"How's everything looking?" Mason asked behind me.

I glanced over my shoulder and gave him the same smile I had just given Heidi.

He shut the door and joined me by the desk. "There's something you haven't told your friend, isn't there?"

I shook my head. "It's nothing. I'm just tired."

"That doesn't surprise me, but I know that's not it. Financially, will you be okay while the store's closed?"

Inwardly I cringed because he'd nailed it so easily. Instead of looking at him I fixed my eyes on the papers in my hand. "Look, Mason, you're not my boyfriend and you're not my brother," I bit out, the reality of everything crushing me under what felt like a ten-ton boulder. "None of this has anything to do with you. I'm not even sure why you're still in Desert Springs."

God, why are you being such a fucking bitch? a snippy voice in my head asked.

Because he was leaving anyway, I reminded it. And more than likely I'd never see him again. That was what we had agreed to in the beginning, back before we had sex the first time. Our days of playing house should've ended already.

"Fine," Mason said, his tone harsher than I'd heard over the past few days—harsher but also heavy with regret. "I'll go."

As his booted feet moved slowly to my office door, shame lashed me.

Blinking away the sting of tears, I peered up. "I'm sorry. I shouldn't have said that. It's just that you've got more important things to deal with than my problems. And that's exactly what this is—my problem. But don't worry, I'll be fine." Somehow I'd make it work. I could always take on a few new website-design clients, if it came to that.

Mason took a step toward me. "Look, I know I'm not your boyfriend, and I'm definitely not your brother. But what I am is your friend, Nicole." He took another step forward. "I've enjoyed hanging out with you—especially since we have no expectations between us. I can't remember the last time that happened. These days, most people want something from me."

His last words didn't surprise me. I guess being a celebrity came at a cost.

The small smile I gave him held more meaning and emotion than any of the words I'd hastily spoken.

"Does that mean it's okay with you if I hang around a few more days to help out?" he asked. "As your friend?"

I nodded. "I would like that."

Mason and I returned to the main part of the store, where Heidi was standing at the front counter sorting through the contents of a cardboard box. She looked up.

"One of the fridges is still working, but the other one is dead. Luckily, most of my tools are still okay," she said, doing her best to sound strong, but the slight wavering of her voice betrayed how she was really feeling. "I just have to clean them so they don't rust. And I found enough supplies for next week-end's wedding, so I won't have to place an emergency order."

"Will there be enough room in the working fridge to store the flowers?" The shipment was due a few days before the wedding, and there was no way the flowers would stay fresh if left in my house. Not unless I cranked up the air-conditioning —and even if I did, I didn't think it would get cold enough. Like everything else in the house, it was an old model. I was surprised it still worked.

"There should be," Heidi said.

We spent another two hours sorting through the debris. Mason found a broom and swept the shattered glass and destroyed flowers into a pile in the corner.

By the time we were finished, our feet were wet, we were filthy and reeked of smoke, and our bodies were ready to call it a day. A few hours of sleep wasn't enough. And I'd had more sleep than Mason, who had dealt with Bernie first.

I glanced over at him and my heart did a flutter kick at the sight of him, dirty and carrying a box. He could have bailed this morning while I was sleeping and headed back to L.A. He didn't have to be here in the store with me. He didn't have to help me with assessing the damage. And he certainly didn't have to walk Bernie . . . but he had.

"You ready to go?" I asked him. We said our goodbyes to Heidi and Chris and drove back to my house. "I'm going to have a shower and then walk Bernie."

Carrying the paperwork I'd brought home with me, I climbed the stairs, each step feeling as though I were wading through a vat of drying glue. In my room I dumped the paperwork on my desk, grabbed clean clothes from the closet, and went into the bathroom.

After turning the shower on full blast, I stripped out of my clothes and stepped under the spray. I closed my eyes, but the memory of the destruction in the store was too much, and a sob broke free.

Unable to hold it back any longer, I let the tears fall. With the water raining hard against the tub, I could cry without Mason hearing me.

Suddenly the shower curtain moved to the side, freaking the hell out of me, and I shrieked. Before I could say anything coherent, Mason stepped into the shower—fully dressed.

His T-shirt was instantly wet from the water pelting him. The soaked fabric clung to his body, showcasing his perfect muscles. Normally I would've been turned on. This time an unexpected laugh bubbled free. "You were that eager for a shower, you couldn't wait long enough to take your clothes off first?"

"I heard you crying."

"So you figured you would climb in with all your clothes on, to make me laugh?" If that had been his plan, it had worked. I giggled uncontrollably, so overwhelmed by everything that had happened that I was unable to stop laughing.

"I was thinking that you should join me on tour." He said it with such a straight face, I couldn't help but laugh some more. He was obviously kidding.

"I don't think that will solve any of my problems," I said after I'd calmed down and taken a breath. "Besides, I need to stay here to help with the store renovations."

"Actually, it's a perfect solution. The band needs a social media person to travel with us and post regularly on our social media sites. With your background, you'd be perfect for it. And just so you know, I'm asking you as a friend, not because we've slept together."

"But I have a job."

"You can do this one while you wait for the store to reopen. Tour with us for a few months. Once it's ready to reopen, you can come back here and the band will find someone new to take over the social media job."

"I can't be gone that long. Heidi will need my help."

"For what? I thought she was the one who does the floral arrangements, and you stick to the business and marketing side of things. You can always do that on the road with the band. We have computers and Wi-Fi on the bus."

Was he for real? Or just plain crazy? I had a life here. And by life, I meant I had a job that took most of my time. A job that was for the most part on hold for now, thanks to the fire.

But what he was suggesting did sound tempting. I had always done the sensible thing. The boring thing. And look where that had gotten me—nowhere but a string of boring dates that Heidi and Cindy kept setting me up on. Before that, I'd been busy with college and working part-time. I'd never done anything adventurous. What would it hurt to do something different for once? It wasn't like I was running off to marry Mason. And it would be great job experience.

Plus I wasn't ready to say goodbye to Mason yet. In the few days he'd been here, I'd had more fun with him than I'd had in the past year. We'd taken Bernie on walks several times a day, cooked together, watched movies, and worked on projects around the house. And unlike with my recent boring dates, none of it had felt awkward.

The object of my thoughts pushed a wet strand of hair from my face, reminding me I was naked in the shower and he wasn't.

"So what do you think?" he asked.

"I don't need a job 'cause you feel sorry for me."

"That's not what this is. You're smart and talented, and I figured you'd be perfect for the position. I mean, if you don't want it, fine. We'll find someone else."

"It's not that . . ." God, what he was offering did sound amazing—a once-in-a-lifetime opportunity.

"So what will it be, then? I already told you the job offer has nothing to do us sleeping together. If I didn't think you could handle it, I wouldn't have asked."

I believed him, even if I was standing in the shower naked. "I have to talk to Heidi first."

"But you're thinking about it, right?"

"Yes. I'm thinking about it."

That got a smile from him, and his entire face lit up. "I swear you won't regret it, Nicole. It will be fun."

"Well, it would definitely be an experience to one day tell my kids about." My gaze wandered down his wet clothing. "Enjoying your shower?"

"If you say yes to coming on tour with me, then yes, I'm enjoying my shower."

I laughed. "Doesn't take much to make you happy, does it?"

He glanced down at his body. "Well, getting out of these wet clothes will make me happy too."

I smiled slyly at him and reached for the hem of his T-shirt. "I think I can help you there."

A few moments later—though it took a lot of tugging,

because wet clothes tended to be reluctant when it came to being removed—Mason stood in front of me naked.

Despite everything that had happened in the past twelve hours, my entire body buzzed at seeing Mason like this, and begged for a whole lot more. I needed to escape the memories of last night's fire and of the damage left behind. I needed to escape my churning thoughts, even if just for a few minutes.

And I needed to do whatever I could to keep from going numb.

"Thanks again for doing that." I pointed at the showerhead he had installed the other day.

"You're welcome." A smug smile slipped onto his face, along with a wicked spark in his eyes, but there was also an edge of uncertainty.

"Maybe we should christen it," I said.

"What do you mean?"

"You know . . ." I reached up and ran the tip of my tongue against the edge of his ear, and smiled at his answering moan. "So, how exactly do we do this?" The romance novels I read always made shower sex sound easy, but I couldn't quite figure out exactly how to do it—the mechanics sounded complex.

Mason stepped closer to me and traced his fingertips up my rib cage. "Are you sure about this?" His voice was a low, sexy rumble in his chest.

"Very."

He cupped my breasts and I released a small whimper. His thumbs brushed against my now perky nipples. The whimper became a moan, and I leaned forward slightly, pressing my breasts against his warm, wet palms.

My fingertips caressed the ridges and valleys of his abs as I explored the sexy terrain. "Do you have any condoms with you?"

He had bought a box yesterday, since he'd already used the condoms he'd had stored in his wallet.

"In my jeans back pocket. Give me a second." He slid the shower curtain to the side and stepped out of the tub, allowing some of the spray to follow him. He returned a moment later with the foil square. The man was a Boy Scout . . . always prepared.

He slipped a hand between my thighs and traced my folds with his fingers. At his touch, my legs practically buckled under me. I leaned back against the cool tile wall to keep from making nice with the floor.

"Look at me, Nicole. I want you looking in my eyes when I make you come. I want to see the effect I have on you."

"As if you don't already know." I settled my hands on his shoulders as his fingers teased my clit. I moaned again as a warmth ignited between my legs.

"Eyes open, Nicole."

I hadn't even realized they were closed. I opened them and was met by Mason's warm brown eyes, sparkling with challenge and lust. His mouth was close enough that if I stretched my head up slightly, I could kiss him. And I really wanted to kiss him.

Mason's skilled fingers continued stroking me . . . until the warmth between my legs flared into a white-hot heat. "Oh God!" The heat commenced low in my belly, then quickly radiated outward, turning me into molten liquid.

And forget about keeping my eyes open. My head fell forward against Mason's shoulder and I dug my fingers into his flesh.

Once the tremors had subsided, I glanced up at the man who knew how to turn me inside out. "Wow."

The word was barely out before his mouth was on mine and we were kissing. His cock pressed against my stomach, letting me know that it yearned for its turn. I rubbed my body against it, eliciting a groan from Mason.

Pride rushed through me at the effect I was having on him. It made me feel strong and sexy. It made me feel desirable.

It made me want to harness this feeling for the next time I went out with a man. Maybe then my dates wouldn't end the way they always did, with me unable to get away fast enough.

I paid no attention to the annoying voice that pointed out the guys weren't the only ones to blame when it came to the dates being duds.

Mason gently turned me around so my back was facing him. "Do you want to stop or keep going?" he asked.

"Keep going."

"Place your hands against the wall and bend over," he growled in my ear, and a shiver of desire shimmied through my body.

I parked my hands on the wall opposite the shower and walked them down until my torso was parallel to the tub. Hot water would have rained against my butt, but Mason was standing behind me, blocking it.

I heard the crinkle of the condom wrapper as the steam from the shower hugged me. A moment later, the tip of Mason's cock teased my entrance, then he slowly pushed himself inside me. He kept going until he was fully seated, filling me in more ways than I'd ever imagined possible.

His finger found my clit and teased it again. I gasped and my body rejoiced. As I came close to falling off the edge once more, he removed the finger from my happy zone and thrust his cock in and out of me.

It didn't take much work on his side before the softest part of me clenched around his hardness, as if it wasn't interested in ever letting him leave. And considering how the bathroom's tile walls amplified my cries of ecstasy, I figured that everyone down the street now knew I'd just come hard. Again.

But if I was loud, that was nothing compared to Mason. As

he came apart he let out a guttural noise that would've impressed a bull.

Afterward I expected him to pull out of me right away, but he didn't. Instead, he bent over and rained kisses on my back. "Christ, that was hot," he said, and no way was I going to argue with that.

His hands gently caressed my body before he finally pulled away. "Don't go anywhere," he said, then stepped out of the tub to dispose of the condom.

He returned a moment later, and with his strong hands and a vanilla-scented body wash thoroughly cleaned every part of me.

I couldn't remember the last time a guy had made me feel this alive and this safe.

14

MASON

Two days after the fire, Nicole and I drove to L.A. in my car. Heidi had been all for the idea of Nicole traveling with the band for the next three months. The two women had spent the remainder of the time Nicole and I were in Desert Springs planning out every detail of the new store. Heidi would keep Nicole updated on what was happening, and forward anything Nicole needed to deal with while she was away.

Now I just had to tell the band about her. I'd spoken with Nolan yesterday but hadn't mentioned Nicole or what I had been doing while I was away. I had been telling the truth when I told her the band needed to hire someone to handle our social media. Until recently Jared and Aaron had been responsible for it. Our publicist had suggested we hire someone to take over the task, but I hadn't exactly given the guys any choice when it came to Nicole. I had hired her without consulting them first.

I'll admit that when I came up with the idea, I hadn't really been thinking things through. I'd just known that for the past few days, before the fire, I'd been having fun. Sure, I loved touring and I loved my life in L.A., but something was missing. I still didn't know what it was, but in the time I'd spent with Nicole, even after the fire, the feeling that something was missing was less intense than it had been before.

I didn't know if it would vanish with her joining us on tour, but what I did know was that I wasn't ready to walk away from her just yet. Eventually I would have to when she returned to her life in Desert Springs, but in the meantime we might as well enjoy ourselves.

We spent the rest of the journey talking and joking around and listening to my favorite rock station. I pointed out when the band's latest single was on.

"Do the guys know I'm not some huge fan of the band?" she asked while we were stopped at a red light, and then blushed. "I mean, because, you know . . ." She gave a quick shrug.

"I haven't told them. It's actually better that you're not a huge fan. Female fans tend to get all giddy around us. It's impossible to even talk to some of them. It's fine when they just want an autograph, but it wouldn't be so great if they were working for us."

"But eventually they'll realize you guys are nothing more than regular people, and won't act that way anymore."

"One would hope. But in the meantime they'd be pretty useless. With you, we skip all of that."

She laughed. "You do realize if I bumped into Luke Bryan, I'd be exactly like the fan you just described."

"Who the hell is Luke Bryan?" The light turned green and I pressed my foot on the accelerator.

"Oh my God, you don't know who Luke Bryan is?" she practically squealed.

"Not a clue. He's not a singer from some lame boy band, is he?"

She laughed again. "He's just one of the hottest singers in

country music. He's won numerous awards. I can't believe you've never heard of him."

I lifted one hand from the steering wheel and smacked my palm flat against my chest. "I must admit, Nicole, I'm heartbroken. You've never gushed over me that way."

"You poor baby. I'm sure you'll get over it." Laughter filled her voice, reminding me once again why I'd asked her to join the tour. She enjoyed teasing me, but it wasn't like she was attempting to get into my pants. Not that she hadn't already been in them. Nor would I complain if she tried to get into them again.

We pulled up in front of Nolan's house an hour later. The rest of the band had already arrived, their cars either on the driveway or parked in the street.

Nicole climbed out of the car, and I took the moment to enjoy the view. She was wearing a dark sundress covered with tiny pale pink flowers. The short, flowing skirt was the kind that would flash her ass and panties if a wind caught hold of it. She wasn't wearing much when it came to jewelry, other than a narrow beaded bracelet in black and teal. But it was the short black cowboy boots with the rope design etched in the leather that gave it away—she wasn't your usual Pushing Limits fan. She looked like she'd be more comfortable at a country music concert than she would be at a rock concert.

But either way she looked hot.

We walked to the front door, and I rang the doorbell. Rocky's small yet determined bark answered from the other side. The door opened, revealing Nolan holding on to the collar of the eager eight-month-old golden retriever.

At seeing me again, Rocky yipped excitedly.

"Oh, aren't you just adorable?" Nicole said, her voice pitched higher than usual. She knelt in front of the puppy and offered him her hand to sniff. Forget sniffing—he was more interested in jumping onto her lap, his front paws already there.

"Not quite Bernie, is he?" I said, smiling at Nicole's excitement at seeing Rocky.

Nolan lifted his eyebrow in a question.

"Nolan, this is Nicole. She's the sister of a friend of mine." Who would kill me if he found out what we'd been doing the last few days. As it was, Nicole had made me promise not to say anything to Zack when it came to the fire. She didn't want him to worry when there was nothing he could do.

He hadn't even suspected that I would do the deed with his sister. But why would he? He didn't know me as well as he thought he did. To him, I was probably the guy who had once been dragged down by a gambling addiction and drug abuse. Neither of those activities had given me the energy or drive to have a sex life.

And no, I hadn't switched from one addiction to another—I hadn't become a sex addict. If I went without sex for a period of time, I didn't get the shakes and I didn't get moody. I could survive.

Whether I *wished* to go without sex for a period of time was another thing. If it was offered, who was I to say no?

"She's our new social media person," I explained to Nolan.

A furrow formed between his eyebrows, unseen by Nicole, who was attempting to extricate herself from Rocky's enthusiastic welcome.

When she finally succeeded, she stood up and held out her hand to Nolan. "Hi. It's nice to meet you."

"Nice to meet you too," Nolan said politely, but I knew him well enough to understand what he was really thinking . . . and it didn't bode well for me.

I mentally shrugged it off. We needed someone to help us manage our social media, and we couldn't do better than Nicole. The guys would quickly realize this and would be thanking me in no time. Or at least I assumed they would be.

"Everyone's out back," he told us, pulling Rocky away from the front door.

I stepped into the house. Hailey had been busy while her boyfriend was touring. From what I could see, the inside had been repainted a light brown and the furniture seemed like a modern version of rustic, with lighter colors and clean lines. The only reason I knew those terms was because my aunt was an interior designer. Or at least she had been the last time I'd seen her and the rest of my family.

"Place looks good," I said.

"Definitely an improvement over my old apartment," Nolan replied, smiling in the same goofy way he always did whenever he was thinking about his girlfriend.

"Rocky!" Logan said from the kitchen doorway.

The puppy barked at his favorite five-year-old and bounded toward Jared's son. Logan kneeled and let Rocky lick him. Nothing was cuter than a little boy giggling over puppy kisses, as he liked to call them.

Taking hold of Nicole's hand, I led her over to the pair.

"Hi, Uncle Mason," Logan said and signed, still kneeling. He held up his fist to me.

I fist-bumped him. "Hey, Logan, this is my friend Nicole. She's going to work with the band while we're on tour. Nicole, this is Logan, Jared's son."

"Nice to meet you," she said to him.

"Do you curse like Uncle Mason?" he said, a hopeful expression on his dirt-smudged face.

I laughed. "Hate to disappoint you, buddy, but I've yet to hear her swear even once. Besides, I don't think the dollar-per-swear-word rule counts for her. She's a guest."

Nicole's gaze darted to me. "Dollar-per-swear-word rule?"

Nolan snickered. "Jared wasn't thrilled when Mason cussed around his son, especially when Logan started repeating the words. So Aaron suggested that Mason had to cough up a dollar every time he cursed."

I let out a mock huff. But I couldn't complain. I would've felt the same way if our places were reversed. Although at the time, when Jared first adopted the payment rule, he'd had no idea Logan was his son. Probably just as well—otherwise he might have charged me five dollars per word.

"Let's play, Rocky." Logan charged outside with Rocky close on his heels.

"Logan's hearing-impaired?" Nicole asked.

"No, deaf. But he has a cochlear implant, so he can hear a lot of what goes on around him. He just doesn't like listening to music with it. He prefers to feel the vibrations through the floor."

"Jared is the band's guitarist, right?" At my nod she added, "That's so heartbreaking that his son can't listen to you guys play."

I shrugged. "It is what it is."

Outside, I introduced Nicole to everyone else in the backyard, including Hailey and Callie. Beckie was also there, standing next to Kirk—close enough for me to wonder if something was going on between them.

Like Nolan, the guys looked less than impressed when I introduced Nicole as our new social media person and said that she'd be joining us on tour. But also like Nolan, they managed to keep Nicole from guessing that something was wrong.

Food and drinks had been set up on the patio, and Aaron had returned to manning the grill. I grabbed a beer for myself and was pouring Nicole a glass of wine when Nolan approached the table.

"Band meeting in the living room," was all he said before heading inside.

Nicole was busy talking to the three other women, all of them laughing at something one of them had said. I handed her the glass of wine. "The band is having a brief meeting to get me up to speed since I've been away for a few days. I'll be right back."

She smiled sweetly at me, and my cock twitched at the thought of those luscious lips on it.

Keeping that erotic thought in my head, I entered the house, braced for the interrogation I was about to face.

15

MASON

I entered the living room to find Nolan, Jared, Kirk, and Aaron taking up all the available seating—leaving me with no choice but to stand. On the mantel, the antique clock counted down the seconds until they would deliver my sentence. Tick. Tock. Tick-you-are-royally-screwed. Tock.

"Did I miss anything while I was gone?" I asked, doing my best to buy time before the shit hit the fan.

Nolan's gaze jumped from Jared to Kirk, then to Aaron. They nodded for him to speak. "You didn't. But apparently we did," he said. "What's this crap about you hiring your friend's sister without consulting us first? This band is a democracy. Which means we all get to vote on the person we want to hire —not just you."

Knowing I wouldn't be able to joke my way out of this, I held my hands up, surrendering to my fate. "Look, I'm sorry I didn't tell you about Nicole sooner. Her brother is overseas, serving with the navy. He was worried about her when he couldn't get hold of her, and asked me to see if she was okay."

"I gather she was fine," Jared said, sitting next to Kirk on the couch, his arms folded across his chest. "So why did it take you so long to get back?"

I snorted. "I would've thought you'd be too busy screwing your new wife to notice I was gone. Obviously you've got your priorities fucked up."

He huffed a laugh. "Don't worry about me, Mas. I've got my priorities figured out just fine. Kirk filled me in on your absence."

"So if Nicole was fine," Aaron said, "why not return to L.A. as soon as you figured it out?"

"Because I needed a break before we started touring again, so I decided to stay there for a few days."

"What you're really saying"—he leveled his gaze at me—"is that because you were too busy fucking your friend's sister, you couldn't be bothered to return until today?"

Ouch. Guess I deserved that . . . mostly because it was true. "Actually, that's not the reason. She needed help fixing things around the house, so I stuck around to help her out." At least it wasn't a complete lie. "She and her friend own a floral business, but there was a fire in the building a few days ago. Their store suffered major smoke and water damage. It will be a few months before they can open it again, and since we'd already agreed to hire someone to handle our social media, I thought Nicole could do it in the meantime.

"And she is a great choice," I added. "She does the social media for her business and has a marketing degree. She knows what she's doing."

"So the only reason you hired her was because of her qualifications, and not because she's a nice piece of ass?" Aaron asked, one eyebrow raised.

Tick. Tock.

"Her being pretty has nothing to do with it." It didn't hurt, though.

"And where's she going to sleep while we're touring?" Nolan

asked, still not looking thrilled about the situation. None of the guys did.

"The same place as us. On the bus."

He leaned forward in the armchair, elbows on knees. "Our bus?"

"Of course. How's she going to pretend to be us on social media if she's not around us?"

"What Nolan is asking," Kirk said, "is where are you planning for her to sleep on the bus? If she's our employee, that means you can't be fucking her."

Tick. Tock. Tick. Tock.

I bit back what I had planned to say, because that wouldn't help the situation. Besides, I didn't want them to believe that was the real reason I'd brought Nicole back with me. I also didn't care to admit that something about her had gotten under my skin and I wasn't ready to walk away from her just yet.

"She can stay in the back room." In addition to the narrow bunk beds in the middle of the bus, there was a small back room with a larger bed, where Hailey and Callie stayed whenever they visited Nolan and Jared. But other than that, the room remained empty. And because of that, it had become an unofficial storage room.

"And what happens when Hailey or Callie join us?" Kirk asked.

"Then Nicole can bunk on whichever bed is vacated when that happens. It's not like Nolan and Jared stay in their bunks whenever Hailey or Callie visit." Although in Jared's case, Logan usually took over his bunk so his parents could spend some private moments together without the five-year-old. Not that he knew it.

"And she's okay sleeping on the bus with us?" Aaron asked, sounding somewhat doubtful a woman would want to do that if she wasn't involved with one of us . . . unless she had other motives. Like when the last girl Aaron had hooked up with had joined us on tour with the goal of exposing us in ways we didn't wish to be exposed.

"Why wouldn't she be? It's not like we're going to hurt her. And she'll be our employee, which means we have control over what she can say. It will be in the contract." The same confidentiality clause all employees of Pushing Limits and Endless Motion had to sign. Anyone who violated the agreement would be facing a lawsuit.

"All right," Nolan said. "I'm fine with it if everyone else agrees to hiring her. But"—he gestured at me with his finger—"like Kirk pointed out, if she's our employee, then you can't fuck her. At all."

The loud, crisp chime of the antique clock intruded on the meeting, as if to voice its opinion. I had a feeling its vote wasn't in my favor.

For a second I considered reminding them that she was my friend's little sister, but while Zack might have believed I wouldn't do something as low as fuck her, the guys clearly thought otherwise.

"Fine." But since she wasn't our employee yet, technically I could have sex with her one more time before we hit the road. I kept that to myself. It was bad enough they'd already guessed what she and I had been up to. I just hoped they didn't hold it against her.

The women were still chatting when we joined them outside. Hailey and Callie wrapped their arms around their guys' waists, making the most of the time with them before our tour bus would pull away tomorrow.

My fingers itched to touch Nicole, but I suspected this would also be a violation of the upcoming contract. And although it wasn't an issue until the contract actually arrived, there was no point flaunting the fact that I planned to ignore the no-sex rule for tonight.

"Hey, Logan," I said, needing to find a way to distract my

thoughts from what I intended to do to Nicole tonight. "You want to play soccer?" I signed "soccer."

"Yay!" was his answer. Like at Jared's wedding, we divided into teams, although this time we didn't have as many players.

"I'll play," Nicole said when we realized Logan's team had one less player than mine.

We got into position, Nicole barefoot. Callie, who was officiating the game, threw the ball in. It landed on the grass closer to Logan, and he kicked the ball down the pint-sized field as Callie and Beckie cheered him on. He giggled as he kicked it into the goal past Hailey, who used to play on a women's collegiate team. She pretended to block him but didn't put any effort into it.

Hailey kicked the ball to Nicole. She easily gained control of it and dribbled it toward my goal, which was nothing more than two deck chairs set two yards apart. And damn, was that girl good, especially considering she wasn't wearing shoes.

I saw it on Aaron's face the moment it hit him that Nicole knew exactly what she was doing. Nolan and Hailey weren't the only talented players in the group.

Also realizing this, Jared made a play to stop her, but he failed to block her in time. She kicked the ball and sent it sailing toward the kid-sized goal. Aaron dove at the ball, but he wasn't fast enough. It traveled under his outstretched hands.

"You never mentioned she could play," Nolan said.

"I didn't know. But with her on our team, the roadies don't have a chance of beating us." Like with our last tour, for this tour we'd found roadies who loved playing soccer whenever we all had a chance. And most of them had grown up playing the sport, which left us outmatched.

But not this time.

The guys couldn't fault my decision to hire Nicole now.

"Where did you learn to play like that?" I asked her.

"Zack. As you know, he played soccer in high school and taught me a thing or two."

"I'd say more than a thing or two," Hailey said.

"And there's a chance I might've played it in high school and college," Nicole said, laughing.

"That would do it," Hailey replied with a huge grin.

At one point the teams were tied as Nicole dribbled toward Aaron, who was guarding my team's goal. No way was I letting her score again . . . completely on principle, mind you. I wrapped my arms around her waist, pulling her against me.

Laughing, she kicked the ball to Hailey, seemingly unaffected by our closeness—unlike me. Desire shot through me at the feel of her warm, soft body against mine.

Hailey passed the ball to Nolan and he scored. Callie blew the whistle, signaling the end of the game. We shook hands with the opposition, even though what I really wanted to do was kiss Nicole long and hard. As it was, after tonight I wouldn't get to do that anymore.

The evening wound down around nine o'clock, with Jared and Callie needing to take a very tired Logan home to bed. He could barely keep his eyes open.

"Remember," Jared said to me, "we need to meet at the mall parking lot at seven tomorrow morning. If you're late, we'll have to leave without you."

I snorted. "Right, as if you would do that."

Kirk slapped me on the back. "Just like you'd never tell the bus driver I was napping when I'd told you I was going for a run?"

"Hey, I couldn't help that he misunderstood me." Or that he understood me perfectly and no one had questioned why Kirk wasn't on the bus when we pulled away from the parking lot.

Kirk rolled his eyes but didn't say anything else, having long since gotten over what happened.

Nicole said goodbye to the women and promised to keep an

eye on their men. "Don't worry, I'll fight off the groupies with my bare hands if I have to," she said, smiling.

"What, not only are you our social media person," I said, "you're also Nolan's and Jared's bodyguard?" I grinned and addressed the two of them. "You guys need to develop some fucking balls if a bunch of barely dressed women scare you."

I reached back and removed my wallet from my pocket, then pulled out two bucks and handed the money to Logan. I figured using "balls" in the context that I had would result in a penalty, like saying "fucking" did. Might as well save me time—and a lecture.

I pretended to look remorseful as I gave him the money, but then winked at him. He giggled—with Jared no doubt mentally cursing me for corrupting his son.

"You're really good with Logan," Nicole said as we drove back to my loft.

"He's a cute kid."

With a sigh, like the one all women let out when they're fantasizing about having children one day, she shook her head. "That's true, but you're also a natural when it comes to kids. Just like you were with Bree the other day."

I barked a laugh. "I somehow think Jared and Callie will disagree with you there."

"But not Logan. He looks up to you."

"That's because I'm six-two and he's barely three feet." Although I couldn't see Nicole because I was watching the road, I was certain she was rolling her eyes.

"That's not what I meant and you know it. It's hard to explain, but it's like he worships you."

"That's because I'm unofficially funding his college education with my inability to quit swearing around him."

Nicole's laugh was possibly the hottest sound I'd ever heard, and my dick got excited. Like it normally did whenever she laughed. "I'm sure that doesn't hurt either. But like I said, you'll make a great father one day."

No, my dad had been a great father, even if he did turn his back on me. But that was completely my fault. I couldn't blame him for that. Until I screwed things up for the tenth time, he had always been there for me. If I had a child, I wouldn't be around for him the same way my father had been there for me. The band came first—always would.

As we drove Nicole and I lapsed into silence, but not the uncomfortable kind. The kind that felt like everything was all right with the world, even when it wasn't. "So how come I didn't know you played soccer?" I finally asked. "You impressed the hell out of Nolan."

"I don't know—it just never came up. So, does that mean I'm now in when it comes to the job? That's what the meeting was really about, wasn't it?"

I'd hoped it wasn't so obvious. "I don't know what you mean."

"C'mon, Mason. Are you seriously telling me that tonight wasn't the first time they'd heard that I'd accepted the position?" She didn't sound pissed, so that was good. Actually, she seemed more curious than anything else.

"We did need someone to help us out, but we hadn't gotten around to hiring anyone. I just took the initiative and hired you for the interim. Besides, you're qualified for the job." Other than the part where I'd been fucking her during the past few days. "Your credentials speak for themselves. Plus Callie and Hailey like you, so that made it a done deal in Jared's and Nolan's eyes."

"And it didn't hurt that I could play soccer, huh?" she said, laughter in her voice.

"If you could play hockey, I wouldn't be surprised if Kirk offered to marry you."

"He likes hockey?"

"That would be like asking if penguins like cold weather. Rumor has it he was headed to play in the NHL."

"So what happened?"

I shrugged. "No one knows exactly. He doesn't talk about it." *Time to rip off the Band-Aid.* "There's one thing I should tell you." I briefly tore my gaze off the road and looked at her. She was watching me expectantly, her slightly parted lips begging me to skim my tongue over them and taste her.

I pulled my attention back to the road. "After tonight, we can't do what we've been doing."

"You mean we can't be friends with benefits?"

My ego might have felt a whole lot better if she could've at least pretended to be disappointed at the news. "That's right."

"Why after tonight?"

"I was hoping we can still screw around tonight . . ." One side of my mouth curled up. "For old times' sake."

She laughed. Despite the bruising my ego had just taken, I took this as a good sign.

16

NICOLE

"I was hoping we can still screw around tonight . . ." Mason's gaze was on the road, but in the headlight of the oncoming vehicle, I could make out the smirk on his face. "For old times' sake."

I laughed. How could I not? That sounded just like the Mason I'd already grown to care for—as a friend. But what he said about us not having sex together after tonight made sense. It prevented us from crossing over the line of professionalism, and it gave me a chance to take a giant step back from what we had been together in Desert Springs. And I wasn't talking about the friends part.

A horrifying thought hit me in the stomach with the force of an out-of-control ten-ton truck. "Your bandmates . . . they don't know we've been sleeping together, right?" *Please tell me no.*

The look on Mason's face said it all.

Crap. "You told them?" I squeaked.

"No, I didn't tell them. They guessed."

"That's not making me feel any better." That his band-mates had immediately guessed that I'd had sex with him suggested he'd been with a lot of women during his time with the band . . . and *that* suggested he'd be with a lot of women on this tour, with me knowing about every one of them.

"I'm sorry, Nicole. I didn't mean to hurt you," he said, glancing at me briefly before returning his gaze to the road. His eyes echoed the sentiment. If he could've kept the truth from the band, he would have. For my sake.

"It's okay. You don't owe me any explanations. After tonight, you'll be nothing more than my boss."

Mason gave a small nod.

A few minutes later he pulled into the parking lot of a low-rise building that featured lots of windows. The lawn and garden were well maintained, hinting that the rents weren't exactly low here, but I guessed they also weren't exorbitant, like in some parts of the city.

Unlike on my quiet street back home, a stream of traffic drove past, reminding me that we were no longer in a small town. The less-than-fresh air might have been another clue.

As we rode the elevator to the third floor, the sexual energy between us buzzed like a wire you know you shouldn't touch, but do so anyway. I stared at the elevator door, fighting the craving to throw myself at him. By the time it finally pinged opened, I was bouncing on the balls of my feet, desperate to get moving.

The first thing I noticed when we stepped into his loft a few minutes later was that the place was the complete opposite of my house. The furniture was decidedly masculine and of higher quality. It was also a lot sparser than I would've expected. But who needed much in the way of furniture when you were always on the road, touring?

The walls that weren't glass were either exposed brick or white. At the far end of the open space, a black metal staircase led up to what I figured had to be the bedroom. Black metal railings, like on a balcony, gave the faint impression of bedroom walls.

The kitchen was straight from a magazine, with its shiny stainless steel appliances and black granite counter. The only thing that wasn't out of a home design magazine was the child's drawing on the fridge. I couldn't be sure what it was intended to be, but it made me think of Mason playing the drums. The "Uncle Mason" written in crayon at the top of the page might have something to do with that.

I pointed to the picture. "Who drew this?"

"Logan." Pride lit up his face like a campfire on a cool dark night as he studied the drawing. It was clear to anyone who saw it that he'd make a great father one day. The kind of father who would always be there for his kids, in one way or another.

My ovaries got excited at the thought. Typical. They really needed to read the memo.

Obviously disagreeing with me, they gave me a not-so-subtle hint to kiss him. It was too late to worry about the band and how they had assumed that he and I had already had sex. I had to make tonight count before my sex life hit another long drought.

I stepped into him and brushed my lips against his jaw. "I guess we should make the most of tonight while we still can."

Mason didn't answer with words. But that was because his mouth was too busy kissing mine. It was hard to talk when your tongue was making nice with someone else's.

I wrapped my arms around his neck and pulled myself closer to him, our bodies touching. Every inch of me that brushed against him hummed with need . . . and something else. I would definitely have to make sure I didn't touch him while on tour. My willpower was at an all-time low when it came to this man. I wouldn't want to embarrass myself in front of the band or the roadies.

Or his groupies.

He bent his knees, and the next thing I knew my legs were wrapped around his waist. Our tongues stayed entwined as he walked across the room and up the stairs.

He sat, and only then did I look to see where we were: on a king-sized bed on the upper level. The ceiling, with its dark wooden support beams, stretched high above us. Everything about the loft screamed bachelor. I couldn't imagine him living anywhere but here.

Still straddling him, I gazed into his chocolate-colored eyes and my body practically melted. *Note to self: while with him on tour, do not look into his eyes.* To do so would lead to disaster— and I wouldn't get my work done.

But since I wasn't officially on tour with him yet, I ignored the warning for now and worked on my next goal, which was getting him naked.

Less than thirty seconds later, I had achieved exactly that, but I did have Mason to thank for it. It would seem that I wasn't the only one eager for our last night together.

I slipped my dress over my head. Before I could stretch my arms back to unhook my bra, his arms encircled me. A moment later my bra was dangling from his talented fingers.

"I'm impressed," I said as he dropped the bra onto the floor. "You're like the Houdini of bras."

He chuckled deeply. "Never been called that before."

"No one might have said it, but they were certainly thinking it."

He gave my breasts a light squeeze and skimmed his thumbs against my now perky nipples.

A moan slipped from between my lips. I couldn't help it. It was just as well we weren't going to have sex while on tour. When it came to Mason, there was no way the guys wouldn't know what we were up to. I was that noisy—not that he was much better.

And just to prove it, when he finally plunged into me

several minutes later, the room echoed with our panting breaths, our moans, our not-so-whispered "Oh God" and "Christ, I want to fuck you hard, Nicole." Thank God I wasn't a screamer, or else the entire L.A. police department would've been banging at the door.

Once we were finished, with me sated and limp, Mason disposed of the condom, then rejoined me in bed. He cuddled me as we lay there, my head on his chest, listening to the steady *thump thump thump* of his heart.

The only reason I knew he wasn't asleep was because his fingers were gently stroking my arm. I closed my eyes, drowsiness lapping over me.

"Have you ever been in love?" Mason asked after a few minutes, startling me. Of all the questions he could've asked, that was one I certainly had not been expecting.

I peered up at him, trying to figure out where this had come from. "I had a boyfriend in college. At the time I thought I was in love with him. He graduated a year before me and had a job offer in San Francisco that was too great to turn down. We tried doing the long-distance thing, but it didn't last long."

"What happened?"

"I guess in the end what I'd believed was love wasn't. I cared about him, but I didn't experience an ache in my heart from being away from him like I thought I would. Yes, we talked on the phone and we Skyped, but when he forgot to contact me because he was busy, it didn't bother me. And I'd also forget to contact him. In the end, we realized we were really nothing more than friends and broke up. What about you? Have you ever been in love?"

"Yes, and she broke my heart." For a second his face was a study in pain, but then both sides of his mouth twitched up.

"So what was her name?" I asked, figuring he wasn't as heartbroken as he claimed.

"Meggie Smith. She was nine, I was eight."

I spluttered a laugh. "Ooh, so you prefer older women! So, no other broken hearts after that?"

"Nope. None at all. I'd learned my lesson and wasn't going to risk my heart again."

Despite the humor in his tone, I pushed myself up on my elbows to get a better look at him. Along with humor, there had been something else in his voice.

But whatever it was wasn't on his face. I shifted over him and skimmed my mouth over his.

Which progressed to heavy kissing.

Which resulted in another round of sex.

17

———

NICOLE

A godawful noise blared near my head and intruded on my dream. I groaned, but not in the same way I had in my dream. That sound had been purely erotic.

I pried my eyelids open in time to see Mason lift his hand and slam it down on what I presumed to be his alarm clock. A second later I was rewarded with a glorious silence.

Mason shifted around to face me, and a sly smile broke out on his face. His white teeth gleamed in the dim light of the loft. I couldn't get enough of his smile, especially first thing in the morning when we woke up next to each other. Too bad that was ending as of today.

"Morning." He traced his fingers down my neck to my breasts. I didn't have to look under the sheet to know he was hard and ready for an encore of last night.

Too bad it was an encore we wouldn't get.

I scooted away from his hand. "It's my first day on the job, which means I'm officially off-limits." My girlie parts might have groaned, but they would get over the disappointment soon enough. Or so I hoped.

Before he had a chance to respond, I scrambled out of bed.

"Your first day on the job sucks," Mason grumbled, voice sexy with sleep.

I laughed—because I had to agree with him there—and walked down the steps, the metal cool against the soles of my bare feet.

Downstairs, I opened my suitcase and removed my jeans, white tank top, cowboy belt, and long wraparound cardigan. I might not have looked like a social media specialist for a bunch of rock stars, but at least I would look good and be comfy for our first day on the road.

Using the clothes as something of a shield against Mason's lust-filled gaze, I hurried to the bathroom to shower and get ready. When I emerged a short time later, the delicious smell of breakfast wafted in the air. I was going to miss Mason cooking for me. Something told me there wouldn't be much opportunity for it on the road.

I reached up and kissed him on the cheek, but at the last second he turned his head and my lips grazed his. Mason pulled me against him, his lips opening and welcoming me in . . . and the food was temporarily forgotten.

It wasn't until his hands skimmed down my back to my ass that awareness slipped in and I snapped out of the spell he'd had me under. Yes, I would definitely have to remember for the next time that a handshake was a better way to demonstrate my gratitude to him.

I grabbed a plate and shoved a forkful of omelet in my mouth. "Mmm. This is delicious." Which wasn't a big surprise. Mason really was a good cook.

We finished eating breakfast, and while I cleaned up, Mason showered. So that he didn't have to abandon his car at the mall parking lot for the next five months, we took a cab. Hailey and Nolan were climbing out of their vehicle when we arrived, and my heart instantly went out to her. The next time she would see her boyfriend was at Christmas, when the bands had a four-day break. Unlike yesterday, today she looked like she was barely holding things together. They walked over to us, holding hands.

"Hi." She gave us a small smile and then laughed at my expression. "Don't worry, I'll survive. It usually takes me a day or two to get over him leaving."

Nolan wrapped his arm around her waist and kissed the top of her head—and I came within an inch of sighing dreamily out loud.

"It's not like Nolan's much better," Mason said, impish fire sparking in his eyes. "He usually sobs like a baby for several days."

Hailey giggled. Nolan backhanded Mason's chest.

The rest of the band arrived shortly after, just as the tour bus pulled up. Aaron, Kirk, and Mason helped load everyone's suitcases and bags onto the bus, then the four of us climbed on board, giving the two couples a chance to say their tearful good-byes. Logan wasn't with Callie and Jared, having been dropped off at his grandparents' on the way over.

I didn't know how any of them did it, especially Jared. Not only was he leaving his wife, he was leaving his son.

But it wasn't like the guys were going off to war. They'd be returning home soon, in one piece.

While we waited for Nolan and Jared to join us, Mason showed me around the bus. It was larger than I had expected, and was divided into three zones: the sleeping quarters, with curtains around each bunk bed to provide some privacy; the living space, complete with couches and a small kitchenette; and the work area, which contained a built-in desk and computer. My room was small, but the bed was bigger and comfier than the guys' bunk beds.

Next he showed me the band's social media sites. Kirk gave me the list of passwords for each one. "Just make sure you don't let Mason on any of the accounts."

"And why's that?" I knew Mason had a reputation for pranking the guys, so I was almost scared to find out what he'd do if let loose on their media sites.

Mason rolled his eyes. "I tweeted something inappropriate once and I'm banned for life."

"Once?" Aaron said.

"Okay, twice."

Aaron snorted. "Try six times." To me he added, "We had to change the password after that." He tilted his chin at the list in my hand. "So guard it with your life."

"Will do." I'd stuff it down my bra if I had to.

By the time Nolan and Jared were on the bus, the rest of the guys had given me an idea of what their day-to-day life was like, and showed me their jam-packed schedule for the next month. It was no wonder Mason had needed a few days off to chill before they resumed touring again.

I checked my emails, to see if Heidi had contacted me. She had, and we spent the next few minutes chatting on the phone about the renovations to the store. It would still be two more weeks before the construction company could get started. And before they could do that, Heidi needed to discuss with them what she and I wanted done. But first we had to wait for the insurance company to tell us exactly how much money we would get from the fire claim.

I signed on to the store's social media sites, gave everyone an update, and responded to the comments on the Facebook page. Then I signed on to the band's accounts and sent out updates as to where they were now and where their next show was located. Next I answered the fans' comments, trying not to blush too much at what some of them said.

But those comments were nothing compared to the video one fan sent Nolan. Of her dancing. Naked.

And then there were the fan emails. A few were suggestive beyond reason. I quickly deleted them and scrolled through page after page of messages . . . all unread. God, when was the last time the guys had checked their email?

An hour later, just when I figured I'd be scarred for life, Mason pulled up the spare chair and sat next to me. "How's it going?"

"Did you know some of your fans send you porn?"

I expected Mason to get excited—because what guy wouldn't?—but he just shrugged. "I don't bother with the email. That was all Aaron and Jared. Sorry. Hope there wasn't anything too bad."

I was vaguely aware of him speaking, but he had leaned closer to me and his amazing man scent—a combination of spice, testosterone, and pheromones—had turned my brain fuzzy.

He rested his hand on the back of my chair and his fingers lightly brushed against my shoulder blade. At his touch, the neurons in my brain went berserk, and I had to do everything in my power not to lean in and kiss him.

"Nicole?"

I blinked. "Huh?" *Real smooth, Nicole.* I mentally collected myself and logged out of the account.

"So how does everything look?" He gave the standard chin nod, directed at the computer, which I took to mean the social media sites and not the porn.

"You've got some very interesting fans." But none of them seemed too crazy, from what I could tell. I remembered hearing last year that one country music singer had had to get a restraining order against a fan. It didn't stop her from showing up in his hotel room one night . . . where he found her on his bed, naked. The last I heard, she was spending quality time in a psychiatric unit.

"I came to see if you want to join us," he said. "We can discuss this afternoon's interview and your role with that."

"My role?"

"Our handler is sick, so we need you to keep the radio personalities in line."

"Not sure what you mean by that." I'd always figured a handler was someone big and intimidating, and I was neither of those.

"You tell them what topics they're allowed to ask about and which are off-limits. If they venture into the off-limits zone, you give them a warning or end the interview."

"And how exactly do I do that? Charge into the room and make a scene?" Now that would be amusing.

Apparently Mason thought so too, because he laughed. "No, you just do this." He demonstrated a cutting motion of his hand across his throat.

"That seems easy enough."

The guys were lounging on the couches in the middle of the bus when Mason and I joined them. Aaron, Nolan, and Jared were sitting on one couch. Kirk was sitting on the one opposite them.

"What time's the interview?" I asked as Mason and I sat down in the only spot available—next to each other, our hips practically touching. Which meant Mason's scent was still invading my space. I did my best not to inhale it too obviously. I also did my best not to lean into him.

My best was clearly not enough, and I quickly shifted away from him, trying to look casual about it.

"Four-thirty. It's scheduled for half an hour. Then we'll head to the arena for sound check, and the show's pretty much after that."

"What topics are allowed?" I asked, my gaze scanning the guys—anything to keep me from noticing Mason's scent and how close we were still sitting.

"Anything to do with our music, our recent releases, and our upcoming one."

"What about the topic of dating?" I asked. From what I'd

heard on the country music stations, it was a popular topic when it came to hot musicians. No one seemed interested when the musicians weren't so good-looking or had been married for a while . . . unless there were rumors of infidelity or a breakup. But those questions weren't usually brought up during an interview. Not unless you had the urge to piss off the celebrity involved.

"That's fine," Jared said, "but other than confirming that I'm recently married and Nolan is in a committed relationship, the two of us would rather not go there. But these guys"—he gestured at Kirk, Mason, and Aaron—"are fair game."

"Are you two dating anyone?" I asked Kirk and Aaron.

"Maybe," the mysterious Kirk said. The guys all looked at him, waiting for him to elaborate.

"Are you talking about Beckie?" Jared asked. From what I'd been able to tell yesterday, she was Callie's friend. I'd seen her and Kirk talking a few times, but I hadn't been able to tell if something was going on between them.

"Maybe."

"Hey, puck boy, does she at least know you're dating her?" Mason asked, laughing.

Kirk smirked. "Maybe."

"So that leaves Mason and Aaron who are currently single, right?" I asked, looking at Aaron and doing my best not to glance at the guy I'd had sex with at least a dozen times during the past week.

"That's right." Aaron's gaze slid to Mason.

Mason shifted next to me on the couch, accidentally bumping me with his hip. "Yup."

I asked them more questions about what was acceptable and unacceptable when it came to the interview. Then we spent the rest of the drive chatting about this and that, giving me a chance to get to know them better. I knew some things from Mason, especially when it came to Nolan and what had happened to his family. From what Mason had told me, I was glad Nolan had Hailey. It didn't take much to see they were deeply in love. Like Jared and Callie were.

"So when are you planning to finally propose to Hailey?" Mason asked as casually as could be, apart from the amusement creasing the corners of his eyes. "If you don't get on that soon, she might get bored waiting for you and dump you."

I elbowed him in the chest. Hard.

"Owww," he said, rubbing the spot where I'd hit him. "What did you do that for?" The guys cracked up with a we-like-this-girl-already laugh, clearly no longer quite so annoyed at how Mason had hired me without telling them first.

"That's not going to happen," I pointed out. "It's obvious Hailey loves him. So unless he royally screws up"—I didn't think I needed to elaborate on what I meant by that—"she'll wait for him to decide when the time is right." I just hoped he didn't wait too long if she wanted to marry him sooner rather than later.

Nolan rubbed the back of his neck. "Well, actually, I plan to propose to her at Christmas. I'm just trying to figure out the best way to do it."

"How hard can it be?" Mason asked, barely holding back a laugh. "You ask her to marry you and hope she says yes."

Nolan and Jared exchanged looks, which made me curious about what I was missing.

"Do you have a ring?" I wasn't an expert on the topic of proposals, but this part seemed like a given. If he didn't already have one, it would be a little more challenging to get one while they were touring.

He nodded.

"Here?"

Again he nodded. "It's in the safe."

"Can I see it?" Yes, I was a tad bit curious about what kind of engagement ring a rock star would buy his future fiancée.

He pushed himself off the couch and headed to the back of the bus, then returned a short time later with a black velvet box, which he handed to me. Inside was a platinum ring with a large diamond in the center. On either side of it, the shiny metal split and crossed, forming two small gaps on either side, with a small diamond nestled in each one. It was breathtaking.

My eyes got moist at how lucky Hailey was. She had found the love of her life and survived hell for him, and this was the symbol of how much she meant to him. On top of that, he wasn't a professional and he had tattoos.

Go figure.

I blinked away the happy tears before the guys could see them, then closed the lid and scooted forward on the couch to hand the box back to him. "She'll love it."

He smiled at it as if the ring was Hailey herself . . . and those damn tears started up in my eyes again.

"A wise man once told me to make the gesture big when you propose." Jared winked at Nolan.

Nolan laughed. "And that man was right. Glad you listened to him."

"So Hailey's not going home for Christmas?" Aaron asked, his fingers tapping away on the leather couch he was sitting on, like he was playing a piano.

"No, her family's flying out to join us. They understand why I don't want to go back there, even if my old house has been sold and the ghosts have moved on."

"Which means you either have to propose in front of her family," Jared said, "or figure out how to get her alone and propose."

"Exactly."

"Well, you've got just over two months to figure it out," Aaron said. "Good luck with that." He patted the lead singer on the back commiseratingly.

We chatted for a while longer before the guys went off to do their own thing. Nolan sprawled out on the couch to read a book. Jared fiddled around with his acoustic guitar, stopping every few minutes to write something down. Mason and Kirk were busy playing a video game, with Aaron every so often giving them some not-so-helpful suggestions.

I pulled out my sketchpad and started doodling a simple lily, with a bee. It was a nice flower and a nice bee. Which was another way of saying the drawing sucked. I ripped the page off the pad, crumpled it into a wad, and tossed it next to me on the couch.

"Hey, what's this?" Mason said, snatching the paper up.

I jumped off the couch and tried to grab it from his hand. "It's nothing." *Damn you, Mason, and your long arms.*

He held the paper up so I couldn't reach it and smoothed it out.

"This is really good," he said once he had succeeded. "Why the hell did you throw it away?"

"Because I'm trying to come up with a design for my line of etched glassware—but this isn't it. All I seem to be able to come up with is flowers."

The laugh that erupted from him caused the guys to look over at us to see what was going on. "And you have something against flowers? You should've thought about that before opening a flower shop."

"I just want to come up with something different. Something unique and special. Not something you would expect to see in the store."

Now I needed a miracle to help me figure out what the heck that was.

By the time we arrived at the arena where the bands were playing tonight, I couldn't believe we still had the radio interview and concert to get through. Even though we weren't doing anything mentally or physically taxing during the trip, it was still exhausting.

And when we climbed down from the bus and loaded into the waiting van, I was glad they were the ones doing the interview and I just had to watch.

After another long drive, we pulled up in front of the radio station. Silly me had thought we could walk to the door like regular people. With the exception of a path between the van and the front entrance, the sidewalk was packed with screaming fans.

"Is it always like this?" I asked no one in particular.

"Pretty much," Mason said.

I surveyed the crowd. Just how secure were those ropes? Would they protect us from being trampled if the fans wanted to get closer to the guys? Yes, they had Brian, their bodyguard, who was a former Marine, but how effective would he be against all those girls? Several men, not quite as bulky as Brian, were standing to the side, doing their best to keep the fans back, but they wouldn't be too effective if the crowd surged forward.

"Don't worry," Mason murmured, his breath a warm caress against my ear. "I'll protect you." His arm brushed my shoulder, and the usual buzz that happened every time he touched me zinged through my body, immediately making me forget about the crowd.

Brian, who was sitting in the front passenger seat, climbed out and slid open the van's side door. Excited screams greeted us, which grew to a deafening volume the moment Nolan stepped from the vehicle.

The rest of his bandmates joined him . . . and I was left to follow behind, which, when I thought about it, was the safest place to be. If the crowd swarmed them, I'd be ignored while the girls chased down their favorite band member.

Even though we didn't have tons of time before the radio interview, the guys stopped to chat with their fans and sign autographs. With the exception of Mason, the guys stayed at arm's distance from the girls. Mason was more than happy to pose for selfies with them.

Which was why one girl, who could've easily been a model, swooped in and kissed his cheek. A sensation in my stomach twisted into a knot. Jealousy, maybe? Not that I had a reason to be jealous.

Her lips had barely touched his skin before he took a quick step back. After that he didn't pose for selfies again. But it might've also had to do with Brian hustling the band into the building.

Because I was a few yards behind the guys, I heard some of the girls scream out names of the individual band members, along with "I love you!" I decided I was going to take that as an appreciation of the band's music instead of the men themselves —although in the case of a few fans, the opposite was most likely true.

Mason was the last to step into the building. He glanced over his shoulder and held the door open for me. I hurried past him.

"You don't have to walk so far behind us," he said with that damn sexy smirk he did so well.

"I'm just an employee. And I don't want your fans to get the wrong idea and think I'm romantically linked to one of you." A large number of them were probably disappointed that Nolan's and Jared's hearts had already been claimed. "I wouldn't want to disappoint them."

"I'm sure they can handle it."

I laughed as the other guys stepped onto the elevator. "Never underestimate a girl's heart, especially when it comes to her favorite musician or actor."

He quirked an eyebrow. "And you speak from experience?"

"Hey, are you two coming or what?" Kirk called from the elevator.

"Sure," I said in answer to Mason's question as we strode

over to join the rest of the band. Well, more like Mason strode; I jogged to keep up with him. "I've had my heart broken when my favorite lead singer got married. I had harbored unrealistic expectations that he would see me at a concert and fall undeniably in love with me. His marriage left me devastated for weeks."

Mason stopped abruptly and the guys in the elevator groaned.

"We'll see you upstairs," Kirk said, and the doors closed, leaving us behind.

Mason spun around to face me, his back to the elevator. "You serious?"

The corners of my mouth twitched. "Of course not. I crushed on him and he fell in love with some model. I moved on with my life." And, two months later, so did he—after he and his new wife split up.

I pushed the up button for the elevator. "But the point is, some girls are so infatuated with their crush that they get upset when the guy becomes unavailable. I don't wish to be the cause of some poor girl's broken heart when the reason it broke isn't true."

At his doubtful expression, I laughed. "There's a lot you still have to learn about girls."

"I know plenty." He smiled. It wasn't a happy smile or a panty-dropping smile. It was a smile full of smugness.

Inwardly I rolled my eyes. "I don't mean how to give women orgasms."

The door to the second elevator opened, and a man in a business suit stepped out, talking on his phone. He didn't give us a second glance; clearly his conversation was that riveting.

"I wasn't even thinking that," Mason said.

Maybe I would have believed that if the smug smile hadn't still been on his face.

I stepped inside the elevator. Mason followed, his body too

close for comfort. Damn, how long would it take me to become immune to him?

I didn't even have a chance to think about that question. No sooner had the doors closed than I found myself pressed up against the wall, Mason's mouth against mine.

Turned out I wasn't the only one who had an issue with willpower.

I knew I should stop it. That would be the smart thing to do. But my brain and my body apparently weren't on speaking terms. I parted my lips and let his tongue invade my mouth. If we were lucky, the elevator would get stuck and we would have to stay in here for the next few hours, kissing.

The bell pinged as the door opened. Someone standing outside coughed. And we continued kissing, Mason's fingers knotted in my hair.

The person coughed again. *He really should see a doctor.*

A moment later, the bell pinged a second time. "Fourth floor," announced a voice from beside us.

A voice in the back of my head pointed out that this was important. I couldn't for the life of me remember why.

"You two getting off or not?" This time the voice was laced was impatience—just the bucket of cold water I needed.

I reluctantly pulled away from Mason and flashed the stranger a big grin. "Thanks." Without waiting for my partner in crime, I stepped off the elevator . . . and practically crashed into a woman my age.

Her long blonde hair was pulled back in a perky ponytail. She was wearing a pair of black pants that skimmed her body and an ultra-chic blouse. Her soft suede black ankle boots complemented the outfit perfectly. At least she didn't look like she had been sitting in a tour bus for the past seven hours.

Nor did she look like she'd just been making out in the elevator.

Trying not to look obvious about it, I ran my hand over my

hair, doing my best to fix the mess. The other hand did its best to straighten my clothes.

"Hi, I'm Erin," she said, sounding like a cheerleader on caffeine. "They're waiting for you in the studio." She turned enough for me to spot her intern ID, and she flashed Mason a big grin. She then sashayed down the hallway, leaving us to follow her.

The rest of the band was setting up when we entered the studio. Each man had a microphone and headphones in front of him on the long table. I introduced myself to the DJs, then outlined what topics they could ask questions on and which were strictly off-limits and would ultimately end the interview. I did my best to look intimidating, but it's hard to come across as daunting when you're short enough to have to look up at the people you're talking to.

I really needed to start wearing heels.

18

MASON

In the studio, I took the empty seat between Nolan and Kirk and put on the headphones. The wall behind the two DJs contained autographed eight-by-ten photos of rock bands, past and present. Some of my all-time favorites were there, with the drummers who had inspired my love for the instrument.

"All right, guys," Stacey, one of the DJs said. "I need each of you to speak into your mikes, one at a time, so we can do a sound check."

"What do you want us to say?" Nolan asked, then sat back, his part of the test now over.

"Anything you want," replied Dennis, the other DJ, even though it had been a rhetorical question.

"I'm in the mood for pizza," I said.

Kirk snorted a laugh. "You're always in the mood for pizza." True enough.

"And beer," Jared added, stating the obvious. He fiddled with the base of his microphone.

"I could go for pizza and beer before the show." That was from Aaron.

"That's good, guys," Stacey said. "And we're ready to go live in three . . . two . . ." She held up her index finger, then spoke into her mike. "We're back now with the guys from Pushing Limits. And I'll add that they're looking mighty fine . . . Guys, how about you introduce yourselves?"

We did exactly that. Then, like with all our interviews, she asked about the album, the latest single, the tour—the standard stuff we could answer in our sleep, we'd been asked it so many times. I glanced out the studio window, to the hallway where Nicole was standing. She gave me a thumbs-up and smiled.

I nodded at her, wishing this interview was over and she and I were back in the elevator, alone. It was less than twenty-four hours since I'd last had her in my arms—if you didn't count what had happened on the way up in the elevator—and I missed the closeness and having her to myself. I had lusted over women before, but it had never felt like this. Maybe this was advanced-level lust, saved for special occasions.

"Let's get a question from one of our listeners," Dennis said. "Melody, you're on."

"Hi," a young female voice squeaked in my headphones. "I was wondering which of the guys has a girlfriend."

"Okay, guys," Stacey said, "the females of America want to know which of you are still available."

"I have a girlfriend," Nolan replied, which everyone was aware of after what had happened earlier this year. He'd been romantically linked to the actress Alyssa Graham, but that had been a sham the record label had arranged. It was later revealed that he was in love with Hailey.

"From the reports I've heard," Stacey said, "you two are pretty serious. Is that true?"

"More like *very* serious," he replied. "There's no other woman for me." For a second I wondered if he was going to say more, maybe blurt out a clumsy proposal on the air, but he leaned back in his chair and waited for the next person to answer the question.

"I'm married," Jared jumped in.

"Recently too," Stacey said. "Congratulations."

"Thanks!"

"Wow, popular with the female fans and already settling down," Dennis piped up. "How do you do it, Jared? I mean, if I were in your shoes, I wouldn't bother with settling down. I'd continue to enjoy dating."

While he didn't say it, we all knew what he meant. He wasn't referring to actual dating. He was referring to what I'd been doing while touring—enjoying backstage sex with anyone interested in going there. But now that Nicole was touring with us, I wasn't interested in being with anyone else that way—even if, for professional reasons, she and I weren't allowed to have sex.

"It's easy," Jared said. "I love my wife and can't imagine being with anyone else."

Dennis didn't look so convinced. Fortunately, Stacey stepped in before he could say anything else. "What about the rest of you guys?" While she might have been asking the question of all of us, she looked specifically at me.

I had to fight the urge to glance at Nicole standing in the hallway. The moment I did that, one of the DJs might very well jump on it and force me to say something I didn't want to say—either a lie that would hurt Nicole or the truth. What was going on between us wasn't up for discussion.

"I'm currently single," I replied after a heartbeat.

"You have quite the reputation of being a ladies' man, Mason," Dennis said. "Are you happy to be back on the road?"

I wasn't sure what he was implying, since there was plenty of ass back in L.A. that I could've hooked up with. My lays weren't strictly confined to touring. But it was a lot easier dealing with them then, because after the show finished, the band moved on and the girls were left behind.

"I'm always happy to be on the road," I said. "Playing live to the fans is where it's at. It's why we tour."

"It's how we all feel," Aaron said, saving me from more questions about my dating life.

The interview continued until Nicole finally indicated it was time to wrap it up so we could get ready for tonight.

"Thank you for being on the show," Stacey said before playing another of our songs and signaling we were off the air.

"Great interview, guys," Dennis said. "You handled it like real pros."

I wasn't sure what he had expected. We'd been doing this for well over a year now. We *were* pros.

As much as I wanted to ride the elevator with just Nicole and resume what we had been doing earlier, it didn't look like it would happen. There was no reason for us to not get on with everyone else.

The elevator door opened, and we all piled in, along with two interns. Nicole and I stood in the back. Everyone else faced forward, waiting for the doors to reopen, exchanging words about the interview, and generally not paying attention to us.

Encouraged by Nicole's sweet scent, I rested my hand on her lower back. She stiffened slightly, then her muscles relaxed and she leaned into my touch. I caressed her back with my thumb. She sucked in a small breath, too quiet to be heard by anyone but me. I'd screwed a lot of women over the years, but this was the first time one had left me uneager to walk away from her anytime soon.

The fans were just as noisy when we left the building as when we arrived, maybe even more so, their screams building in crescendo. We stopped for a moment to sign a few more autographs. Fans from behind surged forward, wanting their chance to get closer to us.

I scanned the area and spotted Nicole climbing into our van. I let out a relieved sigh that she was safe should something happen. We'd had a few close calls in the past, although nothing the guys and I couldn't handle. But there was a huge difference between Nicole and us when it came to size and strength.

Fans reached out, eager to touch us, straining against the ropes designed to hold them back. Sensing things could get crazy soon, we waved goodbye and hustled to the van. As I sat next to Nicole in the back row, the relief I'd experienced a moment ago once she was safely inside the vehicle was now mirrored on her face. I reached for her hand and threaded my fingers with hers. She gave them a light squeeze, her attention focused on the fans outside the window.

Excitement buzzed in the van as we drove to the arena, and continued to grow as the van entered the parking lot where the tour buses were parked. This was typical before a concert— except usually before our part of the show, I'd fuck a groupie or two to keep the edge off. Some people did yoga to help them relax. Some went for a jog. I couldn't see myself as the yoga type, and as much as I enjoyed running to keep in shape, it didn't do much to help me get ready for a show. But since I didn't want to disappear for fifteen minutes to screw a groupie while Nicole was with us, I didn't know what else to do.

We exited the van, Nicole and I no longer holding hands, and entered the arena through the back door. The security guard checked our IDs, which hung around our necks on lanyards, and let us past. For now, Nicole had only a visitor ID, but it permitted her access to most places in the arena the band was allowed to go.

We were directed to the stage, where the roadies were fiddling with last-minute adjustments to the setup. A huge black banner formed a backdrop, separating Endless Motion's equipment from our smaller part of the stage. That was the disadvantage of being the opening act: we didn't get as much room to move around in. Nothing like for the main act. It didn't matter to me, since I was the drummer. It wasn't like I could go anywhere. But Nolan loved to move around when he sang, making the most of the stage.

The guys and I jumped up onto the platform while Nicole watched from the arena floor. We took our positions, and after the sound guy made the necessary adjustments, we played the set's opening song.

While drumming, I watched Nicole dance around, moving to the beat I was creating. Over the years I'd seen how the fans responded to our music, but seeing how much she was enjoying it caused a ripple of pride inside me. It was the first time I'd felt anything like that. And it was the same pride I'd experienced after playing on the piano the music I'd created that no one had heard before . . . except for Nicole in that moment.

I could've easily played the rest of our set if it meant getting to watch her move like that some more.

With the sound check finished, we went backstage to prepare for tonight. We changed into our stage clothes and headed for the area designated for the meet-and-greet. This was our chance to visit with the fans who had won the opportunity to meet Pushing Limits and Endless Motion. When we first started touring after the release of our debut album, only a few individuals would trickle into the room set up for the band. Some had come into the wrong room, looking for Crazy Piper instead of us. But by the time we'd finished touring with them, our designated room had been packed each time. Because of that, the record label had decided we needed a bigger room on this tour. Even so, it was still packed.

We stood side by side near the exit, with the fans herded toward us like cattle. While it wasn't my favorite way of doing things, at least it gave them a chance to meet us.

The large room smelled like a nightclub, minus the booze, with an extra helping of perfume. And it wasn't easy to hear over the chattering of fans as they waited their turn, or the occasional individuals singing our songs in the background, as if auditioning to replace Nolan in the band.

"Can I get a picture of us together?" a woman asked, her long black hair styled in hundreds of tiny braids. She was hot in a tight T-shirt that clung to her sexy curves. She was the type of woman I would've been more than happy to screw before the show.

But instead of flirting with her, I glanced around for Nicole. Disappointment kicked me in the nuts when I couldn't find her.

"Sure," I said to the fan.

She stepped up to me, pressing her large tits against my arm, and shot the picture, her head close to mine. She checked how it looked and grinned, happy with the results, which was a relief. Some girls weren't happy just to get a picture with a member of the band. The photo had to be worthy of the cover of *Rolling Stone*.

She thanked me and moved on to Kirk.

The girl behind her approached me, bouncing up and down like a cheerleader who had to take a piss. "OMG! I love you so much, Mason!" she shrieked. I managed to hold back a grimace. As much as I loved meeting the fans, there was a level of fangirling that was hard to take. She was approaching that line.

I smiled at her, but then had second thoughts about doing that when it looked like she might faint. *Note to self: hold back on patented panty-dropping smile whenever dealing with fangirls who shriek.*

"I can't believe I'm actually meeting you," she gushed, her words coming in a hurry. "You're, like, the sexiest man alive."

I laughed. "Tell that to *People* magazine."

She nodded, the jerky movement reminding me of a grinning bobblehead. "I definitely will." From the way she said it, I wouldn't be surprised if she did, even though I'd been joking.

The parade of fans continued. Some were excited to meet us and tell us how much they loved our music. Some wanted selfies with us. A couple of girls tried to kiss my cheek when I posed with them; by the third time, I had to preface the photo with a no-kissing rule—something I'd never felt the need to do before. Others required only a quick autograph. A couple of individuals tried to give us their demo CDs to pass on to our record label. Those were always filed away in the trash can after the meet-and-greet—as were the bras and panties flung at us while we were onstage.

The guy who had just handed me his demo moved on to Kirk . . . revealing Nicole. My heart did a rapid four-beat pattern. That was new. My heart had never responded that way to a woman before, clothed or unclothed.

For a second I cursed my no-kissing rule. At least then I could've persuaded Nicole to give me one, even if it was a quick peck on the cheek.

"Can't wait to see you in concert," she said with a smile.

I shifted closer, my mouth an inch from her ear. "Can't wait for you to see what I can do with my hands," I murmured.

She laughed, and not for the first time I wished we were back at her house, alone. Having fun. Being ourselves. "I already know how good you are with your hands," she said before stepping away. She winked at me and moved on to Kirk.

I didn't hear what he was saying to her, because in that moment, while I was no longer paying attention to anything other than Nicole, the next person in line swooped in and planted a kiss on my cheek. "Hey, babe," she purred. "Do you remember me?"

The worst question you could ever ask a touring musician was if he remembered you, especially if he saw thousands of people a night. Chances were great the answer was no. And how was he supposed to respond when he was at risk of hurting your feelings? Because no girl *ever* asked "Do you remember me?" and wanted the answer to be no.

"How're you doing?" I asked, nimbly avoiding the question. Which of course she took to mean that I did remember her.

"I'm going commando like last time." Too bad she had to announce it loud enough for Kirk and Nicole to overhear, and both turned to look at us. Judging from the hurt on Nicole's face for a fleeting moment, she no doubt assumed I would be disappearing with the fan right after this, for a little pre-concert stress release.

I was so busy paying attention to Nicole, I didn't notice the woman lean into me. "Are you free after this? I've got some new moves I wanna show ya." Her tongue forged a trail along my jaw.

My head jerked away from her as if a killer bee had stung me. "Thanks, but I'm gonna be busy after this."

"What about after the concert?"

"Then too . . . that's when we leave."

She pouted, much the way Logan did whenever he was disappointed—a definite mood killer, if I'd been in the mood. "Even though Endless Motion hasn't gone onstage yet?"

"Our bus driver likes to get an early start." Maybe that would have been true if the driver had had a choice, but it didn't matter—the buses all left at the same time, once the venue was packed up.

"That's too bad. Maybe next time."

"Yes, maybe next time," I said, without really meaning it.

She moved on to talk to Kirk. I glanced at him to see how much Nicole had overheard, but she wasn't with him or any of the other guys.

19

NICOLE

The woman who had just declared to the room that she was going commando licked Mason's face like a dog licking her prized bone.

I didn't need to see any more to know what would happen next. Luckily for me, Kirk had no issues with confirming my suspicions. "Sorry, Nicole, but this is who Mason is. He always gets restless before a concert. He goes off, has a good fuck, then he's ready to go." He really did sound sorry, but it didn't take the sting out of his words.

I gave him my best Mason-is-just-my-employer-nothing-more smile. "It's getting a little claustrophobic in here. I'll wait for you guys outside the room." I didn't give Kirk a chance to say anything before I bailed. Aaron, Jared, and Nolan were too busy with their fans to notice me leaving.

Outside the room, I checked to see if I had missed any calls or texts. I sent Heidi a text, telling her that I couldn't believe how crazy things got on tour, but so far I was enjoying it.

I shot a few backstage photos that I figured the fans would be eager to see. What better way to get the fans involved than by showing them a taste of the band's day-to-day life on the road? I'd already taken a few photos during the radio interview. I checked their media sites to see if anyone had responded to them, and was met by tons of variations on "They're soooo hot," "Wish they were coming to my town," and heart-eye emojis. Nothing said it better than a heart-eye emoji.

I posted the new pictures I'd taken at the meet-and-greet. People were still trickling out of the room, so I leaned back against the wall and brainstormed an idea for a giveaway to help increase the band's exposure on the sites. The other thing I wanted to talk to them about was setting up a newsletter. It was easy to miss things on the social media sites unless you lived on them 24/7.

By the time the last of the fans staggered from the room, I had come up with several ideas. The guys appeared a moment later, and we headed to the room set up with food and drinks for everyone involved in the show. Some people were already there, eating and drinking, enjoying a short break before returning to work.

We grabbed paper plates and loaded them with food. I selected a bottle of water, while Mason pulled a bottle of beer from the cooler. I sat on the ugly green vinyl couch. Mason didn't. Instead, he paced while eating his food. Back and forth. Again, and again, and again. I was getting nauseated just watching him.

The guys didn't appear to notice. Maybe this was what Kirk had been referring to earlier. Which meant after Mason finished eating, he would meet up with Miss Commando.

I chewed on a slice of pizza while I contemplated what I should do. Obviously I wouldn't be the one to help him with his "problem," because that would be crossing the line of professionalism.

Not that making out with him in the elevator was standing on the right side of the line either.

I checked the time on my phone. The band would be

playing soon, and he still hadn't left to hook up with the woman from the meet-and-greet.

"Mason, can I talk to you in the hallway for a minute?" I said it loud enough so no one would think we were sneaking off for a quick fuck. At least I hoped they didn't, because it was the truth.

"Sure," he said with a shrug, obviously perplexed that what I needed to tell him couldn't be said in front of everyone. He set his plate down on the empty plastic chair next to the couch and followed me out the doorway.

I led him down a hallway that didn't look like it got much traffic.

"So what's up?" he asked. The distant sounds of cheering could be heard coming from the arena, where the audience was getting ready for the show.

An uneasy energy buzzed from him that was hard to explain. It seemed like a combination of the excitement a child experiences the night before Christmas and exam apprehension. "Are you okay?" I asked.

"Sure. Why wouldn't I be?"

His comment would've been more believable if he hadn't been fidgeting.

"Well, for starters, you were pacing in there. I haven't known you for long, but I've never seen you do that before."

His shoulders hiked up in a quick move. "I'm always like this before a concert."

"Kirk mentioned that."

His eyes narrowed. "What else did he say?" His tone was sharp enough to cut, yet not sharp enough to inflict serious damage.

"Not much else, other than that you usually burn it off before the show by . . . um . . ." I could feel the heat of my face increase to a new record temperature.

"By fucking some random chick?" The edge was still there, and I cringed.

"He didn't go into specifics, but it was kind of obvious." *After the woman you were talking to announced it to the room.*

"What are you getting at, Nicole? Are you offering to find me some random chick to screw?"

"Of course not," I bit out. "But there must be something I can do to help you." At his suggestive grin, I added, "Something in the realm of my contract." Which the label had forwarded to Nolan while we were on the road, and I had printed off and signed.

"So you're telling me a blow job is off the table?"

I harrumphed. "Of course it's off the table."

Mason threw his head back with a laugh, and I couldn't help smiling a little at how my words had sounded. Finally I gave in and laughed too.

Mason closed the distance between us, his warm beer breath stroking my face. "More than anything, I want to be buried deep inside you, Nicole. Or have your hot lips around my dick."

His voice—deep and rough and bursting with pure male sexiness—went directly to the spot between my legs and turned my panties damp. *Damn him.*

"But I'll settle for this instead." His lips blazed a path along my jaw to my mouth . . . then those talented lips consumed me. And I let him. I ignored the nagging voice in the back of my head pointing out this was still unprofessional. Nowhere in the contract had it mentioned that my job responsibilities included kissing him to help him deal with pre-show restlessness.

But maybe they could amend the contract.

Pushing everything to the side, I focused on the kiss and nothing else. What I was doing was strictly for the audience's benefit. They'd paid good money for a great show, and this was my way of making sure the Pushing Limits part of the show was exactly that. And ultimately it would benefit album sales. It was a win-win for everyone.

Yes, keep telling yourself that, a voice in the back of my head said with a sarcastic laugh.

We continued kissing for several minutes, until I became so riled up I came close to dropping my no-sex stance. But before I had a chance to cave, Mason pulled away and rested his forehead against mine. "Thank you," he murmured, voice still rough. "I needed that."

"Anytime."

"We could write it into your job description."

I smirked. "We could."

"I should probably go join the guys."

"You probably should."

Instead of leaving, though, Mason kissed me once again. But not a heavy, all-consuming kiss this time. It was nothing more than a light brushing of the lips—which made me want him even more.

Then we joined the rest of the band near the stage so they could prepare for the show. I stepped back to give them a chance to do their pre-show ritual without me getting in their way. While they did that, I tweeted and posted on their behalf that they were getting ready to go on. Within seconds, I received responses from people who were disappointed they couldn't be here . . . or from people at the show who were excited for it to start. They had come only to see Pushing Limits.

Five minutes later, I knew exactly why they had come to see the band. The guys were onstage, and from where I was standing I had a pretty decent view of them. Well, their backs, at least. But it didn't matter. Their music and their presence filled the space and had the audience screaming with joy, singing along with the lyrics, dancing. Nolan was amazing up there. I could see why he was the band's front man, and it wasn't just because of his good looks. His charisma and talent had the fans hungry for more.

From what I could see, it wasn't just a few people who felt this way. It was the majority of the arena. I wouldn't have been surprised if the people who'd responded to my tweets and posts weren't the only ones who'd come just to see Pushing Limits perform.

They shouldn't be an opening act. They were bigger than that.

Eventually their set came to an end. Nolan thanked the crowd for coming and the guys walked off the stage, waving to the audience.

I'd been to a few country music concerts, and after the main act left the stage, the audience would go wild, demanding an encore. The opening band, not so much.

But that wasn't the case with Pushing Limits. Based on the volume of the audience demanding an encore, you'd have thought they *were* the main act.

"Are you guys going back out there?" I asked.

Nolan shook his head, sweat dripping down the sides of his face, his hair dark with wet strands. His T-shirt was also sweat-drenched—the same look the other four men shared. "Our set's done. The roadies need to finish setting up for Endless Motion."

"Even though the audience wants more?"

"Doesn't matter," Jared said. "It's not our concert. We're just the opening act."

My gaze slid to each guy. "Does this happen often?"

"Pretty much at every show," Mason said, "but there's nothing we can do about it." A hopeful smile appeared on his sweaty face. "So, what did you think? Did you enjoy it?"

I returned his smile, partly because I had enjoyed it and partly because of Mason's expression. He was actually nervous about what I thought. "I loved it. You guys are amazing. It's no wonder everyone wants an encore." Heck, never mind what everyone else wanted . . . *I* wanted an encore.

Jared and Kirk handed their instruments to the roadies. Relief brushed Nolan's face when a roadie handed him his guitar case.

"You guys want to hit the sports bar around the corner and get in a few rounds of pool while we wait?" Kirk asked.

"Let me guess, puck boy," Mason said. "The L.A. Kings are playing tonight."

"Maybe. Or maybe I'm not ready to get on the bus yet."

The guys agreed with that. All were still buzzed from their amazing performance.

The security guard was less concerned about us leaving than he had been about us entering the arena. But it also could've been because the man was busy with two groupies who were attempting to seduce him into letting them sneak in. Either the man was a dedicated employee or he just wasn't interested. Before the doors closed behind us, I caught him telling them, "No backstage passes, no entry."

Since we didn't have tons of time before the show ended, we ran across the parking lot in the direction Kirk remembered seeing the bar. As we ran, water droplets splashed against me. Not many at first, but by the time we got to the other side of the parking lot, the rain was coming down hard and the air had a brisk nip to it.

Which meant two things when we entered the bar—my peasant blouse was now wet and clung to my body, and my nipples were tight buds, pressing against my thin cotton bra. And thanks to the state of my top, you couldn't miss my situation.

The leers of the two men standing at the bar entrance confirmed this. "Hey, sweetheart," one said. "How about you and me get acquainted?" His gaze dropped to my chest and got stuck there.

"She's with me," Mason growled, doing his best angry-bear impression. I'd be scared if I were those two jerks. He parked his hand on my lower back, marking his territory. At least he didn't try to piss on me.

"We're willing to share," the man said, who had consumed way too many beers over his lifetime. Think Santa, minus the jolly.

"Well, I'm not," Mason ground out, jaw clenched. I could practically hear his perfect white teeth grinding.

"Thanks for the offer," I said to the not-so-pleasant-to-look-at men, "but he's more than enough man for me." Without waiting for their reply, I rushed into the building, my heart pounding a little harder and a little louder from the confrontation. It also pounded a relieved rhythm at the way Mason protected me.

The air inside the bar was warmer than outside, but not enough to warm up my nipples or dry off my white top. I crossed my arms in front of me, taking in the inside of the place and doing everything I could to avoid eye contact with the other members of band. Humiliation burned inside me when I thought about how the four of them would interpret what I'd said to the jerks at the entrance. Nolan, Jared, Kirk, and Aaron already knew Mason and I had screwed each other before I joined them on tour.

Kirk made a beeline for the other side of the bar, glancing at a large TV screen with a hockey game on it as he walked past. Mason indicated for me to follow, his hand still on my lower back.

It didn't take me long to realize where we were headed. Kirk parked himself at one of two unoccupied pool tables. Jared and Nolan claimed the other one and began setting up the balls.

Kirk removed a stick from the wall and handed it to me. "Nicole, you're with Mason."

I vehemently shook my head. "Oh, I'm not playing. I'm the worst at this game."

"That's okay, so is Aaron." That got a "Hey" from the keyboardist. Kirk threw him a well-you-are look that left me giggling. "This way we're evenly matched."

"We're not betting, are we?" I couldn't handle the pressure of that, even if the stakes were low. And given my family history with gambling addiction, it wasn't something I even wanted to risk.

Kirk's gaze flicked briefly to Mason, then back to me. "No betting. It's just a friendly game."

"Okay, then—I'm in."

Kirk had been right: Aaron sucked at the game as much as I did. I wasn't even sure why he and I were playing, other than for the comic relief. Instead of tension cramming the small space, we were laughing and having fun. The guys teased each other mercilessly, which had me laughing harder. And this, of course, caused me to mess up my shots even more than I normally would. Wow, who'd have thought it was even possible?

The waitress who had taken our orders returned with our beers. She clearly knew who the guys were, and she hung around for a few minutes, flirting with them. Or at least she tried to. Jared and Nolan were involved in a heated game and pretty much ignored her. Not that I believed for a second they would've flirted back even if they weren't playing. Even with the most brazen of fans, the two men were polite, but that was about it.

She didn't have much luck with the rest of the band either, which surprised me. Other than being polite to her, they were more interested in playing pool than in living the stereotypical life of a rock star.

"You're up, Nicole," Aaron said. The waitress heaved a sigh and walked away.

I gulped down some of my beer. Maybe the secret to nailing a shot was being a little buzzed. I didn't actually believe that, but it was worth a try.

I walked around the table, pretending to survey the situation. All the shots looked impossible to my untrained eye. I settled on one possibility and got into position.

Before I had a chance to tap the white ball, Mason came up from behind me and grabbed the end of my cue.

"Hey, that's cheating," I said, coming close to pouting and glaring at him over my shoulder.

"It's only cheating when I'm trying to beat you. We're on the same team, in case you've forgotten. I wanted to give you some pointers."

I started to straighten.

"No, stand like you were, and I'll adjust your hold on the stick." He leaned over me, his hardening length pressing into my backside. I gasped softly and accidentally shifted my body, causing my butt to rub against his length. It hardened some more. If he wasn't careful, everyone would see just how turned on he was.

Luckily for me, the truth about *my* predicament wasn't so obvious. The party between my legs was my secret and my secret alone.

He adjusted the stick and gave me a few pointers, all of which were lost on me as I focused on the wrong thing—him.

I pulled the stick back slightly, then gave it a well-aimed jab. It hit the white ball where I had intended, and set it in motion. Somehow the white ball nailed the red one and sent it rolling toward the corner pocket. I held my breath, willing the ball to keep moving . . . keep moving . . .

Then it stopped. On the edge of the freaking pocket.

I groaned and inwardly cursed the traitorous ball. Even Aaron couldn't miss the shot. I had set it up perfectly for him.

We continued playing until the alarm on Kirk's cellphone indicated it was time to head back. Nolan paid the bill and we left the bar, me with a happy buzz.

As we approached our bus, the music from the arena grew louder.

"That's Endless Motion's final encore," Jared said. "We'll be heading out soon. Have you ever slept on a tour bus before?" he asked me.

"Nope. Virgin tour bus rider here. Why, is there something I should know? Like, the beds are rock hard?"

"It takes a few days to get used to it, but it's not all that bad. And you're lucky."

"How's that?"

Jared opened the bus door. "You get to sleep in the separate room. You don't have to listen to Mason snore." He winked at me.

I bit back what I itched to say—that Mason didn't snore. I knew this from experience.

We piled onto the bus and got ready for bed, which felt weird. I was used to having a brother, but this was nothing like that. Fortunately, as far as I could tell, they weren't slobs, so bonus points to them.

I entered my room, and by room I meant a cubicle with a bed and not a lot of space to move in. You wouldn't want to be in here if you were claustrophobic. I'd already put my stuff away earlier, so there was nothing to do but go to bed.

I lay down, and instantly missed Mason. Over the past few days we had spent every night wrapped in each other's arms. The bed felt empty, and I had to fight the urge to sneak to his sleeping compartment and cuddle up to him.

After half an hour of tossing and turning, I flipped on the

bedside lamp and started reading the romance novel I had begun the other day. But then I got to the hot sex scene . . .

Tomorrow I would buy a different book to read. Maybe a nice scary Stephen King novel.

I'd bet those didn't have steamy sex scenes.

20

NICOLE

It didn't take me long to get into the rhythm of touring. The days were all pretty much the same. Long hours on the bus. Interviews. Screaming fans. Late nights. Random soccer games between the band and the roadies whenever we could squeeze them in. The sole difference was that each night was spent in a new city. But as Mason had warned, we never got to see much, rushing from one location to the next.

Not that I regretted my decision to join the guys. Even after nine weeks on the road with them, I was having a great time. Nolan, Jared, Kirk, and Aaron had become like brothers to me.

Mason, not so much.

We still hadn't had sex since September, on the last night of the band's break. Instead, before they were due onstage Mason and I would disappear for a few minutes to make out—all for the benefit of the fans, mind you. Even though Mason was still restless compared to when he was staying at my house—especially since I knew he wasn't hooking up with groupies or anyone else—the kissing seemed to help. And given that it was the only time I allowed us to kiss, I craved the moment like a flower craved the rain—more so with each passing day I spent touring with them.

The hallway we'd disappeared down was empty, like every time we slipped away from the band to do this. His hands rested on my waist, and every nerve in my body felt alive.

This wasn't the same feeling you got when the man you lusted for touched you, and all you wanted was for him to fuck you until your body shattered around him. No, this was more than that. It was like being cocooned in a warm, soft blanket on a cold winter day. It was heaven.

I sank into him, and let him consume me as I consumed him. Our kisses weren't pure hunger anymore. They were now sweeter. Sweeter, but at the same time still hot.

My tongue glided against his, and I moaned. I was completely done for. The man who didn't have all of the characteristics on my list of what a perfect man needed—other than that he was kind and sweet, had a great sense of humor, was honest, and had no bad addictions—had become the man I was in love with.

Fine—maybe I was willing to ignore the parts about him not being a professional (like a dentist or a doctor or an accountant) and having tattoos.

But there were two things I couldn't ignore. First, he wasn't the kind of guy who'd settle down and have a family. And second, his life revolved around his job. Thanks to his touring schedule, I wouldn't get to see him much. It wasn't easy for both Hailey and Callie when it came to the men they loved, but they made the best of the situation. They were better people than me—I knew I could never live like that.

Not that it made a difference. Other than our kissing, there was nothing to indicate that what we had between us was going anywhere.

"Break a leg," I murmured, my lips so close to his, we were sharing the same breath.

He laughed. "I'll try not to, but thanks for the sentiment."

We returned to the room where the band and Callie were waiting. She had flown in that afternoon to join Jared for the weekend, since the tour was spending two nights in New York City and we were staying in a hotel. Logan was with Jared's parents in L.A.

Callie was sitting on Jared's lap, and he didn't look like he was ready to let go of her anytime soon, his arms tight around her. He'd been restless for the past week, unable to wait any longer to see his wife.

Mason and I sat next to Nolan on the couch, Mason took his smartphone out of his back pocket and opened the crossword-puzzle app he had downloaded a few weeks ago. "Five-letter word for 'snooze,'" he said to me. Nolan, Kirk, and Aaron were busy debating where to eat after the show.

I pulled my feet onto the couch and wrapped my arms around my legs. What I really longed to do was straddle Mason's hips, but that hardly seemed professional.

Not that the narrow gap separating us could be considered professional either. We were in each other's personal space . . . just so I could help him solve the crossword puzzle. Or so I liked to tell myself.

"Sleep," I replied, after working through a few possibilities in my head.

He entered the word into the app. "Correct."

"And the crowd goes wild at my sheer brilliance." I faked a fanfare.

"As if there was any doubt." Mason's dazzling smile had my heart doing a quick little happy dance. That was the same reaction his smile always got whenever it was leveled in my direction.

My life would be so much emptier once that smile was no longer part of my day.

He bumped my shoulder with his, and my body buzzed

with need. In the nine weeks I'd been touring with the guys, that hadn't changed. If anything, the more time I'd spent with him, the more my body reacted to him. I'd never felt this way about a guy before—comfortable around him and at the same time hyperaware of everything about him.

We continued working on our crossword puzzle until it was time for the guys to go onstage. Then Callie and I escorted them to the stage entrance. We hung back as they climbed up the metal steps, and had to cover our ears at the screams and cheers as the first beat of Mason's drums filled the arena.

"If this is what it's like when they're just the opening act," I said, "can you imagine what it will be like when they're headlining?"

She laughed. "I'm afraid to."

From our location offstage, we could pretty much see the show. Despite how many times I had seen it during the past nine weeks, I had yet to grow bored of watching them in concert. If anything, I'd become addicted to the nightly performance.

"The guys have a TV interview tomorrow," Callie said at one point, loud enough for me to hear her over the music. "Do you want to go shopping with me?"

"You don't want to be there for the interview?"

"Not really. I've been to them before in L.A. I love watching the guys, but that whole scene just isn't for me. Besides, I want to go lingerie shopping and get something special for Jared."

I pressed my lips together, doing my best not to laugh. "Jared likes to wear sexy lingerie?" I knew what she meant but couldn't resist.

"Ha ha. Very funny. But you have to admit that guys love their women in sexy underwear. It's a massive turn-on for them. And you could get some for Mason to . . . um, admire."

My eyebrows shot up to my hairline. "Why would I want to get Mason underwear to admire?"

"Seriously? You have to ask? It's obvious you two have a thing for each other."

"We don't have a thing for each other."

She laughed shortly. "So how is it in Delusional Land? Is the view nice?"

"Honestly, there's nothing going on between us. He's my boss. Nothing more." A boss I kissed before every concert, but that was in my unwritten job description as his personal assistant, a responsibility I had acquired after the first week on the job.

"Oh, please. I've seen how you look at him and how he looks at you."

"And how is that?"

"You're in love with him and he's in love with you."

I vehemently shook my head. "He's not in love with me."

"I knew it!" she practically squealed.

"Knew what? That he's not in love with me? That's kind of a given. Did you forget the part about him being my boss?"

"That's not what I meant. You were quick to mention that he's not in love with you, but you never said anything about not being in love with him."

Busted. "You didn't give me a chance," I quickly pointed out.

"Give me some credit, Nicole. I've seen the way you are together. And I'm not the only one. Even Jared's noticed. Mason looks at you like you're his sun and he can't imagine a day without you."

I rolled my eyes. "You're crazy. He doesn't look at me that way." But that made me wonder: was that how I looked when I was around him? The last thing I needed was to let him know how I felt. This gig wasn't going to last much longer. Renovations to the flower shop were moving along rapidly, and we were expecting to reopen in six weeks—too late for the Christmas season, but in plenty of time for Valentine's Day.

"I'm not crazy," Callie said. "When are you going to admit to yourself you feel the same way about him that he feels about you?"

"It's not that easy."

"Sure it is."

I glanced back at the stage, where Mason was doing the thing he loved most—his job. "You're okay with the man you love doing this." I gestured at the stage. "But this life isn't for me. I love traveling with them, but that's because I know it's not going to last forever. It gets tiring with all the long hours on the road. The rushing to interviews. The late nights." The screaming fans who hung out at the radio stations, eager for a glance at their favorite musicians. The living on the bus with five men and not getting much privacy.

"I know that you and Hailey don't tour with the band," I continued. "You have your lives back in L.A. But I couldn't do that either. I couldn't stay home and only see him every month or two, and even then just for a few days. I admire you two for being able to balance it all and still be there for the men you love. I wish I could be like you."

Callie let out a sigh that I had no idea how to interpret. She watched the guys for a moment before saying, "It's not easy. None of it's easy. But I love Jared, and I couldn't imagine him giving any of this up for me. It's his life. . . . I know Logan and I are his life too, but I want him to have this for as long as he can. I had to give up my dreams once, when Logan came into my life. I never want that to happen to Jared. And as long as we can make it work, I'll do what I can to be the supportive wife he deserves."

She smiled at me, the gesture warm and filled with understanding. "But I also know what you're saying. It is tough, and this life isn't meant for everyone. But when it comes time to leave the band, will you be able to walk away so easily?"

I laughed, the sound more bitter than amused. There would be nothing easy about leaving Mason, but it was something I had to do. And eventually I would move on and find love again . . . hopefully . . . maybe. "No," I admitted to her. "But I'll have to."

I could feel my heart starting to splinter, and had to remind myself that I was being ridiculous. Anything to keep the damage from becoming too great. Despite what Callie had claimed, Mason wasn't in love with me. Whether or not I was willing to be the ideal girlfriend to a rock star was irrelevant in the end.

All I could do was focus on my job and enjoy my final weeks with the band and with Mason.

21

NICOLE

Later the next morning, while the band was at the TV station, Callie and I took a cab from the hotel to the lingerie store she'd been dying to visit. She was glowing the entire way—and it had nothing to do with where we were going, and everything to do with what she and Jared had no doubt been doing last night.

Which was more than I could say about Mason and me. We'd stayed in our own separate rooms. The way it was supposed to be.

Only that wasn't what I now wanted.

I missed him. I missed sleeping with him, and I missed waking up in his arms. I missed the warm feeling I got when I drifted off to sleep, knowing he was there and would still be there in the morning.

On the drive over, Zack sent his daily text, checking up on me. After the first week of touring I had confessed to him about the fire and how I was working with the band until the store was ready to reopen. Once I told him the guys in the band were nothing more than brothers to me, he had been less freaked out about me doing something completely out of the norm for me.

It also helped that we still talked on the phone at least once a week.

How's my crazy sister doing?

He'd been calling me that ever since finding out what I was doing.

Great. And how's my jealous brother?

And I'd been calling him that ever since I realized how envious he was that I was the one touring with the band instead of him.

Missing real American pizza.

I laughed. Every day he told me what American food or TV show he missed while he was overseas.

Shopping with friend. Will talk to you later.

The cab dropped Callie and me off in front of the store, and we entered. The upscale boutique was nothing like the one back home where I usually bought my underwear. The lighting was softer than in your typical store, and the air smelled sweet, like the gentle caress of freshly cut roses. Classical music played in the background. If there was one word to describe the store's goal for its customers, it would be "romance." Although from the look of some of the lingerie adorning the mannequins, hot sex also came to mind.

The other difference between this store and the one back home was that I wouldn't be surprised if a thong cost more than a week's groceries. Everything was of super-high quality.

"Is there anything I can help you find?" a woman in her late forties asked. She was wearing a business suit with a skirt and heels, her hair wrapped in a chic bun. Definitely not the same as the girls who worked in the lingerie store back home.

"I'm not sure," I said, and with a surprisingly straight face added, "I'm looking for something sexy that will turn my husband on." I tucked my left hand—the one without an engagement or wedding ring—behind me. "But nothing sleazy. That's not my style."

She gave me a long look, implying that nothing in the store could possibly be called sleazy and that she was seriously considering spraying me with sanitizer for even suggesting anything so vile.

I bit back a giggle and smiled sweetly at her before joining Callie next to a rack of short satin slips.

She pulled out a navy one with ivory antique-style lace along the low neckline and the hem. It was sexy without being overly revealing. "What do you think?" she asked.

"It's gorgeous," I said in an awed whisper.

"I think I'll try it on." She scanned the store. "But first we need to find something for you." Before I could say anything, she grabbed my wrist and dragged me to a rack of baby doll nighties not far from where we had been standing.

She immediately pulled out an incredibly sexy and utterly revealing raspberry pink outfit. The panties were nothing more than a string bikini, and the bra was covered with intricate lace. The rest of the outfit was created from a fine mesh that would show off everything beneath it.

It was so not me . . . yet at the same time it was perfect.

"I can guarantee Mason will love it," Callie said, still inspecting the baby doll.

"Didn't realize I was buying it for him to wear. But he might need a larger size."

"Very funny." She handed it to me. "You should try it on."

"You do realize nothing's going on between him and me, right?" We'd already had this discussion last night, but I felt like it needed to be repeated in case her hot husband had distracted her while he'd been onstage and she hadn't heard me.

"So you've mentioned. You can lie to yourself all you want, Nicole, but you're in love with him and nothing will change that. Besides, wasn't the point of you joining the guys on tour that you could be adventurous and do something different?"

I grinned until my face hurt. "And buying sexy lingerie is adventurous?" Okay, maybe the one she had picked out for me was on the adventurous side.

She shook her head. "No, but taking a chance on Mason is. What do you have to lose? You've only got a few more weeks left with the band before you'll be heading home. Live life. You never know when it will be your last chance." A brief look of pain flashed over her face, but it vanished in a heartbeat. "My sister and parents taught me that the night they died."

My heart squeezed in on itself, knowing the pain of losing a parent. "I'm so sorry. I had no idea."

"It's okay. It happened almost five years ago. I'm better now."

We grabbed a few more items to try on and started heading for the fitting rooms, browsing as we went.

"It doesn't matter if I'm in love with Mason or not," I said. "He doesn't fit the list of what makes a perfect husband."

"There's a list?"

I explained the purpose of the list and the criteria I had painstakingly come up with. "And he can't have any piercings or tattoos," I added at the end, although the part about tattoos might have come out more mumbled than clearly enunciated.

Callie laughed. "You do realize a lot of professional men have tattoos these days, so you've just reduced your list of possibilities by a large amount?"

I guess she was right about that. For all I knew, my last two dates had been heavily tattooed under their dress shirts.

"And based on your criteria, Jared would fail as perfect-husband material, but I can tell you that he's an amazing husband and father. I wouldn't change a single thing about him."

She did have a point there too.

While we were searching through a rack of teddies, Callie's phone pinged in her hand. "Jared," she said, smiling softly, reading the text. "He and Mason will meet us in Central Park in an hour for lunch."

The saleswoman unlocked the fitting rooms. I stepped into mine and changed into the baby doll Callie had found for me. It was sexy as sin and made me look equally sexy. But when on earth would I get a chance to wear it?

A persistent voice in the back of my head told me I deserved something feminine and pretty, especially after spending so much time on the bus with a bunch of men. Not that any of said men would ever see it.

I tried on the other outfits, but none appealed to me the same way the first one had.

Once I was finished changing back into my jeans and sweater, I came out of my room at the same moment Callie stepped out of hers. "So?" she asked.

"I'm getting this one." I lifted up the raspberry baby-doll outfit.

The way Callie's face lit up, you'd have thought I had announced that Jared was taking the next year off from touring. "It's perfect. I guarantee you won't regret it."

I just hoped she was right.

22

MASON

Jared and I waited at the counter of our favorite New York City deli for our food. It had been his idea for Nicole and Callie to meet us in Central Park for lunch—even if the temperature was chilly. Although I wouldn't have been too surprised if he had come up with the idea as an excuse to cuddle with his wife some more.

"Having a wife and kid has made you go soft," I told him with a laugh. "Since when do you do picnics?"

"My family used to have them all the time when I was growing up. Still do, especially since Logan loves them."

My parents used to love them too when I was a kid. Back before I was too cool to hang out with them. Back before my family disowned me.

"Anyway, you're going to thank me for this," he said.

"How so?"

"You need to make the most of the time you two aren't on the bus with the rest of us, and this is the perfect way to do that."

I chuckled, the sound a little forced, as were my next words. "What's that supposed to mean?" Except I knew exactly what he meant. I'd been living under the delusion that no one, including Nicole and the band, had figured out that I'd been falling for her since day one, even before I realized it myself.

He leveled his gaze at me, as if the answer to my question was so obvious that only an idiot wouldn't see it. "It means you're in love with Nicole."

"I have no idea what you're talking about." My gaze darted around the crowded deli, searching for anyone who might have overheard him. I didn't need to find myself suddenly engaged on the front page of whatever trash some asswipe paparazzi worked for.

"Right," Jared said, his voice heavy on the skepticism. "When was the last time you hooked up with a groupie?"

I shrugged. "A few weeks." More like two and a half months.

"My guess is you haven't screwed around with anyone since before my wedding, with the exception of Nicole. And it's not just that. Before she joined us, we always had to be on the lookout for you pranking us. You haven't done anything since she joined us on tour."

"That doesn't mean I'm in love with her. It just means I'm tired from all the touring and haven't had the chance to fuck a groupie." And it meant I was too distracted by Nicole to even think about pranking the guys.

He raised his hands, palms out. "All right, you're not in love with her . . . so why do you keep looking at her like you are?"

"I don't . . ." The words faded away at Jared's I-don't-buy-it-and-neither-will-the-guys expression.

"So when are you going to tell her how you feel about her?" he asked, apparently not ready to drop the topic of my love life anytime soon.

"I'm not telling her," I grunted, "because I'm not boyfriend material."

A couple of teenage girls stepped into the deli, giggling.

One glanced in our direction, and her mouth flopped open as she stared at Jared and me.

"How do you know you're not boyfriend material?" Jared asked, oblivious to the girls. "It's not like you've ever had a girlfriend."

"Maybe I don't want to be a boyfriend. I like being single. It's simpler." What was the point of having a girlfriend if you had to worry about her walking away because you were always on the road and were never there for her? My music was all I had left after everything else that had happened in the past. It was the only thing that had never turned its back on me.

Jared didn't say anything for a moment, and I figured he had dropped the topic. But then he spoke again. "It has nothing to do with whether or not you think you're good enough to be someone's boyfriend. This has to do with what happened with your family."

My gaze slid back to the girls still standing near the entrance. All three were now staring at us, prepared to let out a fangirl scream at any second . . . or maybe implode from seeing us here. Fortunately, they were too far away to hear our conversation.

"It has nothing to do with that," I grumbled, already regretting that I'd let Jared talk me into this picnic.

"You're not a gambling addict anymore, Mason," he said, dropping his voice so that there was no chance of anyone overhearing him. "You haven't gambled in years. Maybe it's time you let go of the past and move on with your future. Tell Nicole how you feel about her."

I snorted a laugh. "When did you develop a pair of ovaries?"

"When did you become such an idiot? Look, I know what I'm talking about. I screwed things up big-time with Callie, in case you've forgotten. Don't make my mistake, and don't make the same mistake Nolan made. We both nearly lost the women we love. At least learn from our mistakes."

"Order for Jared," the blonde at the counter called out, ending our conversation, for which I was thankful.

He was right, though. What was the point of him and Nolan almost fucking things up with the women they loved if I couldn't at least learn from their mistakes?

But it wasn't as easy as that. Nicole had said she couldn't be with an addict. True, I wasn't an addict anymore, but did she feel the same way if the person was a former addict?

We grabbed the bags with the food in them, and after chatting briefly with the teenagers (who looked ready to faint at any second) we walked to Central Park. After searching for a few minutes, we found a spot on the grass far enough away so no one would disturb us, yet easy for Nicole and Callie to find. He texted Callie with the exact location. Fortunately, while we waited Jared didn't bring up the topic of Nicole and me again.

But the moment I saw her, I realized he was right. I'd been too afraid to tell her how I felt because I didn't wish to go through the pain again of what I'd experienced with my family. Plus I had no idea how she felt about me. After I revealed my feelings for her, she might bolt across the park, screaming, unable to get away from me fast enough.

She dropped onto the grass next to me, a couple of bags in her hand. She was wearing the pair of jeans I liked best on her, cowboy boots, and a warm cream-colored jacket with brown buttons down the front. She had recently bought it because of the cooler fall temperatures she now had to deal with on the road. Between that and the light sweater underneath, it didn't look like she needed me to warm her up anytime soon.

It didn't take long before Jared and Callie were busy kissing, and I knew from experience they would be occupied for the next few minutes. Suddenly unable to wait another second, I shifted around and my lips were on Nicole's, our tongues proving how much we both needed this.

I threaded my fingers in her hair, pulling her head back,

which allowed me to deepen the kiss. She leaned into me, as if melting at my touch. She tasted and smelled like I'd remembered—like a piece of heaven. A piece of heaven that I wasn't sure I could walk away from once this was all over.

I removed my lips from hers and rained small kisses along her jaw to her ear. "Are you gonna show me what's in the bag?" I murmured. Her breath caught in her throat, and it was one of the sexiest sounds I'd ever heard—along with her laugh.

"It's nothing," she whispered.

I licked the shell of her ear. She made that sexy sound again, and my dick twitched with interest. "Since when did anything from a lingerie store amount to nothing?" I asked.

I grabbed for the bag, but she jerked it out of my reach at the last second. What she hadn't counted on was that I had the upper hand when it came to size and strength. Not to mention that my curiosity had spiked, fueling my determination to discover what she had bought while shopping with Callie.

I lunged again for the bag, which she was holding behind her. Giggling, she tried to scramble away, but I was faster and pinned her down with my body.

"I win," I said, laughing at her adorable pout, and gave her a quick kiss before grabbing the bag from her outstretched arm.

I climbed off her and peered inside the bag. "Doesn't look like nothing to me." From what I could tell, it was the opposite of nothing. I just didn't want to know who the lucky man was who would get to see her in it. The way things were going between us on tour, it wouldn't be me. That much I was certain of.

Smirking at her, I handed the bag back to her, then removed the food and drinks from the deli bags, placing everything on the blanket Jared and I had picked up after the interview. He and Callie were still in their own world, cuddling and talking in murmurs.

As I watched them, jealousy struck me in the heart. Not that

I was jealous of them—they'd been through so much already that they deserved to be happy.

No, I was jealous of how Jared had put his heart out there, risking it all, to tell Callie how he felt about her. In the end, it had worked out for them, and they were even more in love than they had been back in the spring.

"This all looks amazing," Nicole said, checking everything out.

I handed her the turkey sandwich I'd ordered for her, figuring that she would love it. Based on the bright smile on her face when she saw it, I'd been right.

Jared gave Callie her sandwich, and we enjoyed ourselves for a while, eating our lunch and catching up on our mornings. The sun shone down on us, as if smiling at our cozy little picnic for four. At one point I slipped my hand under the hem of Nicole's sweater and stroked my thumb against her lower back, enjoying the feel of her soft skin and wishing it was more than just her back I could touch.

I leaned closer to her, so only she could hear my next words. "I want you in my bed tonight, Nicole." My voice came out as a husky rumble in my chest, and my breath brushed against her cheek.

She inhaled sharply, the sound a soft gasp. "I want that too, but we shouldn't—"

"Yes, we should. I can't take it anymore. I . . . miss you."

"I miss you too. Are you sure?"

My thumb paused against her skin. She hadn't thrown out the that-would-be-unprofessional card, the way I'd half expected. I took it as a positive sign. "I'm sure if you are."

She gazed up at me, and I could've sworn the love I had for her was reflected right back at me. I leaned down and brushed my lips against hers. I wanted to tell her right then how I felt about her, but now wasn't the best time for that— not unless I wanted Jared and Callie to witness me being rejected if Nicole didn't feel the same way about me as I felt about her.

"You wanna play soccer?" I asked after we had finished eating. During lunch Nicole had been eyeing the ball we'd brought, the same excited gleam in her eyes as when the band was about to play against the roadies.

Nicole snatched it out of my hand and scrambled up. We split into two teams—boys versus girls. And there was a reason for this. With the two women involved, Jared and I turned it into a physical game, if you get what I mean. There was a lot more touching involved than was normally called for.

Nicole tried to dribble the ball around Jared, but I swooped in, wrapped my arms around her from behind, and swung her out of the way. She laughed, not at all upset that I'd prevented her from scoring on our makeshift goal, constructed out of the coats we'd shed. Not that she was much better. At one point while I was trying to get the ball away from Callie, Nicole came up behind me and murmured in my ear, "I don't suppose you have handcuffs for tonight?"

That was enough to distract me from the game. I spun around to see if she was serious. She laughed, and did her best to block Jared from using one of his dirty tricks on Callie. Callie went on to score.

We eventually headed back to the hotel to get ready for tonight's performance. There was a notable change between Nicole and me, a shift in our relationship. What surprised me the most was Jared's earlier comments. He didn't care if Nicole and I were involved—not like in the beginning, when the band made it clear that Nicole and I couldn't fuck each other while she was working for us. But maybe the rules changed when love became part of the equation.

Nicole's room was further down the hallway from mine. Callie and Jared had already disappeared into theirs. As we approached my door, I took hold of Nicole's hand, making it clear I wanted her to join me. We still had time before the concert, and I intended to show her how much I loved her—even if I wasn't ready to tell her with words just yet.

"Let me shower first and get my stuff from my room," she whispered, leaving me to fist-pump the air in gratitude.

23

NICOLE

Mason still had some time before we had to leave for tonight's concert, but would he want to spend it with me? Normally we did. But that was different. That was while we were on the bus or going to an interview. That was part of my job. Going into his room and showing him how much I loved him? Not in my job description.

I spent the entire ride to our floor wondering if I should say something to him. If I was a groupie, I'd have an advantage when it came to seduction. But being seductive was a skill that had always eluded me. I was sure that if I attempted it, I would come off as laughable at best.

My question was answered a moment later when we reached Mason's bedroom door and he grabbed my hand. It was clear that he desired me, and he wanted me before we left for the concert. Another emotion—one that wasn't so clear—also stirred in the depths of his eyes.

"Let me shower first and get my stuff from my room," I whispered.

He released my hand and I hurried down the hallway. In my room, I quickly showered and changed into the baby doll lingerie, my heart pounding loudly in my chest. I wouldn't be surprised if the people in the room next to mine could hear it. No, this wouldn't be the first time I'd had sex with Mason, but for some reason everything felt different. This time my heart was on the line—and it made me nervous as hell.

I pulled on my jeans and a Pushing Limits T-shirt and grabbed my favorite long wraparound cardigan. My new look, which I had adopted while on tour, was a fusion between rock music and country-western chic.

As I started toward the door, my phone rang. It was Zack—and he was a day early for our usual chat.

Despite knowing that Mason was waiting for me, despite my body attempting to shoo me over to his room, I accepted the call. "Hey, is everything okay? Or are you confusing Monday with Tuesday?"

"Everything's fine. I just have a second to talk, but I wanted to wish you an early happy Thanksgiving. I won't have a chance to talk for the next week because of a training mission."

I smiled at hearing his voice even though it made me miss him more than normal. Our mother had died shortly after Thanksgiving. But instead of letting ourselves wallow in our grief the following year and every year after that, we had done whatever we could to make Thanksgiving still special—the way Mom would have wanted. "Happy Thanksgiving to you too."

"How are thing going with all the touring? Still having fun?"

"Definitely. But I couldn't imagine doing this for the rest of my life."

"How's Mason doing?"

"He's doing great." Although he would probably be doing better if he wasn't still waiting for me to show up. "All the guys are doing great." I glanced at the clock.

A muffled sound came through the phone, like Zack was talking to someone but had his finger loosely over the mike so I couldn't hear what was being said.

The talking stopped. "Sorry, Nicole. Duty calls." We said our goodbyes as a text came through on my phone. I ended the call and checked it.

> Mason: Are you still coming? Or rather, are you still planning for me to make you come?

> Me: Sorry, Zack just called. Heading over now!!!!

I opened my bedroom door and poked my head out, then glanced down the hallway in both directions. Although I'd gotten the sense today that Jared didn't care if something happened between Mason and me, I had no idea if the rest of the band shared the sentiment.

And this wasn't the time to find out their opinion on the topic.

The hallway was empty, other than the housekeeper parking a cleaning cart a few doors down from Mason's room. Without giving me a second glance, she removed supplies from the cart and disappeared into one of the rooms. I slipped out of my room, shutting the door behind me, and scurried to Mason's room. I knocked on his door, still keeping an eye on the hallway.

The door opened and Mason gave me a once-over, as if he had X-ray vision and was checking to see what I was wearing under my cardigan and jeans. His mouth shifted up to one side, giving him the rapid-heartbeat-inducing smirk I loved so much. No man could pull off a sexy smirk the way Mason could.

"Weren't you supposed to wear the sexy outfit you bought today?" he asked as I entered his room.

"Maybe I am." I winked at him, then let the cardigan slip away from my shoulders and pool to the floor. He stood there, waiting appreciatively for the show to begin.

With one of my favorite Pushing Limits songs playing in my

head, I hooked my fingers under the hem of my T-shirt and dragged my fingertips up my body. Inch by slow inch, I revealed the mesh camisole that covered my stomach but did nothing to hide it.

Mason's eyes turned dark with desire, and my confidence grew with each exposed inch of my body. I might not have been a skilled seductress, but that didn't matter to him.

Which was a good thing. I now understood why strippers didn't wear T-shirts. It was difficult to come off as sexy when yanking one over your head. At least guys could do the cool trick where they grabbed the back of their collar and pulled the T-shirt off that way, revealing their sexy abs in the process.

But when a woman tried it? Not so sexy.

While moving my body in time to the ballad in my head, I removed my T-shirt without ruining (too much) the effect I was going for. Bonus seduction points for me.

If I'd thought Mason's eyes were lustful before, that was nothing compared to now. And I still had my jeans to go. I slowly undid the button, my hips swaying to the beat in my head. Then I ran my fingers along my hips and my waist and up my ribs, briefly cupping my breasts. Mason's heated gaze turned my panties wet, which was nothing new. Judging from the bulge straining against the zipper of his jeans, my strip show was turning him on as much as it was me.

My hands continued their upward journey, ending in my hair, which I pulled back into a messy ponytail. With my hips still swaying and my hands in my hair, I lowered myself until my butt was only inches from the ground . . . and, surprisingly, I did it without landing on my ass. If Heidi's and my business didn't take off after the renovations the way we hoped, I could always become a stripper. *Or not.*

Releasing my hair, I straightened up and traced my fingertips down my body and the see-through baby doll.

"You know you're killing me, right?" Mason said, his voice thick and sexy. He swallowed. Hard.

I winked again.

He groaned, and it took everything inside me to keep from giggling.

With the same teasing slowness as before, I unzipped my jeans and shimmied them down my legs. I had barely stepped out of them before Mason's hands were all over me, his self-restraint finally lost.

The kisses started out hungry . . . for both of us. But then they dissolved into something that was more tender yet at the same time consumed me to the core and almost melted me on the spot.

Mason pulled away ever so slightly, and my lips immediately missed him. But there was also something else of his I was missing. "Hardly seems fair," I said, "that you're dressed and I'm wearing nothing but this." I gestured to my body, then bunched the fabric of his T-shirt in my hands and pushed it up, exposing those fine abs I hadn't seen in a while.

He got the hint and hastily removed the T-shirt. I reached for the button at his waistband and slipped it through the opening. My hand might have accidentally-on-purpose brushed against his hard length. The resultant growl deep in his throat almost had me coming. Oh, who was I kidding? I was pretty close to falling apart at his feet. He really wasn't playing fair . . . but then neither was I.

I unzipped his jeans, but unlike when I'd undone mine, there was nothing slow and deliberate about it. I craved to touch him—*now*.

Mason didn't wait for me to help him with the rest of his clothing. He yanked it off in one efficient move. He then stroked his warm hands over my body, as if worshipping me. Each and every nerve buzzed with the need to love him, and for him to love me in return.

He reached behind me and his nimble fingers unhooked my baby-doll top. The bra and mesh slipped forward, aided by Mason sliding the thin straps down my arms. His hands gently cupped my breasts, then his thumbs traced circles around my nipples. I arched back, pressing the full globes into his palms.

He ran his lips against my jaw. "I don't want to fuck you, Nicole." My legs quivered at his husky, sex-starved voice. "I want to take my time and make love to you." I gasped softly at his words. "But first I want to taste you and make you come hard against my mouth."

I barely heard the second part, my fuzzy brain still stuck on his earlier words. But I didn't have time to further question what he meant—my body was more interested in the part about the promised orgasm.

Mason kissed me again as he guided me backward onto the bed. I sat down, then lay back with Mason still kissing me. His hot, naked body pressed down on mine.

Before I could wrap my arms around him to keep him from leaving, he pulled away and peeled my lacy panties down my legs. He lifted my legs onto his shoulders, revealing my aching core.

It had been only nine weeks since the last time Mason had touched me this way, but it felt like it had been forever. I'd experienced sexual droughts lasting much longer, but this time it seemed different.

His tongue lashed against my happy place. It couldn't have been more thrilled that now the drought was over. And because of that, it didn't take long before the warmth in my lower belly became all-consuming. A wave of euphoria rushed through me, taking me over the edge. I arched my back and released a cross between Mason's name and a moan. I really hoped Kirk wasn't in his room next door. Or, if he was, that he had no idea it was me serenading him with the loud, erotic noises.

I drifted back to earth and smiled drowsily at Mason. He sat down on the bed and opened the nightstand drawer, then removed a box of condoms and pulled out a foil package.

"You have condoms?" I said, stating the obvious.

"After spending last night alone in bed, I was hoping I could convince you to stay with me. That's the only reason I have them. Like I said before, I want to make love to you, Nicole. You and only you." He gave me a small, hopeful smile.

And I nodded. Nodded because I longed to make love to him. Nodded because I loved him and only him. Nodded because I had lost all ability to speak after what he had just said.

He rolled the condom along his length, then leaned down and kissed me. Like the earlier ones, the kiss was tender and filled with love. I shifted my body to straddle his hips and lower myself onto his thick length.

With our gazes locked, I moved my hips slowly, taking him in deep. The heat in his eyes told me he was more than happy with this pace, with this level of intimacy.

We stayed like this, the buildup to the apex a slow burn. When the softest part of me eventually clenched around him, the climax was more intense than I ever remembered it being. After Mason, no other man would ever come close to satisfying me the way he did.

Remaining inside me, Mason flipped me onto my back and thrust deep, again and again and again, until he joined me in an earth-shattering orgasm, calling out my name—which ended any chance I had of keeping our relationship anonymous when it came to his bandmate next door.

After a few moments he lifted himself from me and discarded the condom in the trash. Before I had a chance to miss him, he was back in bed, cuddling me against him.

He kissed my forehead, then shifted so that he was looking down at me, my head on his pillow. "This is probably not the best time to tell you, but I'm in love with you, Nicole."

I parted my lips to respond, to tell him that I loved him, but he settled his finger against my lips, halting my words.

"I know I don't fit your list of the characteristics you're looking for in the ideal man," he continued, "and that's okay. I just needed to tell you how I feel about you." The vulnerability in his eyes was staggering. It was similar to when he had shared a piece of himself in the music store back in Desert Springs, when he had played his song on the piano for me.

And that made me love him even more . . . and wonder at the same time if someone had once hurt him.

He lowered his finger from my mouth, and I brushed my lips against his. "I love you too. I don't know what it means for us, but my heart wants what it wants. And right now it wants you." *Damn, stubborn heart.* I had a feeling that at some point I'd wind up cursing that vital organ.

We continued kissing unhurriedly, confirming our love for each other. We stayed like this until we were ready to make love again. This time, as we got closer to when we had to leave for the concert, our movements were less tender but nowhere near less satisfying.

We then showered and got ready, both of us avoiding the one topic we weren't ready to discuss: what our love for each other meant for our future.

24

MASON

Nicole was still asleep next to me when I woke up late the next morning. Thanks to the thick curtains, the room was dark except for a strip of sunlight sneaking its way in through the narrow gap between them.

The curtains were useless against the car horns that blared every few minutes, though. Welcome to New York City.

I listened for a while to Nicole's soft, even breathing before finally making a decision. I had no idea what our future held for us together, but one thing was certain: before I could move on, I needed to make one final attempt at fixing things with my family.

I owed it to myself, and to them, to at least try.

The last time I had spoken to any of them was three years ago. I had no idea if my parents were still living in the house I'd nearly cost them three years before that, and I had no idea where to find my brother and sister.

I slipped out from under the covers, careful not to wake Nicole, and sat on the desk chair. I pulled out my phone and Googled my father's name. At the top of the results page was the link for an obituary. Frowning, I clicked on it and scanned the article.

"*Fuck*," I said, louder than I had intended.

Nicole stirred in bed and slowly opened her eyes. "What's wrong?" Her voice was husky with sleep, but for once my body didn't react to it. She pushed herself up to a sitting position, causing the bedding to slide off her. It pooled around her waist, leaving her breasts exposed. Normally that would be enough to distract me. But not today.

"My father's dead," I said. To my ears, my voice sounded hollow, broken.

"Oh God." She scrambled out of bed and wrapped her arms around me. Never before had I needed someone's touch as much as I needed it now. Or maybe that had to do with the woman holding me, showing me how much she loved me. "I'm so sorry, Mason."

She pulled away after a beat, her expression free of pity and heavy with understanding. Both of her parents were already dead.

I sat down heavily next to her on the bed. For a second I just stayed there, unmoving, at a loss as to what to say or do. Nicole rested her hand on my thigh and soothingly stroked her thumb against my bare skin.

I closed my eyes and let my shoulders slump forward, the pain of everything overwhelming me.

"What happened?" she asked, her voice a whisper of concern.

What did I tell her? Nicole would hate me if she found out what I had almost done to my family and how low I had sunk at one point when it came to my gambling addiction. Her father's own addiction had come close to destroying *her* family. I knew I should tell her the truth about being a recovering addict, but I just wasn't ready to go there. Not yet. Not now.

I inhaled deeply, then let out a long, slow breath. I opened my eyes and stared at the painting on the far wall, unable to look at Nicole. In it, a lone couple stood next to what could be a fountain in Central Park on a rainy day. You couldn't see their faces, thanks to the red umbrella obscuring them. It was the sole splash of color in the otherwise monochromatic picture.

"I told you I'm not close to my brother and sister. They aren't the only ones I haven't been close to in a long time." I swallowed back the pain, which had formed a bass-drum-sized lump in my throat. "I decided this morning to try to contact my family again. But when I looked up my parents' address back in L.A., I discovered my father's obituary." I scrubbed my hands against my face. It wasn't enough to erase the words in the obituary from my mind. "He died four days ago from cancer, and no one thought to tell me he was dying. His funeral is tomorrow."

And had I waited a few more weeks before looking, I might never have known—the obituary long since buried way down on the search-engine page. Fortunately, because Dell was a common last name and I had been estranged from my family well before Pushing Limits was formed, I didn't have to worry about the media finding out about my father. Not unless a family friend or relative leaked it. My father's memory didn't need to be caught up in the media circus that would no doubt follow.

Nicole didn't say anything at first. She took my hand and held on to it, sharing her own strength with me. "What do you need from me, Mason? I love you, and whatever you need, I'm here for you."

The emotion behind her words almost knocked me over. I couldn't remember the last time anyone had loved me enough to care about me. At least not since her brother stepped in and saved my sorry ass. For years the guys in the band had known me as the prankster, the guy you didn't take too seriously. That was the man I had pretended to be when I checked out of rehab. It had been easier that way once I'd realized how alone I really was. Even Zack hadn't been around at that point. He had been stationed on the other side of the country.

I wrapped Nicole in my arms and held her for a few minutes. "Thank you," I whispered, emotion clogging my words. I kissed the top of her head, doing my best to keep things together. Nicole didn't need to know the truth: how I felt like a wild animal had clawed me from the inside out and left me to bleed to death.

She glanced up at me, her beautiful face filled with sincerity. I kissed her mouth, but mere kissing didn't fill the cavernous void inside me, and I pulled her onto the bed. . . .

Once our breaths had finally returned to normal and the memory of my father's death broke through the euphoria-induced haze, I grabbed my phone. After the concert tonight I could take a red-eye to L.A., then grab a flight after my father's funeral to Atlantic City, where we were playing the following night.

But I couldn't do it alone.

"I'm going home after the concert tonight to attend his funeral tomorrow," I said. It was the least I could do to show that I still loved him, even though he had been unable to love me in the end. That had all been my fault, not his. "Would you go with me?"

"Of course." She stroked her fingers against my jaw.

I grasped hold of her hand and kissed her fingertips. "Thank you."

Without her, I would never survive tomorrow. Now I just had to hope bringing her with me wasn't a big mistake—one I would forever regret.

25

NICOLE

The twenty-four hours after Mason discovered his father's obituary rushed by in a blur. After learning of his father's death, Mason had become more restless than he'd been the first day back on tour—back when I had kissed him before the show. How he made it through the concert last night was beyond me.

As it was, none of the guys in the band knew about his father. His rationale for keeping quiet about it was that he didn't want to worry them. So instead he told them simply that he needed to fly back home and would join them in time for the concert in Atlantic City.

Based on the weird looks the guys kept shooting me before we left, it was clear they didn't suspect the real reason he was leaving. Although I wouldn't have been surprised if they thought we were flying off to Vegas to get hitched.

Mason parked his car in the funeral home parking lot, not far from the entrance to the squat brick building. Unlike in the movies, where it often rained during funerals, as if the heavens also were in mourning, the sun shone down from the faded blue sky. Despite the lack of rain for the past few weeks, the lawn and decorative flower garden on either side of the building looked fresh and inviting—or would, under any other circumstance.

Mason cut the engine but made no move to leave the car. He just sat in the driver's seat, staring at the stream of people in black suits and dresses filing into the building. Tension and sadness sat between us. I reached out and threaded my fingers with his. My heart broke seeing him like this. I remembered how lost I'd felt when Zack and I buried our mother. All I knew about Mason and his family was that they were no longer on speaking terms, but I didn't know why. I had no idea how to ask him, and this wasn't the right time to try to get him to open up. He needed me to support him. The rest could come later, when he was ready.

"It's going to be okay, Mason."

He tore his gaze from the front entrance, and my heart broke some more at the sorrow in his eyes. "How can you be so sure?" he asked.

That was the thing—I couldn't. I had no idea what demons he was facing by being back here, other than they were big enough that he didn't wish to deal with them alone when he was at his most vulnerable.

"You just need to take small steps," I said. "Go in there and say goodbye to your father. Otherwise you'll spend the rest of your life regretting it."

The moment I said the words, I realized how true they were. My father had died a few years ago. Suicide. A side effect of his gambling addiction. Zack had been away on a mission, and I couldn't bear the idea of facing the man—even if he was dead—to say goodbye. He had hurt my mother and he had hurt Zack and me, and I had let the pain block out the happy memories of him from before our lives took a turn for the worse.

And now a part of me regretted that decision. Despite

everything, he had been my father and I had loved him. I was only understanding that now.

"After you say goodbye to him," I said, "then we can leave if you want."

Mason thought about it for a second, then nodded. "And you'll stay with me?"

"If that's what you want."

"I do." He glanced back at the funeral home and nodded again, this time with a little more conviction. "Whatever happens in there, thank you for coming here with me . . . and thank you for not asking any questions. I promise I'll explain everything another time. When I feel brave enough. I just can't deal with it now."

He turned his head back to me, and the vulnerability in his eyes brought the sting of tears to mine. "Okay." I reached out and lightly squeezed his hand, which was gripping the steering wheel.

He loosened his hold on it, then exited the car and waited for me to join him. Once out of the car, I straightened the short black dress I had bought yesterday afternoon in New York City for the funeral. The outfit, with the ballet flats, was simple and classy enough for a funeral. Mason also looked good. Unlike me, he'd been able to go home before heading here and change into one of his black suits.

He slipped his fingers between mine, and we joined the mourners heading into the building. A gentle sob broke out behind me, bringing tears to my own eyes. It didn't matter that I'd never met Mason's father or didn't know anything about him. It was enough that his death touched so many people who *had* known him.

At the dark wooden doors leading into the building, Mason came to an abrupt halt, and part of me was grateful for that. The memory of the last time I'd been in a funeral home was still too fresh and I could barely breathe, so I imagined how much worse it was for Mason. I had at least been there for my mother during her final days. She'd died knowing I loved her.

My palms grew damp, but despite how much I longed to turn and run, I couldn't. The man I loved needed me to help him get through this. I opened my mouth to say something, anything, to encourage him to keep going, but before the words could form, Mason resumed walking.

Inside the building, the cloying scents of a large white floral wreath, burning candles, and furniture polish greeted us. I was instantly transported back to my mother's funeral, except in her case the wreath had been much smaller, because Zack and I couldn't afford the size she had deserved. I closed my eyes against the sob building in my chest. *She died five years ago,* I reminded myself. *She's not the one lying in the coffin.*

Organ music spilled from the open doorway, beckoning us to enter—or maybe it was warning us that we should leave while we still could.

We stepped into the room. The beautiful yet haunting melody was now accompanied by the murmur of hushed voices with occasional sobs and sniffles. I scanned the rows of seats, searching for a spot to sit. The chapel was crowded, with well over a hundred people already seated, leaving us with few options.

I was about to ask Mason if he wanted to sit up front, where some empty seats still remained, possibly for family members, when I noticed his gaze was fixed on something ahead of us. I couldn't tell if he was looking at the closed coffin with the massive red and green floral arrangement on it or at the two men standing up front.

A man a few years older than Mason was talking to a man with gray hair. As if sensing us standing there, the younger man looked in our direction and scowled. Mason stiffened and his hand tightened its hold on mine.

The man, who looked too similar to Mason to be anyone

but his brother or other close relative, continued glaring as he walked toward us. My breath became shallow, my heartbeat rapid. I wasn't one for confrontations, especially in a funeral home with so many people there to pay their final respects. A bad feeling settled in my gut that nothing good could come from us being here.

"You have some nerve coming here, Mason," the man said. The intensity of the anger in his voice forced me to take a step back. Mason didn't so much as flinch.

People sitting near the front turned in our direction or peered over their shoulders. Some were also frowning at us, but I couldn't tell if that was because Mason was here or because they sensed a fight was about to break out.

"I have every right to be here. He was my father as much as he was yours," Mason said, his voice low and dangerous. I suspected I was the only one who could hear the edge of hurt in it, but that was because I had seen how broken he'd been upon finding out that his father had died, how torn up he'd been when he realized no one had told him his father had been battling cancer. It wouldn't have been hard to track Mason down. They could have contacted his recording label and had them tell him.

"You lost the right years ago," the man said.

"So you're telling me I can't even say goodbye to my own father?"

The man scoffed. "That's exactly what I'm saying. You fucked up his life, and now that he's dead, you want forgiveness."

A muscle in Mason's jaw twitched. It was a look I wasn't used to seeing on him, and one I'd be happy never to witness again. "That's not true. I contacted him numerous times and apologized. I did whatever I could to make everything up to him. He was the one who walked away, not me."

For the first time since I'd met him, the Mason standing

next to me was nothing like the man I'd fallen in love with. That man was filled with passion and life. This Mason was a mask of the real man.

"Why are you here, Mason?" a petite woman with graying strands in her short, curly black hair said as she came toward us. Her eyes were red from crying and her mascara had smudged beneath them. I shivered at the chill in her tone and at the way she glared at Mason, like she wished it were his body in the coffin instead of the man who was currently there.

"I wanted to pay my respects, Mama." Mason's voice was noticeably softer now, but also wary.

"You don't belong here," she said, voice shrill and easily heard by everyone in the chapel. "Leave before I get security to remove you."

What the hell had Mason done to deserve this? They were acting like he had killed someone. Obviously I didn't know the history behind all this, but that didn't prevent me from wanting to comfort the vulnerable man standing beside me, his hands shaking.

"Look," I said, somehow finding my voice, even if it did sound rusty from lack of use, "he's sorry for what he did, and he just wants a chance to say goodbye to the man who raised him. He flew all the way from New York City last night to do that. Can't you just give him a chance?"

The woman turned her chilly regard on me. This time I stood my ground, ready to do whatever was necessary to defend him.

"I don't want you or your . . . your hussy here," she bit out. "It's as simple as that."

"Nicole isn't a hussy," Mason said, his words strong and certain. He might've been hurting from everything else, but his love for me pushed that aside for the moment. "She's a sweet and loving woman, and no matter what you may think of me, she doesn't deserve to be called that."

The way his mother studied me warned me that no matter what either Mason or I said, she would see me as someone I wasn't. She would see me as someone well beneath her.

"Son," a man said behind me, "you should leave."

I turned to find a cop standing there. Great—they had called the police to have him removed. Unlike with Mason's mother and the other man, the cop's tone was free of anger. If anything, it held a note of compassion.

Mason nodded, the fight now burned out of him. His head dropped forward slightly and he made a move to leave. I tried to blink away the tears threatening to fall, but one broke free. I sniffed and wiped it away as we walked out of the chapel and through the main doors.

"I'm sorry, Mason," the cop said once we were outside. I started at hearing him use Mason's name. "I'm sorry no one told you about your father. And I'm sorry 'bout what happened in there."

Seeing the confused expression on my face, Mason said, "Nicole, this is my uncle T.J."

"Nice to meet you," the hulking man said, holding out his beefy hand for me to shake.

"Nice to meet you too," I said, hoping he didn't notice I was trembling slightly from what had transpired a few minutes ago.

"Are you staying in town long?"

Mason shook his head. "We have a flight to Atlantic City in two hours."

His uncle raised an eyebrow. Mason answered it with an almost negligible shake of his head.

"So, are you two dating?" T.J. asked.

Good question. We might've said the "love" word to each other two nights ago, but otherwise nothing had changed between us. And after discovering that Mason's father had died, we had been too focused on that to discuss us. He was still my boss as far as I was concerned. A boss whom I was now offi-cially having sex with.

"Nicole manages the band's social media accounts," Mason said, "and has been organizing a few promotional events beyond what our label does for us."

His uncle chuckled. "I have no idea what you said, but it sounds good to me." He looked back at the building. Gospel music now drifted from the open doors. "I should go back inside. I just wanted to make sure you're okay."

They gave each other a one-armed man hug. T.J. wished us a safe flight and told Mason not to be a stranger anymore as far as he was concerned. There was a message in the look he gave Mason as he said it that was lost on me.

"Is everything all right?" I asked Mason once his uncle was inside and we were walking back to Mason's car. "I mean with your uncle."

"Considering he's the only member of my family who can stand the sight of me . . ."

I waited for the remainder of the sentence, but was met by the click of the car doors unlocking instead.

"What happened to make your family act like that?" I asked, temporarily forgetting what he had said about telling me everything once he was ready. But as soon as the words were out of my mouth I regretted them. "I'm sorry, Mason. Forget I asked. I know you'll tell me when you're ready." He had gone through so much in the last twenty-four hours, he didn't need me interrogating him.

"I just can't right now. . . . I'm sorry. I made a mistake and have been trying to make up for it. They obviously will never forgive me, and it's about time I accept that." He turned the key in the ignition, making it clear that whatever had happened in his past wasn't up for discussion.

26

MASON

Don't fuck things up, son. That's what my uncle had been telling me. He wanted me to confess the truth to Nicole about what had really happened between my family and me. If he had known about her father, he might not have felt the same way. Or maybe he would've been even more adamant about me telling her the truth.

When my family had initially turned their backs on me six years ago, my uncle knew how upset I was, and he'd eventually checked on me a few months later. It had taken him that long because he too had been pissed at me. I'd promised him I would turn my life around.

And I did. Temporarily.

But then I lost everything I owned and then some on a bad deal, which meant I was royally fucked—as in the if-you-don't-pay-us-by-the-end-of-the-day-you're-dead type of fucked. So I'd overdosed on alcohol and painkillers. Zack had found me and called the police—and my uncle had been the cop sent on the call. The cop responsible for telling my family the news.

I can't imagine they were too upset when they heard it. More likely they were upset that Zack had saved my miserable ass. His photo was probably on some family dartboard, along with mine.

As much as my uncle clearly wanted me to tell Nicole everything, I couldn't. Besides, what was the point? That wasn't who I was anymore. Plus, who knew how long Nicole and I would be together? I longed for it to work out between us, but I had no idea if that was the same future she also saw for us.

And right now I wasn't in the mood to ask her.

We drove back to my house and changed our clothes, then took a cab to the airport. Once we had checked in for the flight, we sat down in a restaurant and ordered food and drinks. She had water; I had beer.

Before she was halfway finished with her drink, I was already on my second beer. But it would take a lot more than two beers to push away the memory of what had happened at the funeral.

We didn't talk much. I pretended to watch the game playing on the large-screen TV. Just don't quiz me on what sport it was or who was playing. I could feel Nicole's worried gaze on me. I did my best to ignore it.

The men at the table next to us leapt out of their seats, whooping and hollering. They high-fived, then returned their attention to the TV screen. In the background, a recorded female voice reminded passengers to not leave their luggage unattended, or else it would be removed and destroyed. *Happy Thanksgiving to you too.*

Two teenage girls approached the table, giggling. "Aren't you Mason Dell from Pushing Limits?" the tall redhead asked. Before I could reply, she sat down next to me and asked her friend to take a photo.

"I'd rather not be in any pictures right now," I told them. My voice came out gruff, the opposite of how I normally was with fans, but at this point I didn't give a damn.

"You don't have a choice," she huffed. "It's part of your job."

"What he means," Nicole jumped in, her voice sounding like it had been dipped in honey, despite the mother-bear attitude rolling off her, "is this isn't a good time and he's not currently working right now. He's in a restaurant having dinner."

"Doesn't matter," the redhead said. "I bought his album, which means I bought the right to take a photo of him."

Nicole slowly shook her head. "Wrong. You bought the album, nothing more."

"He's a celebrity. If he doesn't like people taking photos of him, then he shouldn't be one."

I didn't have the energy to argue otherwise. Fortunately, Nicole did. "How would you feel if one of your teachers showed up in the middle of the night, handed you a homework assignment she'd forgotten to assign in class, and told you it was due tomorrow morning?"

"That's not the same thing."

"It's exactly the same thing. Yes, Mason is a celebrity, but he deserves his privacy as much as anyone else. Being a celebrity doesn't mean he gives up the right to privacy. It means it becomes even more important to him."

"God, you're such a bitch."

Nicole gave her a long look that basically said, *Pot, have you checked the mirror lately?* "No, I'm not. I'm just asking you to be more respectful of his wishes."

"C'mon, Em," the redhead's friend said. "It's not a big deal. It's enough that we saw him here."

Em glared at her. "But I want proof. No one's gonna believe me when I say I saw him." More so because I wasn't even supposed to be in L.A. As far as everyone knew, I was heading to Atlantic City from New York with the band. L.A. wasn't exactly in the neighborhood of either location.

"We're going," the brunette said firmly, and took her sister's arm. To Nicole and me she added, "I'm sorry about my sister. She can be a spoiled brat sometimes."

Her sister threw her a dark look. "I'm not a spoiled brat."

"Whatever." The brunette rolled her eyes. "Happy Thanksgiving," she said to Nicole and me before the two of them walked away.

Yeah, happy Thanksgiving to me. Too bad the only thing I had to be thankful for was them leaving.

"Thanks," I said to Nicole, feeling even more drained than before the girls had shown up.

"You're welcome." She gave me a small smile and glanced around at the tables surrounding us. Some people were staring at us. Others didn't care about anything besides whether their flight was still on time. The problem was a storm in the Chicago area. So far our flight hadn't been canceled yet, but a large number of others had been.

I checked my phone to make sure nothing had changed.

"Fuck," I muttered.

"What's wrong?" Nicole asked.

"The flight's been delayed by two hours." For now. There was always a chance it could be delayed even longer . . . or worse.

"At least it's not canceled," Nicole said, doing her best to stay positive, but there was no missing the fatigue in her eyes.

The restlessness that had surfaced when I first discovered my father had died grew. I went back to pretending that I was watching the game and shifted around on my seat. I was also vaguely aware that I was drumming on the table.

A hand touched my knee, and I looked up at Nicole sitting next to me. "Did you want to walk around?" she asked.

I nodded and finished my beer while she signaled to the waitress for the check. We paid for the food and walked around the terminal. Like in the restaurant, my presence gained me looks from fans who recognized me, but fortunately no one else tried to talk to me.

Nicole tugged me down a quiet hallway. There were no shops or restaurants here. Nothing that would attract a steady stream of travelers. She pressed a featherlight kiss on my lips. Then she nipped my lower lip between her teeth and gently tugged on it.

Hell, yes!

I didn't need another invitation. Knotting my hands in her hair, I opened my mouth and let her in. Our tongues glided together, taking, giving, worshipping. Her kiss was a salve on my battered soul.

We kissed for a while. I was vaguely aware of the occasional person walking past. No one said anything—not that I would've cared if they had. I just wanted to arrive at the hotel in Atlantic City and get Nicole in my bed.

Once things progressed from sweet kisses to something more intense, I rested my forehead against hers, both of us panting.

My phone pinged with a text from Jared. *We're in Atlantic City. Is your flight on time?*

It's been delayed two hours, I replied.

Will tell the hotel that you'll be late, he responded a few minutes later. *Don't want them to give away your rooms.*

Not that Nicole needed her room. She'd be sleeping with me. But since I wasn't sure how Jared would react to that, I didn't bother to tell him to cancel hers.

Or more like I didn't know how the band would react. Jared knew about my feelings for Nicole. As far as I could tell, he hadn't said anything to the guys.

An antsy feeling crept inside me, and I drummed my hands against my legs. It wasn't enough. I needed to pound on my drums. That and sex were the only ways to drive away the feeling. But after what had happened at the funeral, I had a feeling sex wouldn't be enough this time. Fuck, I shouldn't have gone—then Nicole wouldn't know how badly I'd screwed things up with my family.

As it was, the clock was rapidly tick-tick-ticking toward those final minutes before she would discover exactly how I had destroyed the people I loved.

27

NICOLE

ason and I stumbled into the hotel after two in the morning. My stomach churned with memories of a lifetime of pain as we were forced to walk through the casino to get to the front desk. The lingering smell of stale smoke taunted me—that was what my father had smelled like whenever he returned home from gambling. I wanted to climb into a shower and scrub the stench off me.

Lights from the slot machines flashed, attempting to lure in the unsuspecting. Even at this hour the casino was busy, with men and women of all ages. Some looked like zombies—pretty much how I felt after attending the funeral and then traveling the rest of the day. The only difference was that my resemblance to a zombie was due to a lack of sleep. The people in front of us had been turned into zombies by the slot machines.

Waitresses wearing stilettos and revealing dresses carried trays of drinks to the tables where patrons were involved in their card game of choice. The men at the nearby table barely gave their waitress a second glance, their attention focused on the dealer and the cards laid out in front of them.

Mason stopped for a moment. I had no idea why. I was too

busy watching a man at the blackjack table who reminded me of the last time I'd seen my father. His dress shirt was disheveled and his short brown hair stuck up at odd angles, the result of him shoving his hand through it too many times. Nausea churned in my stomach when I saw the wedding ring on his finger. This man probably also had kids at home who had no idea what their father was up to. If they were lucky, he didn't live around here; he was just here for a day or two before returning home to his happy family. If they were lucky, he wasn't a gambling addict.

The man lost his last remaining chips and his face paled. My guess was that he had lost more than he'd bargained for, more than he could afford. He removed himself from the table. A woman who looked like she was more desperate to win than to breathe quickly filled his empty spot.

I couldn't watch any longer, and started walking away. I didn't care if Mason was with me or not; I just needed to go to the room and sleep. Preferably for the next ten years . . . or until it was time to leave for the concert.

The benefit of getting in so late was the lack of a huge line at the registration desk. One guest was being served by the clerk, and there was a couple waiting in front of me. Even though they looked like they could fall asleep standing right there, their weary gazes kept shifting back to the casino.

Then their eyes went wide, as did their mouths. I spun around to see what had them so enthralled. Mason was approaching, hot as ever, despite what he had gone through with his family and despite having been awake for close to forty-eight hours. I had at least fallen asleep during the flight, but he'd told me he hadn't.

There was something different about him all of a sudden, but I couldn't figure out why. It was as if he had gotten a second wind.

Then I realized what it must be. We were about to check in

to our rooms, and he was no doubt hoping for sex before hitting the sheets. The way I was feeling right now, I'd probably fall asleep in the middle of it, and not even Mason's talent for giving me orgasms could keep me awake.

The customer at the front desk walked away and the couple in front of me took his place. Mason wrapped his arms around me and pulled me close, his chest against my back. "You're spending the night with me, right?"

"I don't have the energy for sex." My words sounded tired even to my own ears.

"I'm not expecting us to have sex tonight. I just want to wake up with you next to me." He nibbled the shell of my ear, and despite my state of near collapse, my body sat up and paid attention. "Then we can discuss the matter of sex when we're both awake. Deal?" He glanced over his shoulder at the casino before his warm breath was on my ear again.

I leaned back against him, letting him momentarily support my weight. "Okay. Deal."

After what felt like a lifetime, Mason and I stepped up to the registration desk. I checked in first. Then it was Mason's turn, and he asked for two key cards for his room and handed one to me.

"I'll meet you in the room," he said. "There's something I have to do first."

"What?" I couldn't imagine him having the energy to do much more than drag himself onto the elevator and stumble down the hallway to our room.

"It's no big deal. Just something I have to quickly do. I promise I won't be long." He fidgeted with his key card, a sheen of perspiration glistening on his face.

"Are you sure it's nothing?"

He kissed the end of my nose. "Promise."

I nodded, because what else could I do? He didn't want to tell me and I had to trust him. "All right, I'll see you upstairs." I took from him the duffle bag that we had been using as luggage for the trip to L.A. It contained the only clothes I'd have with me until I returned to the tour bus.

I walked down a short hallway to the elevators and pushed the button. I didn't even have the energy to glance back to see where Mason had gone.

The ping of the arriving elevator had me doing a happy dance . . . in my head. The doors opened, and I entered and pushed the button for my floor, struggling to keep my eyes open. Naturally the god of irony thought it would be funny to make my room a good hike from the elevator once I got to my floor. I prayed the entire way there that he wouldn't be cruel enough to render my key card useless.

Luckily for me, he listened. The door opened and I stepped into what had to be the sweetest sight for my poor exhausted body and brain. The king-sized bed beckoned to me, and I walked over to it, thinking I would lie down for just a moment or two—to test it out, nothing more.

But after traveling on the tour bus for the past nine weeks, and after everything that had happened in the last forty-eight hours, the bed's pull on me proved to be stronger than I'd expected. My eyes drifted shut.

When I opened them, it took me a moment to remember where I was. The lack of the tour bus engine humming in my ear was my first clue.

I was lying on the bed, fully clothed. Daylight streamed through the open curtains, though fortunately it was cloudy outside, so it wasn't as bright as it might have been otherwise. The light by the door was still on, as was my bedside lamp. According to the alarm clock, it was eleven-fifteen. The way I was feeling—which was a helluva lot better than when I'd lain down last night—another few hours of sleep wouldn't have hurt.

I shifted around to see if Mason was awake yet. But instead

of finding him or a hint that he had slept in the bed last night, the bedding on his side was smooth and untouched.

I pushed myself to sit and listened for any indication he was in the bathroom. When I couldn't hear anything, I climbed out of bed and clicked the bathroom light on. There were no signs that anyone had used it since we'd checked in.

I examined the room again. Still nothing to indicate Mason had even come into the room last night. Maybe he had decided to let me sleep, and he'd slept in my room instead of his own. I checked my phone, but he hadn't left me a text, nor had he phoned me.

I grabbed a change of clothes and my toiletries and hit the shower. Once I had scrubbed off the two days of travel and dried my hair, I checked my phone again to see if Mason had tried to contact me while I was showering. Still nothing.

I sent him a text.

Me: Where are you? Missed waking up to you in bed.

When I didn't get a reply, I sent Nolan a text, asking if he had seen Mason this morning. He responded a few minutes later that he hadn't. Neither had any of the other guys when I texted them.

Jared suggested that Mason was still sleeping in his room, since we had arrived so late. I didn't want to admit that I was in Mason's room and he hadn't shown up.

Jared: But if you see him, tell him "Without You" hit #1!!!!

Me: Congrats!

I wasn't too surprised. It was one of my favorite songs from their latest album.

Unable to stand not knowing where Mason was, I grabbed

my purse and went downstairs. My plan had been to ask at the front desk if Mason had asked for a second key to my room after all. But as I walked past the casino, something made me glance toward the blackjack tables, and my breath stalled in my chest.

Mason was sitting at a table with a tall, gorgeous brunette next to him. She was holding what could've been either orange juice or some sort of alcoholic beverage. He had a bottle of beer. She didn't appear to have been there all night; she looked like she was freshly showered and ready to spend the day with the drummer.

Anger surged through me, tempered only slightly by the realization that I could not make a scene. The band didn't need that. It was also kept in check by the fact that Mason wasn't even paying attention to her, his focus instead on the game he was playing.

From what I could tell, he wasn't a novice at the game. But he also wasn't winning a huge amount of money. Just how long had he been here? How much had he lost?

I walked up to him. "Mason? What's going on?" Hurt bled into my words, even though I had been aiming for a casual, non-accusatory tone.

"He's with me," the brunette said, as if that explained everything. Her voice was smooth and sexy, much like her dress, which was a complete contrast to my jeans, lacy white tank top, denim jacket, and cowboy boots. She gave me a once-over, clearly deciding that my outfit was cute but not suitable for hanging out with a rock star.

"Actually," I said, "he's with me."

She peered at Mason for confirmation, but he was too busy to notice her. He nodded at the dealer to indicate that he wanted another card. "Hit me." Three of hearts. "Stay."

The dealer's next card was a ten. He lost; Mason won.

I expected him to keep playing, the way my father would

have, but he just gathered his winnings and turned his sexy smile on me. "What time is it?"

Like it always did whenever Mason smiled at me that way, my heart beat like the tail of an overly excited puppy. "Almost noon. Have you been here all night?"

"Sorry, I didn't wanna upset you, what with your father's history and all. I wanted to play a hand or two, and did better than I expected."

"So you didn't lose any money?"

"Nope. I bet a small amount and got lucky. Don't worry, I'm not like your father." His gaze drifted back to the table for a moment before returning to me. The woman hanging around him continued to stare at him, as if imagining him naked. Couldn't say I blamed her for that. "And I'm finished. Let me just cash out."

"Who's the woman?" I asked as we walked away from the table. By some small miracle, I kept myself from sounding like a jealous girlfriend. I was trying to come across like a colleague who wasn't screwing around with her boss and was curious, nothing more.

Mason blinked and glanced back at the table, as if he had no idea what I was talking about. A sensual smile grew on her face that made me want to step on her toes—purely accidentally, of course. Her smile dimmed at Mason's indifferent expression.

"I have no idea," he said. "I think she was hitting on me at one point, but I wasn't paying attention. She was only interested in me because she recognized me from the band and because I was winning." He flashed me the sexy one-sided grin that made all my girlie parts hum. "Besides, she's not you." That got them really revved up.

While he went to cash in his winnings, I sent Nolan a text, letting him know that I'd found Mason. He replied that the guys were heading over to the hotel's Tex-Mex restaurant and they'd meet us there.

I told Mason this once he returned from the cashier. "I guess lunch is on you," I said with a smirk. "How much did you win?"

"Three hundred and fifty dollars."

I stopped short. "Are you kidding me?"

He shrugged. "Like I said, I got lucky."

"I'd say." It was no wonder my father had gotten hooked on gambling. I could understand how it could easily happen. You win a few times, and once you start losing, you're positive the winning streak will resume soon.

Mason shifted on his feet, and his bloodshot eyes scanned the area. He looked both wary and exhausted, which wasn't too surprising given that he hadn't slept yet.

"Do you want to meet up with the rest of the band for lunch and then get some sleep? You've got time before the interview this afternoon."

He scrubbed his face with his hand, swaying slightly, and I recalled that not only hadn't he slept, but he'd also been drinking beer. "I'm not hungry, and I don't feel like seeing anyone right now. I'll just go to the room and meet up with the guys later."

After what had happened yesterday at his father's funeral, I wasn't too surprised he felt that way. But his bandmates were like brothers to him, and he needed them more than ever.

I laid my hand on his biceps, over the tattoo that said "I am a fighter" in Sanskrit. "Are you sure? They have some great news to tell you."

"What's that?"

"Why don't you come to lunch and they can tell you themselves?"

"I'd rather not right now. Why don't you tell me?"

I grinned, barely restraining myself from jumping up and

down while squealing like a fangirl. "'Without You' hit number one. Congratulations! You guys finally did it." I flung my arms around his neck and hugged him hard, doing my best to ignore the smell of smoke now clinging to him. "I'm so proud of you, Mason."

He hugged me back, but it lacked the level of enthusiasm I would have expected. I chalked it up to his exhaustion.

"Thanks. Can you do me a favor?" he asked.

I released my arms from around him and stepped back. "Sure, what?"

"Don't mention anything to the guys about the gambling. If . . . if Kirk hears how much I won, he'll want to gamble, and that's not a good idea."

"Why?" But then his meaning slammed into me, and my eyes widened. "Kirk used to gamble?"

Mason nodded. "But he doesn't want anyone to know, so don't say anything to him, all right? He'd kill me if he found out I told you."

"Okay."

He kissed me on the cheek. "I promise I'll make it up to you for last night."

"It's okay. Just make sure you get some sleep, and text me when you wake up."

"I will."

Mason headed for the elevators, and I walked to the restaurant around the corner, where I was meeting the guys. They were already seated when I got there, drinking sodas.

"Where's Mason?" Jared asked.

"In his room." I bit my lip, wondering how much to tell them about yesterday. In the end I decided they needed to know. For Mason's sake. "Look, about yesterday . . . Mason's father died last week, and he and I returned to L.A. for the funeral. Something happened there, and I think he's still upset about it."

They all stared at me, shock clearly stamped on their faces. Nolan was the first to recover. "How come he never said anything about it to us?"

"Probably because he was upset when he first found out. None of his family had bothered to tell him his father was dying of cancer. He only discovered what had happened because he saw the obituary."

Aaron glanced at the other guys, then at me. "So how come he told you and not us?" There was no curiosity to his words—instead, he was pissed. They were like brothers to Mason, but by keeping them in the dark, Mason had acted like his own asshole brother, the one who hadn't told Mason about their father's death.

"Because he's in love with her," Jared finally said, his gaze locked on me.

Kirk and Aaron both looked surprised at this revelation. Nolan, not so much.

"What happened at the funeral?" Kirk asked, skipping past what Jared had just told them.

Shit. I guess I should have expected that. "He wasn't exactly welcomed with warm fuzzies."

The guys looked far less surprised by this than they had been about the news that Mason was in love with me. Whatever had happened between him and his family, they knew about it.

And whatever it was had them worried.

"Why is his family so upset with him?" I asked.

"That's something only Mason can tell you," Nolan said, confirming what I'd already suspected they would say. Their loyalty to Mason came first.

"You're sure Mason is in his room?" Kirk asked me.

"He said he was going to bed. I have no reason not to believe him." Just like I'd had no reason not to believe Mason when he told me early this morning he was coming right up to our room after he did something first.

The something that had kept him from coming to bed like he'd promised.

A bad feeling kicked me in the stomach. I shoved it away. Mason wasn't my father. He wasn't addicted to gambling.

Unlike my father, he knew how to walk away.

28

NICOLE

While Mason slept in his room, I spent the time in *my* hotel room, working on my laptop. Updating the band's social media sites. Organizing the Christmas contest for their Instagram account. Finalizing plans for Blooming Love's grand reopening. Sketching possible designs to etch on glassware, none of which so far felt right, meaningful, or special. Nothing that would stand out.

An hour before we were due to leave for the radio interview, I still hadn't heard from Mason. I sent him a text, in case he'd forgotten to tell me he was up. Five minutes later, having still not heard from him, I walked to his room and let myself in with my key card.

At first I thought Mason was still sleeping, because the room was dark. But then the light from the open doorway spilled onto him and glinted off the beer bottle in his hand as he paced. The only clothing he had on were his jeans; his feet and chest were bare.

"Hi," I said tentatively, and entered the room. He didn't appear to notice me. He just kept walking back and forth, like a caged tiger. I'd seen him like this before a concert, before I gave him his good-luck kiss, except this time something seemed really off.

I clicked the door shut. "We're leaving in an hour for the radio interview," I said, flipping on the light switch. Only then did he look up. The caged look instantly changed to heat—and before I knew it, Mason had me on the bed, my clothes on the floor with his jeans.

Unlike the last time we were together, the sex was purely physical. There was no love in his actions, just the desire to bang out his need and frustration. He tasted of beer and the lingering smell of smoke still clung to him.

Once he was finished, his orgasm coming shortly after mine, he collapsed onto the bed, a great divide now between us. His arm covered his eyes, as if he now didn't want to see me. That felt like a stab in my heart. My brain told me to not be so stupid. He was still upset about his father's death and about what had happened yesterday. If he had to use me for sex this one time, that was fine. I would do whatever I could to help him get over his pain.

I scooted over and kissed his chest. Then I rested my head over his heart, as I'd done before. But Mason didn't touch me like he usually did, and that ripped a gaping hole inside me.

I forced a soft, understanding smile onto my face and sat up. "You should have a shower now and get ready."

Normally at the suggestion of a shower, he would try to convince me to join him—usually for another round of sex. This time he just shrugged and said, "I guess." He got out of bed, grabbed the half-empty beer bottle from the nightstand, and headed for the bathroom.

And for the first time since entering the room, I noticed the four empty bottles scattered throughout the room. That wasn't to say he had never drunk beer in the afternoon, because he had. But it had usually been with the guys, and not while he was supposed to be sleeping.

Unable to sit still, I opened the curtains and straightened up the room while I waited for Mason to finish showering.

When he came out of the bathroom, my breath stopped short in my chest at the sight of his muscular, half-naked body. Water drops trailed down his gorgeous brown skin, further emphasizing his sexiness. My gaze followed one lucky droplet as it traveled between his pecs, down his taut stomach, and under the towel wrapped low around his hips.

"Like what you see?" Mason asked, his deep, rough voice the epitome of sexiness. The sound of it short-circuited my brain.

I stepped closer to him, my fingers itching to reach out and yank the towel free. "Maybe."

"How long till we have to leave?" The towel shifted. There was definitely activity happening under it.

I checked the alarm clock on the nightstand. "Twenty-five minutes."

Mason closed the space between us. His beer breath had been converted to minty freshness. "I need you, Nicole. I need to be inside you." His voice was a seductive murmur against my cheek, yet it held a note of tenderness that had been missing before his shower.

His lips skimmed down my cheek and found their way to my mouth. He gently nipped my lower lip between his teeth and sucked on it. My breath hitched and I welcomed him in.

Unlike earlier, he took his time . . . not that we had much. I freed him from the confines of his towel and let it drop to the floor. He had my T-shirt off in a matter of seconds. My bra came off next, thanks to Mason's talented fingers—he could teach a course on how to unhook a girl's bra in less than a second.

Mason palmed my breasts, heating them with his touch. I wrapped my arms around his neck and pressed my breasts into his hands. He pinched my nipples, and the ache between my legs begged for its turn. I rubbed against him, denim against raw man.

He groaned and removed his hands from my breasts, then with a quick flick of his fingers unhooked the button of my jeans and slid the zipper down. I could almost hear the clock mocking me from the bedside table, reminding me we didn't have a lot of time before we had to leave. While Mason wasn't moving as slowly as he had when he'd made love to me, he was definitely moving too slowly given that we had to leave soon.

It was as if he didn't want to go to the interview. Couldn't say I blamed him.

After peeling my jeans off and tossing them to the side, he slipped his fingers between my legs. "Christ, you're already ready for me," he said.

And that was my problem. Spending so much time with him meant I was ready for him most of the time. I just had to look at him and my heart raced, my body begged for his touch.

His fingers cupped my sex and began exploring. I gasped, then let my fingers do their own exploration of his body.

"I need to taste you," he groaned. "Lie down and let me taste you."

Something about his tone gave me pause. "You remember you have the interview, right?"

He mumbled against my neck. It almost sounded like he said he wasn't going.

I pushed him away, knowing I had a responsibility to the band, although my body screamed, *What the heck are you doing?* With my hands still on his chest, I gazed into his eyes, dark with lust and pain and somewhat still bloodshot. "Mason, you have to go. They're expecting you."

"Tell them I'm sick."

My eyes widened. "Are you?" I wouldn't be surprised if he was after everything that had happened in the past few days.

He grabbed hold of my wrists and pulled them away from his chest. "I don't feel like going."

"I don't think you have a choice." Although if I had a say in this, I would tell him to stay here and rest. But if the empty beer bottles were any indication, he wasn't going to take things easy. "Have you slept at all since you left the casino?"

"Why are you asking all these questions? I don't want to go to the interview and I don't want to be interrogated. I just want to make love to you. Is that asking too much?" But based on his slightly pissed-off tone, it didn't sound like he really wanted to make love. He was trying to distract me from getting ready for the interview.

"How are you going to explain why you didn't show up for the interview but were fine for the concert?" I asked.

He grunted and stepped away from me. "It's not like it's a big deal. I'm the band's fucking drummer. Do you think the interviewers really care if I show up? No, as long as Nolan is there, that's all they care about. The rest of the band is just an added bonus."

"That's not true." From what I could tell from the social media sites, the fans loved all the guys. Yes, Nolan was slightly more popular, but that was because he was the lead singer. He was the member people thought of first when you mentioned the band, but it didn't mean the other guys were considered less important. "Besides, if you don't show up for the interview, you'll be fueling rumors that you're leaving the band. That's how these things start." At his disbelieving look, I added, "You're not planning to leave the band, right?"

"Of course not!"

"Then why fuel speculations?" There were already rumors of the band breaking up, due to Jared's recent marriage.

"So you're saying you don't want to fuck before the interview?" was his non-answer.

"I just don't want you to be late." My body was officially

going to kill me. Tough. It would eventually get over it. This was more important.

Mason heaved out a sigh. "Fine. How about after the concert? Can we fuck then?"

A smile fluttered on my lips. "I'm counting on it." I leaned closer and kissed the light stubble on his face. "I love you, Mason. Don't forget that. I'm here for you, and not just so you can deal with your frustrations by fucking me."

He turned to face me and my lips brushed against his. He gently kissed me, his hand cupping my cheek. "Thank you," he murmured. "And just so you know, that's not what I'm doing. Being inside you makes me feel better."

I kissed him back. "Then I'll do whatever I can to make you feel better. But do you know what would make *me* feel better right now?"

"What?"

"If you got dressed so we can meet the guys downstairs." Something dawned on me. "Have you eaten anything today?"

"Not hungry." He turned away and gathered his clothes from the floor.

"But you managed to down five beers since you left the casino?" Plus however many he had drunk before I found him there.

He leveled his gaze at me, and I did my best to ignore that he was still naked. "I lost my father and no one told me about it. Then I was chased out of his funeral. I think I'm allowed some beer while I wallow in my grief." He yanked on his boxer briefs. The man could be an underwear model. He was that perfect and that hot.

And, in his underwear, that distracting.

But I couldn't argue against his point, and given what he was going through, I didn't want to try. I'd give him today, but I would keep an eye on him. It was all I could do.

I had a quick shower, then we went down to meet the guys

in the lobby. The woman from this morning was standing near them, talking with two other women.

She nodded in our direction. I threaded my fingers with Mason's. Not because I felt threatened by her—I wasn't, much—but because I wanted to show him that I was there for him.

Mason's body was stiff, his hands slightly clammy as we approached the band, but I had no idea why. The guys were talking about the upcoming interview. They said hi to him, but none of them mentioned anything about what I had told them. Maybe they were waiting for Mason to bring it up.

The three women who had been eyeing the guys sashayed over. "Hi again," the brunette said. She gave Mason a smile that was a cross between shy and seductive. She also threw in a little lip nibbling for the added effect. Wow, she was good.

"I don't know if you remember me from this morning," she went on to say, "but I'm a big fan." Her gaze drifted to each of the guys in the band. "Of all of you."

"Thanks," Nolan said, ever the spokesman for the band. "Are you going to our concert tonight?"

If I'd ever seen three women who looked like their puppies had been kicked across the state line, this would be them. "We couldn't get tickets. You guys sold out too quickly." Which was why Endless Motion had added another date in Atlantic City. Both dates had sold out in a matter of hours.

"That's too bad," Nolan said. To the guys, he added, "We should get going." Which was my cue to play the role of handler that I'd been thrown into doing again. Their regular handler was temporarily out of commission due to food poisoning.

"Sorry, ladies," I said. "They have to do a radio interview. It was nice meeting you." Always a good idea to be polite with the fans, even if they were lusting over your boyfriend.

"Can we get your autographs?" said another of the women, a dark-haired supermodel lookalike.

"Sure. Do you have any paper?" Jared asked.

Mason was noticeably quiet, which was unusual for him.

The women glanced at each other, then at the registration desk, but the line was so long it would take more time than we had for them to wait in it and ask for paper there.

"You could always check the gift shop," I suggested. From what I could tell from having walked by it earlier, they had just about everything.

The women didn't need to be told twice. They disappeared into the store. I turned back to Mason to see how he was doing. His dazed-looking eyes were directed at the casino. "You okay?" I asked, low enough so the guys couldn't hear me.

When he didn't respond, I gave him a light nudge. He blinked and peered down at me. "Are you okay?" I repeated.

He gave me a slight nod. "Yeah, I'm fine."

The women returned a moment later, running. I must admit, I was impressed. I could barely walk in heels, never mind run in them.

The guys signed their autographs and said goodbye to the women—who I could tell were wishing we had given them backstage passes so they could see the concert.

"Are you guys staying here tonight?" the woman with brunette hair asked, her eyes wide and hopeful. They flicked back to Mason.

"Yes," Aaron said. "We leave tomorrow."

"Maybe we'll see you around after the concert, then."

"Maybe."

And with that I hustled the guys through the casino and to the front doors of the hotel, where a limo was waiting to take us to the radio station.

29

NICOLE

Like in every other city, a large crowd had flocked to the radio station for the interview. Even from within the limo I could hear the fangirl screams building to a deafening volume. I was used to seeing the crowds, but they had been nothing like this. And I suspected they'd be far more common now that the latest Pushing Limits single had hit number one on the U.S. charts.

Brian climbed out from the front passenger seat while we waited for the limo driver to open the side door, then one by one the guys from the band emerged. I winced at the thunderous noise greeting each man . . . and realized how much I missed Desert Springs. My life had been simple back then, if you could call running a business simple. Instead of the loud, enthusiastic fans, the sounds of nature and small-town life had filled my days.

A pang squeezed my heart. I was in love with Mason, no doubt about it. But that love wouldn't bring me happiness. It would bring me only turmoil. My brain understood that . . . but my heart was not so sure. I mentally went through the list of what made a perfect husband. Nowhere on it was a mention of him being a rock star. Nowhere on it was a mention of this kind of life—a life I wasn't so sure I wanted.

Once the guys had exited the limo, I followed behind them. Unlike in the hotel, I didn't hold Mason's hand to show my support. Out here, it was all about the fans. Sure, Mason and I had admitted our feelings for each other, but we still hadn't talked about what it meant. So for now I just pretended that Mason was nothing more to me than a job.

A job that was ending in a few weeks.

Nolan, Jared, Kirk, and Aaron all interacted with their fans the way they normally did. Mason didn't even spare the fans a second glance. He stalked to the building, yanked the door open, and entered. It was like he hadn't even seen them.

I wasn't the only one who noticed his disappearing act. Screams for Mason followed after him. Despite what he had said earlier, the fans' reaction proved he was loved. They wanted to see the energetic, highly entertaining drummer as much as they wanted to see the rest of the guys.

Hearing the frustrated cries from the crowd for Mason, the guys in the band scanned the area. When they didn't see him, they glanced back at me, puzzlement in their expressions. But I didn't have time to answer their unspoken questions. I rushed after Mason.

I found him inside the building, pacing across the tile floor. A twentysomething guy was standing to the side, looking a little lost as to what to do. My guess was he was an intern.

Ignoring him, I joined Mason. "Hey, are you going to be okay?"

"I'll be fine," he mumbled, but his stooped shoulders suggested he was as fine as Anne Boleyn had been just before her beheading.

The main door opened and fangirl screams spilled into the lobby, accompanied by the guys in the band. I could tell his friends wanted to check on Mason, but once they spotted the intern waiting for us, all they could do was follow him onto the elevator.

The interview itself went fine. Mason was more subdued than normal, but the rest of the guys made up for it. It was as if they were doing it on purpose, to distract the radio personalities from zeroing in on Mason's atypical behavior. Anyone who had ever listened to him in an interview knew he was the boisterous one.

With the interview over, we drove to the arena. Mason's knee bounced the entire way as he stared out the window. The moment we'd climbed into the limo, he'd grabbed hold of my hand. Not once did he let go. Even when we arrived and were hustled into the arena through the back entrance, he held on tight.

The bands still had twenty minutes before they had to be at the meet-and-greet. We headed for the greenroom, and Mason immediately went for a beer. He gulped it down like it was water, then grabbed another one. By the time I had to herd them into the other room so they could meet their fans, he had polished off two bottles. While two beers in that time frame would have done me in, Mason didn't so much as sway or slur his words. So I let it go. He was a grown man who was grieving. Who was I to judge, as long as he didn't do anything to hurt himself or anyone else?

I watched the meet-and-greet, making sure things went smoothly. With their handler recovering from food poisoning, I had taken on her role here too. But after nine weeks of watching her manage this part of the concert, I pretty much had it figured out. It didn't hurt to have Brian, the ex-Marine, by my side. No one would dare question my authority with him next to me.

"Is Mason okay?" Brian asked. "He's acting strange."

"His father died the other day." No point discussing the rest of the details, especially since I had no idea how much Mason was fine with me sharing.

"That would explain things," Brian said, and didn't say anything more on the subject.

As soon as the meet-and-greet was over, the guys returned to the greenroom. All grabbed a beer. Like with his first two, Mason downed his in record time. He pulled another one from the ice chest and flopped down on the worn couch. With each second that ticked past, his restlessness grew. He fidgeted, and when someone tried to ask him a question, he didn't reply. It was like he was no longer in the room. After a while, people quit trying to talk to him—and the once outgoing drummer seemed perfectly fine with that.

I expected him to take me down an empty hallway to make out, as per our normal routine, but he didn't. It was a routine that I wouldn't be doing for much longer. Did it mean that once I returned home, other women would be taking over my role?

For a second I was tempted to grab a beer myself, to help me forget that my time with the guys was ending in a few weeks. By the time the band had to go onstage, Mason had consumed five beers since arriving at the arena. Even the guys were throwing him worried glances. It wasn't that they thought he was too inebriated to play—which he wasn't. Maybe if he had finished a sixth beer, things would've been dicey, but as it was, I was confident his playing would be fine.

It was everything else I wasn't so sure about.

I watched the show from my usual spot backstage. They finished the final song of the night and the audience went crazy, which was no different from what had been happening lately at each of their shows. They waved their appreciation and walked off the stage—to the thunderous demands for an encore.

"You should give them what they want," I told the guys. Hell, I wasn't ready for their show to be finished either.

"We can't do that," Jared explained.

"Yeah, I know. They have to set up for Endless Motion." Except it didn't sound like the audience agreed. They continued chanting for an encore.

"Your call," the stage manager said, having overheard our conversation, "but I think you should go for it. It's just one song."

Mason shrugged, then walked onstage and waved at the audience. This only made them more excited, cheering louder than when the band had left the stage. He headed for his drum set.

"I guess we're going on." Nolan grabbed his acoustic guitar from the roadie, and the guys joined their drummer onstage, to cheers from the crowd.

The stage manager grinned. "I was hoping they'd do that. I know opening for Endless Motion is big, but Pushing Limits shouldn't be still playing as an opening act. They're bigger than that now."

As if agreeing with his words, the screams and hollers from the audience grew. The first beats of "My Song for You" filled the arena, and my mouth flopped open. I had already heard the story behind the song, which they never played in concert. It wasn't even on their albums. I lifted my phone and began videotaping them. A moment later, Jared's sexy voice filled the arena, and I was positive the reaction of the audience would cause the roof to cave in. Their excitement at hearing the song was undeniable.

Once the final bars of music faded away, I sent the video to Callie. Then I braced myself for the return of the five extremely sweaty men.

They bounced down the metal steps, their energy level higher than before they'd played the song.

"You guys were amazing," I said, caught up in their enthusiasm. "And they agree with me." I gestured toward the stage and the audience. "That song better be on your next album. I love it." I grinned at Jared. "And I just sent Callie the video."

He whipped out his phone from his back pocket, probably to text her.

Normally I didn't touch Mason once he'd finish performing, at least not until he had showered. But given the past few days and given that the guys now knew how we felt about each other, I didn't hold back this time. I flung my arms around his neck and kissed him, letting him know how much I loved him and how proud I was of him.

He returned my kiss. I vaguely heard the guys chuckling. Then Aaron suggested we go somewhere to celebrate their first encore performance.

"Before Remar finds out about it and chews us a new one," Kirk said.

I unlocked my lips from Mason's and looked over my shoulder at the guys, my arms still around Mason's shoulders, his arms around my waist. "Remar? Who's that?"

"Ronald Remar. The president of the record label."

"Why would he chew you a new one? Do I need to send him the video of how the audience responded to the encore?" I would if it would make a difference.

Nolan smirked. "That might help. Although in the case of Remar, who knows. We've been trying to understand him since we first signed with the label."

"Well, the man's an idiot if he doesn't see why you need to be doing encores." Maybe I should storm the proverbial castle and have a chat with him, businesswoman to businessman. But I would refrain from calling him an idiot, even if he was one.

The guys decided to return to the hotel to shower first. Mason appeared as eager as them to go out and celebrate, which was surprising given how little sleep he'd had in the past few days. I guess the adrenaline high made all the difference.

While Mason showered, I freshened my makeup and

changed into the dress I'd bought while Callie and I were shopping the other day. It was nothing like my usual style. The body-skimming black dress with spaghetti straps hit high on my thighs and was covered in black lace, revealing my arms and a portion of my chest. I got it for New Year's Eve. Heidi had bought us tickets to some gala event back home—the same gala event she had promised flowers for.

Mason stepped out of the bathroom, this time wearing jeans and a fitted black T-shirt. He did a double take when he saw me, then looked around the room as if searching for the real me. "Wow," was all he said, which pretty much summarized what I was thinking about him. The man could make even jeans and a T-shirt look amazing.

An image popped into my mind of what he would look like in a tux. I was certain even my imagination didn't do it justice—and in my imagination Mason was pretty damn hot.

I slipped on my stilettos, meaning that I was at slightly less of a height disadvantage when it came to Mason, since he was so much taller than me.

He flashed me one of his patented smiles that caused all women within a thousand-yard radius to swoon. "Not quite the cowgirl you were when I first met you."

I laughed. "When you first met me, I was wearing panda PJs, eating ice cream, and watching *Die Hard*."

"I happen to think those PJs are very sexy." His arms encircled me and he brushed his lips against mine. I melted at his touch, and at the spicy scent that was all man, all Mason. "And I definitely miss eating ice cream and watching *Die Hard* with you."

I missed those days too. Back when things were simpler. Back when we were close to being my version of a dream couple—only I hadn't realized it at the time.

"I bet Bernie misses you." I laughed softly at the memory of the big, lovable beast gazing adoringly at the equally big, lovable drummer. My heart hurt knowing that none of it was in Mason's future. But that wasn't where he belonged. Doing what he and Pushing Limits were doing . . . that was where he belonged.

I shoved the thought aside—along with the one where I imagined myself by his side on the road for the next twenty or so years.

The guys were waiting for us in the main lobby when we stepped out of the elevator. They were talking to a few people and signing autographs for them.

Mason suddenly stopped, body stiff, palms sweaty. Not far from us, the gambling zombies were busy pouring money into the slot machines. Put the coins in. Push the button. Repeat.

"Oh my God," a young woman at one of the machines screamed, even though her friends were standing right next to her. "I won a hundred dollars!"

A squeal of excitement rushed from the women as they bounced up and down, hugging each other.

Mason's hand tightened on mine. "I need to get some air." He let go of my hand and stalked through the casino to the main hotel entrance. Seeing him leave, the guys pulled away from their fans and we followed him.

It didn't take us long to find him outside. He was leaning against the gray cinder-block wall, looking photo-shoot ready. His head was turned slightly away from us, as if he was staring toward the road, his left knee bent and the sole of his left foot flat against the wall.

I walked to him and touched his arm. He startled, dropping his foot away from the wall. The pain in his eyes sucked the breath out of me.

"Are you sure you want to go out tonight?" I asked.

He gave me another smile, but this time the smile was painted on and I could feel a wall going up between us. I just wasn't sure what to do about it.

"Positive." He didn't wait for me to respond. He strode over to join the guys, leaving me by the wall, perplexed at his odd behavior.

Jared hailed a cab and we piled inside. Mason didn't hold my hand this time, and stared out the window the entire trip. I was sandwiched between him and Nolan, and could feel the lead singer glance at him every few minutes.

The line outside the nightclub stretched halfway down the block. But the advantage of being a rock star and having a number one hit on the charts meant the guys got to skip the wait. And because I was with them, I got to appreciate the benefits that came with their newfound fame.

Inside, the club was no different from the ones I'd gone to in college, with the strobe lights and loud dance music adding to the party atmosphere. We found a table at the far side of the room and ordered drinks from the waitress. While we waited for them, I grabbed Mason's hand. "C'mon, let's dance." I stood up and tugged his arm, not giving him a chance to say no.

He peeled his butt off the chair and followed me. The dance floor was crowded, which was fine with me. It meant I could press my body against his as we moved.

We danced for a few songs—his hands all over my body, making it clear he was with me—before returning to our table. As we made our way back to where the rest of the band members were sitting, people stared at us. Some probably recognized him and were simply in shock at seeing him here. Others might've been debating if he was really Mason Dell or just someone who looked like him.

Several women watched us, clearly deliberating if they should ask Mason to dance. Even though I'd been touring with the band for more than nine weeks, no one had posted pictures on the Internet of me with them. And there were no rumors of Mason having a girlfriend. Which meant he was free to dance with other women, in theory.

A small Asian woman stepped in front of us, blocking the path to our table. She was pretty, her long black hair streaked with chunks of blue. "Hi," she said. "You want to dance?"

At first I thought she was talking to Mason, because why wouldn't she be? But then I realized she was looking at me, dark eyes gleaming with hope.

Mason wrapped his arm around my waist. "Sorry, she's with me."

The gleam in her eyes was extinguished, replaced with disappointment. "Oh, that's too bad." She turned and sauntered back into the crowd.

"Well, that's a first for me," I said, grinning at Mason. "If I never find Mr. Right, maybe there's a Miss Right out there for me."

But while I was kidding, something about Mason's expression warned me he didn't see it that way. There was no amusement in his eyes, no upward tug at the corners of his mouth.

Nothing more than hollowness stared back at me.

30

MASON

"Well, that's a first for me," Nicole said, grinning. "If I never find Mr. Right, maybe there's a Miss Right out there for me."

Her words were a kick-in-the-ass reminder that I wasn't what she was looking for in a man. And while I'd known this from the start, it wasn't a reminder I needed right now. I already knew I didn't deserve her. I'd fucked up when it came to my own family. I didn't need to do the same to her.

And it was going to happen. I was that kind of man. Normally it wasn't an issue because I had become skilled at keeping people out of my heart. But then I'd spent those first few days with Nicole in Desert Springs and been reminded of what I'd lost because of my mistakes and because of my lifestyle. I wanted it all—the band, a family, Nicole—but I had no idea how to make it work.

Hell, I still didn't know how Jared did it.

Besides, I was too ashamed of my past to tell her the truth. Or maybe I was just too much of a coward. I knew I wouldn't be able to bear the look on her face when she found out I'd been no better than her father.

But if I didn't say anything, would it really matter? Nicole was returning home in a few weeks to reopen her store. I couldn't expect her to give it up for me, and I couldn't see myself leaving L.A. That was my home and it was where the band was located. Which meant it was impossible for me to have it all. The question was, what did I really yearn for?

Nicole and I went back to the table, and I finished off my drink. I ordered another. And then another. Before I knew it, the pain that had been clawing at me ever since I found out my father had died had been numbed a bit. And the newfound numbness made it a little easier to breathe.

I returned to the dance floor with Nicole. After which I had another drink. I could feel the guys and Nicole studying me every so often, but since I was still standing and wasn't making an ass of myself (or at least I assumed I wasn't), they didn't say anything.

So I kept drinking.

The smell of smoke and cheap perfume crept into my head, bringing with it memories of hours spent in casinos. I tossed back another beer, hoping to numb those memories too.

Eventually Nicole yawned for the third time in less than four minutes, and the guys called it a night. I walked out of the club, stumbling into people every couple of steps. Hey, I couldn't help it if they got in my way.

We hailed a cab and returned to the hotel. The closer we got to it, the more the craving that I had been holding at bay nudged at me. As we walked through the casino to get to the elevators, the sounds and smells brought back memories of what it felt like to win. It was like in the movie *Titanic,* when Kate Winslet was standing at the front of the ship, arms high, feeling the wind rush through her hair. She felt like she was soaring over the ocean. She felt like she was on top of the world.

That was what it felt like when I won—when I was invincible.

Right now, after my father's death, I wasn't feeling so invincible. The only time I'd felt that way was when I'd been winning at blackjack this morning, before Nicole discovered me in the casino.

Back in my hotel room, the itch to return downstairs burned strong. I kissed Nicole. The itch remained. I fucked her, doing what I could to drive away the craving.

But the call of the casino was too strong. Just one hand . . . then I would be okay.

Once Nicole's breathing had evened out and I was positive she was asleep, I carefully slipped from under the covers and pulled on my clothes.

Then I quietly snuck out of the room and went downstairs.

31

NICOLE

I opened my eyes, my brain slightly groggy from drinking more last night than I normally would, but not enough for a hangover—for which I was thankful.

The space where Mason had been before I'd fallen asleep last night was now empty. I reached out to touch the sheets, and frowned. They were cold.

I strained to hear if he was in the bathroom, but there was only silence. I turned to check the time on the bedside clock. Maybe I had slept in, and Mason had woken up and decided not to disturb me.

Six-thirty a.m.—five hours after we'd returned to the hotel. And it wasn't like we had gone straight to sleep once we entered the room. We'd had sex first.

Mason hadn't eaten much in the past day or two. He could have woken up hungry and gone to get breakfast. I checked my cellphone. He hadn't texted or phoned me.

I sent him a text to find out where he had disappeared to. While I waited for his reply, I showered and got ready. Even though it was early and I hadn't gotten much sleep, I was suddenly not tired. A bad feeling skittered through me. And it only got worse when I checked my phone and there was still no message from Mason.

Needing to escape the room, which was now feeling way too small, I grabbed my jacket and wandered downstairs. The lobby was busy, with the Thanksgiving weekend crowd checking in.

A twinge of homesickness poked at me, reminding me I wouldn't be celebrating Thanksgiving today with my best friend, the way I'd been doing ever since my mother died. It also reminded me how much I missed the time Mason and I had spent together back in Desert Springs, when he had fixed things around the house as if he lived there. When we'd removed the wallpaper together and spent most of the time laughing and joking around. When we'd walked Bernie and shared stories about ourselves and about Zack. When we'd eaten ice cream and watched *Die Hard* movies. When he'd shared with me the music for the song he had written—the song the guys in the band didn't even know about.

That was the Mason I loved most. The Mason I had fallen in love with long before I realized what was happening.

I headed for the front entrance, along the path that cut through the casino. A chorus of groans rose from one of the blackjack tables as I passed not far from them. Without meaning to, I glanced at where the sound had come from . . . and came to an abrupt halt.

Mason was sitting at a table, a stack of chips in front of him. A crowd of onlookers stood around him like vultures observing their next meal slowly die, unwilling to miss when it finally happened.

The dealer dealt the cards for himself and Mason. I watched in horror as Mason lost, then indicated he wanted to play another hand by pushing a large stack of chips forward.

He lost that as well.

I stood there for a few more minutes, ice filling my veins, as the same thing happened again. It was like witnessing a deadly car wreck as it happened, leaving you unable to turn away. You could only pray the sequence of events would suddenly change, and everyone would be okay.

Once more he gestured to the dealer for another round. And, like the other times, he lost.

"What are you down by? Fifty grand?" the man sitting at the end of the table asked. "Maybe it's time to stop before you lose any more."

My heart jumped into my throat, almost choking me. This wasn't the first time he had lost this big—that much I could guarantee. He'd lied the other day when he said he knew when to walk away. Clearly he didn't.

"He's right, Mason," I said, my voice brittle enough to shatter—much like my heart at seeing Mason this way. "You need to stop."

"I'm fine, Nicole," he grunted, and waved at the dealer to deal him in again.

I dug deep, searching for the strength to hold my ground, refusing to give up on him. "No, you need to stop. Now."

"I said I'm fine," he growled. "I know what I'm doing." Those were words I'd heard my father say to my mom numerous times before she finally decided she'd had enough.

This time Mason did win, which meant it would be impossible to tear him away from the game. He believed his luck had turned.

I stepped away from the table and called Nolan, praying he would answer his phone. A few seconds passed before he mumbled a sleepy "Hi," and I almost collapsed with relief.

"Nolan, it's Nicole. I found Mason in the casino, and he's already lost fifty grand. I can't get him to leave." The words came out in a panicked rush.

"Fuck! I'll be right down." The call ended abruptly, leaving me to wonder about things I would rather not have dwelled on.

Five minutes later—though it felt like an hour—both he and Jared arrived, both looking grim.

"Mason," Jared said, none too gently, "you've got to stop this. You know you'll never make back everything you've lost tonight. You never do."

"What are you going to do about it?" Mason muttered, pain lacing his words. Not once did his gaze leave the cards in front of him. "Cut me out of your life like my family did?"

I staggered back at this revelation. So that was why his family had turned their backs on him. And why Mason hadn't wanted me to tell the band about his win yesterday. Kirk wasn't the one with a gambling addiction. It was Mason.

He'd lied to me, like my father had lied to my mother.

"We're not going to cut you out of our lives like your parents did," Nolan said, leaning a hip against the blackjack table. "We all care about you. We're your brothers, which is why we need you to stop this."

"I'm fine," Mason huffed. "You don't have to baby me."

Jared parked his hand on Mason's shoulder. "I know we don't. And we're not. We just don't want you going down that road again. We can't afford to lose you. You're important to the band."

The way they were speaking to him, you'd have thought Nolan and Jared were trying to talk him out of jumping off a bridge. But given where my father had eventually ended up due to his gambling addiction, maybe that interpretation wasn't so far off.

"Are you still in?" the dealer asked.

Mason hesitated for a moment, then glanced over at me. He nodded, but I had no idea whom he was nodding to—the dealer, his bandmates, or me with my unspoken questions.

He stood up, removed his few remaining chips from the table, and handed them to Jared. "Cash them for me."

Jared gave him a chin nod and walked to the cashier while Nolan and Mason headed for the elevator. Nolan's hand was resting on Mason's shoulder, as if the lead singer was worried Mason would make a break for it and head back to the blackjack table.

And I just stood there, lost, broken on the inside, and uncertain what to do. I loved him, but my love wouldn't be enough to help him. He needed to do it himself. I couldn't afford to be pulled down the way my mother had been with my father. That was why I had my list. It was to save me from following in her footsteps.

Instead of returning to our hotel room, I hurried to the exit, my mind numb with everything I'd just witnessed. Outside, the icy wind bit my face and hands, and chewed its way through my coat. I didn't care. I wasn't ready to face Mason, at least not until I knew what to do.

I wandered along the beach for a long time before I dropped onto the frozen sand and hugged my knees to my chest. At some point I'd started crying, and my face stung from the salty tears freezing on my face.

The frigid wind did its best to turn my heart to ice, numbing it against further pain. A shiver overcame my body, but I couldn't find the strength to get up and return to the hotel. I needed to be on the beach, a place where I felt oddly at home. Not that the beaches in Southern California ever got this cold.

I'd been staring out at the stormy ocean for who knows how long when Nolan plunked himself down next to me. "Aren't you cold?" he asked. His tone was casual, but there was no denying the strained emotions underneath the words.

I wiped away the remnants of the frozen tears from my cheeks. "Maybe a little," I said through chattering teeth, but made no move to get up.

Nolan removed his jacket and attempted to wrap it around my shoulders. I shook my head and shrugged the jacket off. He needed it as much as I did, and it was my fault I was out here instead of back inside the warm hotel.

"He didn't tell you about his past gambling addiction, did he?" Nolan asked.

I laughed, the sound dry and brittle. "No, but I told him all about how my father's gambling addiction destroyed my family." He had known about it well before things had progressed from having fun to falling in love. He'd had plenty of time to tell me the truth before deeper emotions became involved.

"I'm sorry," Nolan said. "None of us knew about that, otherwise we would have been more honest with you. But we thought he had gotten past his addiction. Or maybe we just hoped he had."

I gave him a faint smile. "I know."

Nolan was quiet for a couple of minutes as we watched the waves crash against the beach. "You're leaving us, aren't you?" he eventually said.

"This job wasn't permanent. I'm just leaving a few weeks earlier than planned."

"When?"

"Today." My heart and stomach hurt at my saying that. Gambling addiction or not, leaving Mason would be hard. "I love him. I really do. But I'm not sure if my love will be enough."

Nolan didn't try to convince me to stay and finish the job I'd been hired to do, and for that I was grateful.

"I'll take care of the Christmas contest," I added, "but that I can do at home." There were a few other marketing tasks I had taken on, but those could easily be completed at home too. "I wish I could stay, but I can't. Mason and I live two very different lives. Heck, even before I knew about the gambling addiction, I had no idea what would happen between us once I returned home."

"You guys never talked about it?"

I let out a strangled laugh. Apparently there was a lot we hadn't talked about. "It never came up. He might love me, but music is his life."

I reminded myself that after my last boyfriend had moved away, my feelings for him had faded with time. But an inner voice pointed out that what I felt for Mason was nothing like the love I thought I'd had for my ex-boyfriend. Not even close.

I wiped away a new crop of tears.

Nolan pushed himself to his feet and held out his hand for me. "We should head back before you turn into an ice sculpture."

I giggled, possibly slightly delirious because of the cold. "Just add lights to me and I'll fit in perfectly with this city."

Instead of walking back to the hotel, Nolan insisted we take a cab. While we drove back, I pulled out my smartphone and booked my flight home. Even though it was Thanksgiving weekend, I was able to find something—not everyone in the United States was traveling from Atlantic City to Desert Springs.

At the hotel, Nolan escorted me down the hallway to the room Mason and I were staying in. "Thanks," I told him. "I'll be fine." I hugged him and asked him to say goodbye to the other band members for me. It was hard enough for me as it was without having to say goodbye to them too. I would miss them . . . and I would miss Hailey and Callie. Even in the short time I had known them, they had all become like family to me.

Using my key card, I entered the room, only to find Mason pacing, the way he'd been doing the other night. I couldn't tell if the pacing was because of what had happened downstairs or because his addiction was pleading for him to return to the casino.

Hearing the click of the door as I entered, Mason snapped his head in my direction. An array of emotions paraded on his face—regret, shame, sadness, love. Then they were gone. He didn't move or say anything. He just continued to watch me, now with a guarded expression.

My mouth went dry as my brain scrambled for the words I needed to say.

"You're leaving, aren't you?" The indifference in his tone nearly gutted me.

I nodded, the only thing I was capable of, and gathered up my belongings. I didn't have much time before I had to be at the airport, and I still had to go to where the tour bus was parked at the arena and pack the rest of my stuff.

"I'm needed back home," I said at last. That was partly true. There was still so much to do before Blooming Love's grand reopening, and I really did need to be there to help Heidi.

Or at least that was what I kept telling myself.

Plus I needed to work on my glass etchings . . . the design of which still eluded me.

"Yes," Mason said, rather briskly. "You should go home. I'll let you get back to packing." He turned to leave.

The tears from earlier threatened an impromptu encore. I knew I should just let him go. That would be the smart thing to do. But I couldn't walk out of his life the way so many other people he loved had done to him.

I grabbed his arm. He paused, muscles ready to snap from being so tense, but he didn't turn around. I stepped closer and kissed his cheek. "I'm not your family, Mason. I love you, but you know our lives are so very different. It never would have worked out between us. We both know that." So why did it feel like my heart was shattering into a million pieces?

I stepped back to let him go but didn't get far. His lips crashed against mine. Without thinking what I was doing, I automatically let him in.

The kiss wasn't tender or sweet. It wasn't a goodbye kiss. It was hungry, possessive, mind-numbing. A kiss no other would be comparable to—now or in any other lifetime.

Once it was over, Mason left the room without saying another word.

And my heart shattered some more.

32

MASON

"You sure you can handle the meeting with Remar?" Kirk asked, eyeing the beer in my hand. It had been a week since Nicole walked out on the band, and to make things worse, Remar had arranged a meeting for this afternoon. Which was surprising, considering that we were in Memphis and not L.A. Rumor had it that he had flown out specifically for this meeting.

But that wasn't what had me on edge. I gulped more beer. "Why wouldn't I be able to handle it?"

"Because you've changed. Because half the time you're either drunk or wasted."

"I'm not drunk or wasted right now." Slightly buzzed, maybe. Yes, I was drinking more than I had been a few weeks ago. And yes, I might have taken an illegal drug or two the other day. But that was only so I could perform. My energy level had recently taken a hit, and I didn't want to let the fans down. Most days I barely had the energy to drag my sorry ass out of my bunk bed on the bus. I was positive I was coming down with something. The flu, maybe?

"Are you sure?" Kirk asked.

"Of course I'm sure. This is only my second beer."

"It's your fourth," Aaron pointed out. All the humor that had been in his tone a few minutes ago had leaked away.

"So what can I say? I'm thirsty." Because of the meeting with Remar, we had gone to the arena early for sound check, and I had started pounding on my drums. And had kept pounding on them, even when the rest of the band had stopped playing. It was one of the few times during the past week when I'd felt good, when I'd felt a little more alive.

"I'm not surprised you're thirsty," Nolan said, "after you broke a dozen sticks while practicing."

I shrugged, the movement barely more than a twitch of the shoulders. "I break drumsticks all the time during concerts. That's nothing new."

"Yeah, but you don't normally come close to destroying that many."

I shrugged again and studied my half-empty beer. "So I'm a little moody. I'm a musician. I'm supposed to be moody." Or so went the theory.

I shifted in my seat, itching to get back to the arena for a game of poker with some of the roadies. I'd won a hundred dollars yesterday, which the guys didn't know about. They also had no idea about the underground poker group that I'd discovered while looking for something to give me an extra buzz for the show—which was necessary now that I no longer had the desire to bang groupies the way I used to before Nicole came into my life.

My heart squeezed painfully at the thought of her. I swigged some more beer.

"You're not moody," Kirk said. "You're depressed, Mason."

"I'm not depressed. I'm happy." I grinned. Then stopped because the action hurt my cheeks. And it wasn't just my cheeks that hurt. My entire body ached with exhaustion.

"I believe that as much as I believe in the Easter Bunny."

"I'm sure the Easter Bunny will be happy to hear it." I tried to form a smirk on my face, but the effort wasn't worth it and I gave up.

"My mother used to suffer from depression," Kirk said, ignoring my smartass comment. "I know the signs."

"Well, good for you, puck boy, but I am not depressed. I'm just tired. Touring will do that to you." None of the guys could deny it. They were just as tired from all the touring as I was. Ours wasn't an easy lifestyle. It was the reason Nicole had gone home. It was the reason she and I had never discussed a future together. Our lives were too different for us to make it work.

But no matter how many times I told myself that, I had a hard time believing it. Somehow we could've made it work. It was my past gambling addiction that she'd had an issue with. In her eyes, I was no better than her asshole father. She might have had a point there.

I finished my burger, even though I didn't feel like eating, but if I didn't eat it, the guys would've been on my case for that too, the way they'd been yesterday. We paid for our food, then returned to the arena. The sky had been cloudy when we walked to the restaurant. Now it was pouring, like it was pissed off at the world.

As we passed the security guard standing at the back entrance to the arena, my phone buzzed. I glanced at the screen. Nicole had sent me a text. For the first time since she'd left the tour, my heart came alive in my chest, knowing that she hadn't completely pushed me out of her life.

I opened the text to find a picture of Bernie, the giant English mastiff. Drool hung from his mouth and his face featured rolls of dark wrinkles. My mouth tugged slightly up at the memory of walking him with Nicole, when we resembled a part of the family she had envisioned one day for herself, with the perfect husband, two-point-four kids, dog, and cat.

She had also sent me a message with the photo: *Bernie misses you.* A heart emoji was next to her words.

I miss Bernie, I typed back. Meaning that I missed both the dog and her. More so her.

"What the hell is that?" Aaron asked, peering at my phone. "Is it some sort of genetically modified dog? It's huge . . . and kind of ugly."

I pulled the phone to my chest, as if protecting Bernie from hearing what Aaron had said. "Hey, never let Bernie hear you say that. He's a great dog."

We still had a few minutes before we were due to meet Remar, so we headed to the dressing room first to change into dry clothing. Afterward we walked down the brightly lit hallway to the conference room, all of us suddenly quiet, as if we were heading to a funeral. Hopefully not our own. Other than the heavy tread of our booted feet against the gray floor, the corridor was silent.

We entered the conference room where Remar was supposed to meet us. The sight of him left me craving something to give me a happy buzz. The man was capable of sucking the life out of you, just by being in the same room. He must be fun to be around at the office Christmas party. A real jolly old St. Nick.

I stumbled my way to an empty chair, as far away from him as possible. Then I squirmed in my seat, attempting to get comfy. An urge hit me, like an impossible-to-get-rid-of itch, to leave and find Doug. He was the roadie who had what I needed to take off the edge.

Remar smiled. Holy shit. I hadn't thought the man was capable of doing that. Would miracles never cease?

Next to him was a guy in his late twenties, with very short hair like Remar had. The only difference was Remar's hair was gray while the younger man's hair was black. His dress shirt was an interesting contrast to the hoop piercing above his left eyebrow.

"Congratulations, gentlemen, on the album's recent success," Remar said, still smiling.

We all nodded our thanks.

"In light of this, I've decided to take you off the Endless Motion tour come February and have you headlining your own tour. We'll be announcing the dates next week."

No one spoke for several seconds. We just stared at him, positive we'd misheard him.

Nolan was the first to collect himself. "We'll really be headlining?"

Remar nodded. "It was a ballsy move to do the encore in Atlantic City, but it worked. Fans are demanding that you headline your own tour so they can see more of you. They aren't happy that you're just the opening act."

That news wasn't a surprise to anyone in the room. Nicole had already told us as much from working with our social media sites and from answering our fan email.

"You'll continue with Endless Motion until the new dates, then we'll switch you over. Your new tour manager will fly out on Thursday to iron out details with you for the shows. And in the meantime, let me introduce you to your new social media specialist. Trey will be joining you for the rest of your tour, and will continue with you on the new tour."

The guys and I exchanged looks. Yes, Nicole was gone and wasn't coming back, but weren't we the ones who got to decide whom we hired? The record company wasn't paying his salary. We were.

"Trey has an impressive background," Remar continued, "including a communications degree with a specialization in social media, and an MBA in marketing. Because of that, he will also be working with you to help capitalize on the band's marketing."

Trey sat up a little straighter. "Yes, I was impressed with what you guys have achieved in the way of marketing." What Nicole had achieved. "But there are some other areas you can explore as well."

Kirk swiveled his chair in my direction, a guess-you-won't-be-screwing-around-with-this-one smirk dancing at the corner of his mouth. I mentally flipped him one.

Trey spent the next few minutes enlightening us with his plans for our marketing. I couldn't have told you what they were because I'd tuned him out soon after he started talking. All I could focus on beyond the *blah blah blah* was when the hell we were getting out of here, so I could track down Doug and the poker game.

My leg bounced rhythmically under the table. I had to fight the urge to pound a beat on the edge of the wood. Until I scored something or got behind my drums, I was pretty helpless at keeping the restlessness under control.

Eventually we were released and I located Doug. Most of what happened afterward was a blur. I had some beer. I lost two grand. I drank some more beer and had some pot. I might have gotten into an argument with Aaron. I couldn't be sure.

We went onstage, and as always nailed our performance, even with me buzzed. But the happy buzz faded by the end of our set. Thanks to all the drumming I'd done, I sweated away the benefits.

"I'm beat," I told the guys after we'd finished our encore, which Remar had told us would continue for the rest of the tour. With the adrenaline high the guys had going, they were ready to go out. But it wasn't the same without Nicole. Nothing was the same without her. "I'm just going to head back to the bus and read. Maybe catch up on sleep or play a video game." I wanted to be left alone, something that didn't happen too often on tour.

At first the guys hesitated at the idea of leaving without me, but after I insisted I would be fine and was going straight back to the bus, they decided to go without me.

As promised, I returned to the bus and checked my phone for any more messages from Nicole. Nothing. I sat down hard on the couch and stared at Bernie's picture. But instead of reliving the memory of walking him with Nicole, all I saw was the slobbering dog.

I pushed off the couch and walked back to my bunk, where I had left my sports bag. I unzipped it and pulled out the whiskey bottle I'd hidden there.

Back on the couch, I gulped down a mouthful of the smooth amber liquid and popped one of the pills Doug had given me earlier. The best kind of painkiller around—the kind that killed the pain of a broken heart.

I chased it with more whiskey and stared at the photo of Bernie—remembering everything I could about the few days I had spent living with Nicole in Desert Springs—until I blacked out.

33

—————

NICOLE

"**E**xplain again why I'm doing this?" I asked Heidi as I inspected my makeup in the mirror. Next to me, Heidi was applying a coat of red lipstick.

"Because Simon's a nice guy, fits your criteria perfectly, and is good-looking. And because you've been moping around your house for the past week."

"I haven't been moping. I've been busy finalizing the plans for the grand reopening. And I've been working on my new line of glass etchings." Technically, I'd been staring at a blank piece of paper for the past week, but it was the thought that counted.

Heidi's face brightened. "Can I see them?"

"The final plans for the reopening?" Which hadn't changed since the last time I'd shown them to her.

"No, the designs for the new line."

Yeah, that's what I was afraid of. "They're . . . they're not quite ready for you to see just yet." I applied my pink lip gloss in the mirror—any excuse to avoid looking at her. I didn't want to see if she believed me or not. I just longed for our double date to be over so I could return home to my much anticipated evening of ice cream and any movie on Netflix that didn't have *Die Hard* in the title or any hint of romance in it.

"The guys should be here in a minute," I said, attempting to distract her. The guys were Simon and Heidi's boyfriend, Chris. Simon played on the same touch football team as Chris, which was how they knew each other.

I quickly escaped the bathroom before she could challenge me about the designs. She knew me well enough to know I was stretching the truth when I said I'd been working on them.

Luckily for me, the doorbell rang as my foot hit the final stair. I opened the door, which was a lot easier thanks to Mason's having fixed it when he was staying here. My heart slumped at the reminder of him. After a week of trying not to think about him every second of every day, I'd sent him a picture of Bernie. The pieces of my heart, which I had sloppily taped back together, broke apart again at his *I miss Bernie* reply. He didn't miss me. He only missed the dog.

Not that I could blame him after the way I'd turned my back on him.

I plastered a smile on my face and greeted Chris and the guy who I assumed was Simon. He was tall, muscular, and ruggedly good-looking, with short light brown hair. According to Heidi, he didn't have any tattoos.

The thought of that didn't make me think about Mason's tattoos. Nor was I thinking about how I used to trace my fingers over them after making love to him, as if absorbing their individual messages into my heart.

Heidi bounced downstairs and flung herself at Chris. Fortunately, she gave him only a quick kiss, nothing that would make Simon and me feel awkward—as if going on a blind date wasn't awkward enough.

Instead of the romantic comedy Heidi wanted to see, we went to see some big-budget, action-hero-type movie. Since not a single kiss was exchanged on the big screen the entire time, I had to give the movie a thumbs-up. It was the perfect date movie to see when dealing with a broken heart.

Afterward we drove to Heidi's favorite restaurant for pizza. Heidi kept giving me the so-what-do-you-think look, which left me struggling to not roll my eyes. Simon was a great guy—if you were into gamers.

As he was explaining the ins and outs of one of his favorite games, my phone rang. I glanced at the number. Nolan? A bad feeling slithered down my back. "I need to answer this," I said as I accepted the call, hands trembling. "Hi, Nolan. What's up?"

In the background, I could hear what sounded like "Code blue, room eighteen" and the quiet murmurs of people talking.

He cleared his throat. "I wanted to tell you before you heard it from the media. Mason's in the hospital."

"Oh God. What happened?"

"I'm not sure exactly." The heavy mix of emotions choking Nolan's voice told me that whatever had happened to Mason was far more serious than him needing stitches or having a broken bone. I came within an inch of begging Nolan not to tell me. I didn't think my heart could take it. "Jared and I returned to the bus and found him unconscious. . . . From the looks of it, he might have OD'd."

My blood turned cold at his words. "OD'd?" I asked, voice shaky. I could feel everyone at the table watching me while I stared at the white tablecloth as though it was a life preserver, the one thing keeping me afloat. "Is he okay?"

"I don't know," Nolan said. "They're working on him, but we haven't heard anything. He was barely alive when we found him."

My hand flew to my mouth, and I only just contained the sob threatening to erupt. I didn't know what to do. I just knew I couldn't sit in the restaurant on a date while the man I loved was clinging to life.

Without a word to Heidi or our dates, I stood up and

headed for the main entrance. I didn't want them or anyone else in the restaurant to be part of the conversation. "What happened? I had no idea he was using drugs," I said as I exited through the door.

Nolan mumbled what could have been "shit." "How much did he tell you about his past?"

I leaned back against the brick wall. I had a feeling I would need it to help keep me upright. "Apparently not as much as he should have. I only knew that his family disowned him because of something he'd done, but he wouldn't tell me what it was." But given my history with a father who had been a gambling addict, it didn't take much to guess what he had done to destroy their trust in him. I just wondered how much money he had cost them. "I'm guessing it had to do with his gambling addiction."

"It did. He paid them back with interest, but they wanted nothing to do with him. From what he told us, he struggled with depression several years before that and tried to commit suicide. It was only because your brother became worried about him when he wasn't answering his phone that Mason didn't die."

"Oh God!" That was why Mason had driven all the way from L.A. when Zack had been worried about me. Mason believed he owed my brother for saving his life.

"As far as we know, he only started gambling again while we were in Atlantic City," Nolan said. "His father's death and what happened with his family at the funeral must have caused the relapse. And he started drinking more, especially after . . ." He let the final words hang.

"After what?"

Nolan sighed, long and heavy. "After you left. What with everything else, he didn't handle it so well. We suspected he was also getting high."

"How? Where the hell was he getting drugs from?" Oh, who

was I kidding? He was in a rock band. Drugs were common, even if I had never witnessed anyone use or deal them while I was on tour with them.

"Wish I knew. If something happens to Mason, I'll personally kill the guy he got the drugs from. All we know is that he stayed on the bus when the rest of the band went out after the show. He said he was tired and just wanted to sleep or play a video game. Jared and I returned early and found him unconscious, a half-empty bottle of whiskey next to him. We don't even know what drug he was using."

I closed my eyes, Nolan's words pulling me under, making it hard to breathe. "Do you think he tried to commit suicide again?" The sob I'd been barely holding back finally broke free.

"I really don't know. But we found out today that we'll be headlining our own tour soon."

Even though he couldn't see me, I smiled, although it was weak at best. "Congratulations! You guys deserve it. It was about time your label finally realized it."

"So it doesn't make sense that Mason would try to kill himself," Nolan continued, without acknowledging what I had said. "He wanted this as much as the rest of us did."

"Then it was probably an accidental overdose," I said, praying it was true. Praying he would be all right. Praying that if there really was a God, he wouldn't be offended that I hadn't believed in him, and would still listen to my prayers for Mason.

"You're probably right. Look, I should go now. I just wanted you to know before it explodes on social media."

I would have offered to help them, but this afternoon I'd received a call from their label letting me know that my services were no longer required. They had hired a more qualified candidate. He was taking over the contest I'd been running on the band's behalf. To say it hadn't stung would be like saying a great white shark didn't bite.

"I can be on the next plane out." I needed to be there for him, to make sure he fought for what was important—his life.

"It's best that you don't. It's not like the doctors will let you see him anyway. And he wouldn't want you to see him this way."

If I had thought the call from the label had hurt, that was nothing compared to Nolan's words. I sucked in a sharp breath. It did nothing to dull the pain. "Will you keep me updated on his condition?" I asked.

"Are you . . . are you sure you want that?"

I could feel my face crumple. "I still love him, and I miss him so much it hurts." I covered my mouth with my hand, working hard at regaining some sort of control over my emotions, as futile as the effort was. I took a deep breath and lowered my hand. "I need to know he's going to be okay."

"All right. As soon as I find out anything, I'll let you know."

"Thank you," I whispered. We ended the call, and for the longest time I stood leaning against the wall, staring at my phone. Eventually Heidi came out of the restaurant looking for me.

"What happened?" she asked, voice soft.

I told her everything, then burst into tears. She hugged me and held me tight. Still hugging me, she sent someone a text. A moment later that someone left the restaurant, along with my date for the night.

They drove me home in silence, with me staring out the side window, tears dampening my cheeks, willing Nolan or Jared to phone me with an update—and at the same time willing them not to. I wasn't sure if I could handle any more bad news about Mason.

When we arrived at my house, I apologized for ending the evening so soon, then bailed. Simon didn't say anything, not that there was much he could say. And in the end, I didn't care if I never heard from him again. I would gladly remain single for the rest of my life if it meant Mason would be all right.

Heidi walked me to the door. "I'm staying with you tonight."

I attempted to smile, but my facial muscles refused to obey. "I'd rather be alone, thanks."

Heidi frowned. "I don't think that's a good idea. I'd feel better if I was here with you."

This time I did smile. "I know, but it's not like I'm going to do anything stupid. I'm just tired. I'll probably go to bed anyway."

She looked like she was about to argue, but something on my face must have caused her to change her mind. "Promise me you'll call me as soon as you hear anything."

I nodded and let her hug me again.

Inside the house, I grabbed a glass of milk and sat on the living room couch. The same couch I had made out on with Mason. But instead of letting those memories make me feel sadder, I pulled out the *Die Hard* DVD. As crazy as it sounded, I felt more connected to Mason while watching it. After it finished, I switched to *Die Harder*.

At some point during the third movie, I must have drifted off to sleep. I woke to the vibrations from the smartphone still clutched in my hand.

Nolan had sent me a text. *He's conscious but groggy. The doctor thinks he'll be fine. He'll be here for a few more days.*

Relief flooded me, and another round of sobs racked my body. Never before—other than when my mother died—had I ever felt so lost and confused.

None of the problems associated with gambling addictions were new to me. But, I realized, things with Mason were different from how they'd been with my father. And it wasn't only that my father had shot himself in the head to end his life. After Mason's first ride with a gambling addiction, he had turned his life around. He had been able to control it—until something triggered him and sent him into a downward spiral again. My father had never been able to control the beast, and it destroyed him.

I texted Nolan back, thanking him, and asked him to keep me updated. Then I sent a text to my brother: *Call me!* He deserved to hear about Mason from me and not find out about it through social media.

He called a few minutes later. "What's wrong?" he said, his voice sounding like he would've crawled through the phone line if he could have, just to be with me.

"It's Mason." I told him what had happened and everything Nolan had told me. "The physician said Mason should be all right." I didn't mention that Mason had fallen off the deep end when it came to the gambling and drinking. I didn't want to worry my brother any more than absolutely necessary. He was away on his tour of duty—he wouldn't be able to help Mason this time.

I also didn't 'fess up when it came to my feelings toward Mason. That was the last thing Zack needed to know.

We talked for a couple of minutes more, and then I let him go.

I turned the movie off and went upstairs to bed. I couldn't fall asleep, though. I lay awake until the weak sunlight peeked through the gap in the curtains. Then I plodded downstairs and made myself an extra-strong cup of coffee. Standing at the kitchen window, I sipped the hot drink and stared numbly at the world. Beatrice's kitchen light was also on. Familiar with her morning schedule, and knowing what I needed to do, I took a long sip of my coffee before bolting upstairs.

I returned a minute later in jeans and an oversized Pushing Limits hoodie, shoved my sneakers on, and hurried out the door with my cellphone in hand . . . in time to see Beatrice step out of her house with an eager Bernie. He practically dragged her out the door.

I ran across my small lawn to her adjoining lot. "Hey, do you mind if I take Bernie for a walk?"

Bernie gave me an enthusiastic woof. I took that as a *Yes, I'm fully on board with that plan,* and held out my hand for his leash.

Beatrice grinned at me. "You know you're welcome to walk him anytime you wish, Nicole. But is there a particular reason why you want to do that? Maybe to meet that nice gentleman down the street who likes walking his English bulldog at this time?" She winked at me, and despite everything I giggled. That nice gentleman was about sixty-five years old and had quite the crush on Beatrice, as far as I could tell.

"You've found me out," I said. "I'll be sure to tell him you said hi."

She chuckled. "You do that." She didn't ask about Mason, the way she had when I first returned from touring with the band. If news about his accidental overdose had been leaked, she hadn't heard it yet. Which came as no surprise. It wasn't as if she listened to the kind of radio station that would've given two shits about the rock band.

Bernie and I went for a long walk, checking out the Christmas decorations and lights adorning the houses in the neighborhood. I tried to get into the holiday spirit. But no matter how hard I tried, I couldn't get past how they reminded me of Atlantic City, with its bright lights and over-the-top decorations.

While we walked, I told Bernie about Heidi's and my plans for the store's grand reopening, and he daydreamed about chasing squirrels down the street. My goal of not thinking about Mason was a bust, but that was nothing new since returning to Desert Springs.

My phone chirped in my hand. Bernie stopped and looked over his shoulder in interest. I checked who was calling and my hand shook. I didn't know why. Nolan had already told me that

Mason was conscious and was expected to make a full recovery. Callie wasn't phoning to give me bad news.

At least I hoped she wasn't.

"Hi," I said, forcing the word out like it was a reluctant baby bird, not ready to take its first flight.

Deciding the conversation between Callie and me could take awhile, Bernie plunked down on the grass next to the side-walk and eyed the fake donkey guarding the baby Jesus in the manger near us. Faith and hope—weren't they what Christmas was all about? Too bad I was fresh out of both.

"Hey, I wanted to see how you were doing," she said, her words full of compassion. I took this as a good sign. She would have sounded more broken up if anything had happened to Mason.

I gave a short laugh, the sound more pained than filled with humor. "I'm not sure. I can't believe he would do something like that. And I have no idea what I should do. Do I go there and see him? Do I leave him alone? I just don't know."

"Do you still love him?"

"Yes," I whispered. "No matter what he did, I still love him. I'm trying not to, but so far that's not working too well for me."

"That's what I thought. I figured you might want to know that Mason checked himself in to rehab."

"He did? Aren't the guys still touring?"

"They've canceled the rest of their dates for the next month. Then they'll wait to see what happens. If he's out by then, they'll resume touring." She didn't sound too disappointed that the band would be taking an extended break. And I doubted Logan would be too disappointed either.

"Can I visit him?" I blurted out without thinking.

"Are you sure you want to do that?"

"I don't know," I admitted after a heartbeat. "I want to see him, but I don't want to hurt him either."

Callie let out a long breath. "I know."

34

NICOLE

The Spanish-style building beckoned me with its peaceful exterior, as did the lush green plants grouped along the curved stone pathway. The rehab center didn't resemble the sterile institution I had originally expected. It looked more like a fancy spa. Although from what I'd read about the place, it did offer treatments similar to those found in a spa.

I caught sight of a stray butterfly flitting about the purple flowers on the leafy vines tangled around the tall metal fence between stone columns. The butterfly seemed happy to be here. I only hoped Mason would be that happy when he saw me.

I'd done as Callie had suggested, waiting two weeks before visiting, but as I walked to the front entrance, palms sweaty, I wondered if my being here was a big mistake. Maybe it was too soon to visit him. Maybe I shouldn't have come at all, so he could move on with his life.

I stood in front of the entrance, deliberating whether I should turn around or go in. Mason had no idea I was coming, so it wasn't like he would think I'd abandoned him yet again if I didn't show up. But I also knew that was what a coward would do, and when it came to Mason, I wasn't a coward. He needed to know that I hadn't turned my back on him like his family had. I had done what was best for both of us. Or so I kept telling myself.

I removed my phone from my purse and, with a long sigh, called the one person whose voice I really needed to hear right now. The one person who didn't know about my feelings for Mason.

Zack answered after a few rings. "Hey, sis. How's everything going?"

"Great." *Or not.* "I'm about to visit Mason in rehab." I attempted to sound casual about it, like I would if announcing I was at the grocery store to buy bananas.

Zack didn't say anything at first, and for a second I thought we might have been disconnected. "Is there something I don't know that maybe I should?" he eventually asked. "Or rather something that I've suspected but figured I had to be wrong about, because Mason isn't your type?"

"If you mean do I have feelings for him, strong feelings"— now was probably not the time to tell him that I was in love with Mason—"then the answer is yes. He's my friend and I want to make sure he's doing okay."

"Nicole, this is me you're talking to. You've never been good at lying to me."

True. But usually he had to see me to know I was lying. "So we can save time here," I said, "what answer are you really looking for?"

"Are you in love with Mason?" He didn't sound at all surprised—or too upset.

"Yes. I am."

"Even now that you know about his past?" I had already filled Zack in on what I'd found out about his involvement when Mason had attempted suicide all those years ago. And he knew that Mason had recently relapsed.

"Yes, even though I know about his past."

"And nothing I can say will change that?"

I shook my head even though he couldn't see me. "Nothing."

He let out a long breath. "Well, good luck. Just know that I'm here if you need me."

"Thanks."

We said our goodbyes, with him hinting heavily that I should tell Mason that Zack would come after him if he hurt me. I just rolled my eyes and ended the call.

I opened the front door and stepped into the lobby, which instantly made me think of a high-end hotel. The Spanish-style architecture continued in here too, but the area had also been decorated for Christmas, with a huge fake pine tree covered in white lights standing proud in the corner.

Rich wooden support beams ran across the ceiling, further adding warmth to the place, as did the patterned tapestries covering the white walls and the sconces on either side of the artwork. Classical Christmas music played in the background.

I walked to the reception desk, my heels clicking against the wooden floor. The woman behind the desk looked up from her computer and smiled as I approached.

"Good afternoon. How can I help you?" she asked.

"I'm Nicole McCormick. I was told it would be okay to visit Mason Dell?" I hadn't meant for it to come out as a question.

"Is he expecting you?"

I shook my head. "No." The word came out as a squeak, and I coughed to make it sound like I had to clear my throat.

She tapped on her keyboard and studied the screen. "He's in a counseling session right now, but as soon as he's out, I'll have someone tell him you're here."

"Thanks." Clutching Mason's Christmas present in my hand, I walked over to an empty armchair and sat down.

A variety of magazines lay scattered on the coffee table. I picked up a home decorating one and leafed through it, pretending to be fascinated with the pictures. Pretending not to be thinking about how much I missed the guys in the band, how much I missed touring with them and my old job, and how much I missed Mason.

One page caught my attention. The article contained a picture of dishes with floral and butterfly designs painted on them. Each design was simple yet beautifully elegant.

"Nicole McCormick?" a female voice said as an idea for my glass etchings took shape.

My head jerked up. "Yes?"

"Hello. I'm Suzanne Prescott," said a woman in her forties wearing a long-sleeved knit dress and heels. "I understand you've come to visit Mason?"

Fear reached inside me and silenced my tongue. Fear that Mason had refused to see me. Fear that he was saving the rejection to throw in my face. Not that I didn't deserve it.

When I didn't answer, she said, "He's in the garden. Let me take you to him."

"Does he know I'm here?"

"Yes." I longed to ask what Mason's reaction had been when he found out I was here, but I had a feeling not knowing was a better idea. I was nervous enough as it was. So I got up and followed her down a hallway and out an exit at the back of the building.

The first thing I saw out there was a patio with a large built-in hot tub. Small groupings of wicker chairs surrounded the area. Beyond that, palm trees stood tall against the blue sky.

"As you can see," Suzanne said, her tone easy, as if we were doing nothing more than chatting about the weather, "our goal is to help our clients relax and to find other ways to fill the perceived void the lack of drugs, alcohol, or gambling leaves behind. Depending on the weather, we conduct our early morning yoga sessions out here too."

I scanned the area, feeling as though an army of moths were slapping their wings against my stomach in an attempt to flee. And that's when I saw him.

The moths grew suddenly still, their frantic movements replaced by the desperate beating of my heart. He hadn't noticed me yet. He was standing at the far edge of the patio, gazing off at the mountains in the distance, his back to me. Even from where I was standing, I could make out the muscles under his T-shirt, each one strained with tension. Not at all what you would expect to find in such a relaxing environment. Which meant it had nothing to do with him being here and everything to do with me.

As if sensing me watching him, he turned toward me. An assortment of emotions washed across his face. Happiness at seeing me wasn't one of them.

My heart sagged in my chest, the sadness too much for it. Even after my mother had died, it hadn't felt like this. *I shouldn't have come.*

Suzanne gently nudged my arm, encouraging me forward. Easy for her. Mason was just a client to her. He was the man I loved, the man I had turned my back on when things got tough and I couldn't cope.

I still couldn't cope.

Mason continued to remain rigid. I gave him a tentative smile, searching for a sign that he understood why I'd had to walk away from him in Atlantic City . . . and why I would have to walk away again.

"I'll leave you two to talk," Suzanne said. "If you need anything, I'll be in my office."

Mason and I nodded. I waited for her to be out of hearing

range before saying, "So . . . how's it going?" I smoothed a strand of hair behind my ear.

"Good. You?"

"Great. Blooming Love is almost ready to open. The contractors did a great job with the renovation. The store looks even better than before." I was babbling, but I couldn't help it. It was that or fling myself into Mason's arms, and from the cautiousness in his tone, I didn't think he would appreciate me doing that.

I shifted on my feet, the Christmas present suddenly heavy in my hand. I held it out to him. "It's a few days early, but . . . merry Christmas."

Mason didn't move for a second, then took the small box and freed it from the wrapping. He opened the lid and removed a man's bracelet, which consisted of a string of small purple amethyst and black onyx beads. A tiny silver butterfly charm dangled from it.

"It's a healing bracelet," I said, immediately feeling stupid for giving it to him. According to the website I had ordered it from, the gemstones were supposed to support recovery from addictions. I had no idea if it was true or not . . . just as I had no idea whether Mason would throw the bracelet in the trash once I left.

"Thank you." His voice was low, without a hint of emotion. To me it felt like a blunt knife thrust into my gut. I reeled back a half step.

He slipped the bracelet on. "I wasn't expecting you. I didn't get you anything," he said, still studying at it.

"You don't have to give me anything. You being alive is enough of a gift." My voice cracked on the word "alive," and I blinked away the tears threatening to reveal how much his reaction hurt.

His head snapped up, eyes narrowed to slits. "I didn't mean to overdose. I wasn't trying to commit suicide."

"I know," I said softly. "It was an accident." I wrapped my arms around myself.

Mason turned his head toward the mountains, the tension in his muscles even tighter now. He stayed like this for several seconds before releasing a heavy breath, as though the weight of the world was sitting square on his shoulders and he had no idea what to do with it.

Suddenly he turned back to me and closed the distance between us. Before I could react, his arms encircled me. At first his hold on me was loose, his arms slightly stiff, as if he was afraid to touch me, but then he pulled me against his body and relaxed into me.

He kissed my temple. "I still love you, Nicole." His voice was gruff with emotion, yet his words felt like a soft caress. "But we always knew this would never work between us."

My heart ached at his words, but he was right. Our lives were moving in different directions. Once he was released, he'd be back to touring, possibly putting himself at risk again. There would be no place in his life for me.

I hugged him back, head on his chest, tears leaking onto his T-shirt. "I love you too," I managed to say past the lump in my throat. Sucking in a sharp breath that bordered on a sob, I pulled away. "I just wanted to make sure you're okay." I smiled, the expression genuine although a little shaky, my body already regretting the loss of him against me. "By the way, congratulations on becoming a headlining band. The band deserves it. You deserve it."

"Thanks," he said, his tone once again free of emotion. I couldn't tell if he was excited or not. But in the grand scheme of things, I supposed, it didn't really matter. He was alive to witness his success—that was more important.

We talked for a little longer after that, avoiding discussing the band and what had happened on the night he'd OD'd. He told me about his time in rehab, how he was actually enjoying yoga (I had to laugh at that), and how he got to play the piano in the rec room. His face lit up when he shared that, and a warm feeling snuggled up inside me. I told him about the upcoming reopening and how Bernie missed him, but there was no escaping how much I missed him too, even though I didn't say the words. I also told him that Zack said hi, but kept what else he had said on the phone to myself.

Eventually I knew I couldn't stay any longer. I needed to walk away, and I needed to do it now, before it was too late.

As much as I craved the feeling of his lips on mine once more, we didn't kiss. We hugged like friends who were saying their final goodbyes. Somehow I kept from crying, though barely. That was a small miracle in itself.

We didn't say "I love you" either. It had already been said, and that was enough.

Walking away was the hardest thing I had ever done. My body and my heart begged me to turn around and stay with him. Even my brain was having a hard time knowing what was the right thing to do.

I returned to my car and climbed in. But instead of starting the engine, I let my grief consume me—and cried enough tears to turn the desert into an ocean before I finally drove away.

35

NICOLE

"Look at this, Margie. Isn't it gorgeous?" the woman said to her friend as they stood next to the display in Blooming Love. They were studying a set of drinking glasses with one of my designs on them.

As soon as I'd returned home four months ago after visiting Mason, I'd spent the following week sketching and creating my new line of glassware. Each etched design had a different butterfly and a symbol to represent music, usually a treble clef and floating musical notes. The butterfly symbolized change, hope, and life. And, well, it wasn't too hard to figure out what the music represented.

There had been no shortage of customers once news got out about my designs. I had recently begun selling them on Etsy and eBay, and had created a line of T-shirts too. To say I was busy was an understatement.

Being busy had been necessary if I was going to move on after leaving Mason that day at the rehab center. Except I was still waiting for my heart to realize it was time to move on. Maybe it would've been easier if I hadn't designed a line of glassware that had everything to do with the man I still loved.

"Ten percent of the proceeds are donated to a charity that helps families dealing with addictions," I told them, and gestured toward the small sign on the shelf that provided more information about it and my work.

The bell above the door jingled, and as usual I glanced over to see who had entered the store. When I saw Hailey, my eyes widened to the size of one of my glass plates. The last time I had spoken to her was a few weeks ago. She and Callie called me every so often to see how I was doing. Both avoided the topic of Mason, and I was always careful not to mention him, afraid that if I even said his name, I would break down in tears. Again.

Hailey spotted me and smiled. Unable to contain my excitement at seeing her, I rushed over and hugged her in congratulations. Nolan had proposed to her on Christmas Day. Naturally, she had said yes.

"Let me see the ring," I gushed, and checked it out even though I had seen it when Nolan first showed it to me. It was as beautiful as I remembered. Tears of joy blurred my vision, but I didn't care. Hailey had found love and I couldn't have been more thrilled for her. "When's the big day?"

"September twenty-fifth. And I'm hoping you'll be there."

I smiled at her but didn't say anything. I wanted to be there for her and Nolan's big day, but it would also be hard seeing Mason there. Possibly with a date.

"So, are you seeing anyone?" she asked, not looking at me but studying the black-and-white mural on the wall. Vinelike tendrils floated behind the large butterfly and transformed into fine lines like sheet music, complete with musical notes. I had painted it on the wall between the two shelving units containing my giftware. Below the mural was a shorter shelf with even more glassware.

I laughed. "I don't have time to date. The store's keeping me busy." After much convincing on my part, Heidi and Cindy had stopped trying to set me up on dates—although my last disastrous date, which had been three months ago, might've had something to do with it. The part where I cried because my date was everything on my list but he wasn't Mason could've had something to do with it too.

"It looks amazing." Hailey strolled over to the giftware and checked it out. She picked up a glass serving plate. "Wow, you made these?" she asked, referring to the design etched on them.

"Yes. That's what's kept me so busy. But it's been worth it."

Without missing a beat, Hailey said, "You still love him, don't you?"

I traced my fingertips over the butterfly and musical notes on a lavender T-shirt. "It doesn't matter if I love him or not"—or if my heart ached every time I thought about him, which happened more often than I would've liked—"because he needs a woman who can handle him being away while he's on tour. And he needs someone who loves living in L.A., not someone who is more comfortable living in a small town more than two hours from there."

Unfortunately, even in the short time Mason had been in Desert Springs, his presence here had woven itself into every part of my day-to-day life. No matter where I went, what I did, I was bombarded by memories of him.

"I know it's not easy," Hailey said. "I often wish Nolan had a regular nine-to-five job. But I know how important his music is to him. It's what got him through the years of abuse and helped him deal with his grief after his mother and sister were killed."

"And that's why I would never ask Mason to leave the band. Music is his life." Which left my pathetic heart no choice but to love him from afar.

Delving deep, I finally found the courage to ask the one question I craved the answer to: "How's he doing?" My limited knowledge about what he'd been up to since leaving rehab came from what I'd seen online, but I knew from experience that meant little, if anything.

"Much better. The guys have done everything they can to support him, and he regularly contacts the online Gamblers Anonymous and Alcoholics Anonymous support groups. The band has been selling out the few shows they've scheduled. The label wanted to see if they could pull off being a headlining act. They'll be touring for another month, and then they're off for several weeks." She grinned, no doubt already counting down the days until Nolan was home again.

"That's great." All of it was. After what had happened last time, I was positive the guys would make sure he didn't fall back into his addictions. They were family. A family who would do anything for each other.

"It *is* great." She glanced down at the serving plate in her hand. "I'm buying this. It will be perfect for the wedding." She looked back up at me, smiling. "And don't forget I really want you to be there. Nolan and I really want you to be there."

36

MASON

The arena dressing room was empty, other than the lingering smell of sweat. I rolled out my yoga mat on the carpeted floor and began what had become my daily routine before each show. A few months ago I'd have scoffed at the idea of doing yoga. But after finding out during my latest stint in rehab what it could do for me, now I couldn't imagine a day without it—twice a day when we had a show.

Now I no longer fucked groupies to help with the pre-show buzz. After being with Nicole, I had lost all interest in females that way. She was the only one I could think about, even though I hadn't seen or spoken to her in four months.

After getting into the right mental space for the show, I returned to the greenroom with my mat and grabbed a sports drink from the ice chest, ignoring the beer that was also there. The temptation to have one still tormented me daily, but the bracelet on my wrist that Nicole had given me reminded me why I couldn't have it. I had hurt too many people when I'd struggled with the depression that had almost cost me my life. I had no intention of ever going there again.

The downside of the bracelet was that it provided a daily

reminder of the woman I still loved. But the bracelet wasn't the only thing to have that effect on me. My last memories of Nicole were of us together on the Endless Motion tour. Everything around me each day and each night was a constant reminder of her.

Nolan was busy texting on the couch, a goofy expression on his face. I laughed. "Let me guess. Hailey?"

"What makes you so sure it's Hailey?" he asked, still grinning. Like he had been doing ever since he proposed to her and she said yes.

"Oh, please. Who else would it be? You always have that lovesick puppy dog expression on your face whenever you're talking to her. Like puck boy does whenever he's talking to Beckie." Who had joined us on tour a few times since she and Kirk hooked up at Jared's wedding.

"Hey, I never look lovesick," Kirk said. "It's not in my genes." Then his phone played the song he had programmed for Beckie, and his face lit up.

With my tongue lolling from my mouth, I panted like a puppy. Kirk flipped me the bird. Jared and Aaron cracked up laughing.

I flopped down next to Nolan on the couch and caught a glimpse of the picture on his phone. "Wow. You really have been domesticated. Now Hailey's sending you photos of plates?" Not just any plate. It was glass with a butterfly and musical notes etched on it.

As if he were holding state secrets I wasn't supposed to be privy to, he jerked his phone away and set it upside down on the couch so I couldn't see the screen.

I chuckled. "Didn't realize plates were such a secret matter." Suddenly my amusement fizzled. "Nicole made it, didn't she?"

Nolan nodded and picked up his phone, the screen now black.

"Where did Hailey get it from?" I asked, my tone lacking

any hint of emotion—the exact opposite of how I felt. Although I had never come out and said I didn't want to talk about her, the topic of Nicole had been off-limits ever since I was released from rehab. Which was why Nolan looked uncomfortable at my question.

"She wanted to see how Nicole was doing, and drove down to visit her," he said. "She bought the plate at Nicole's store."

The door to the room opened, and our tour manager stuck his head in. "Showtime, guys."

Nodding, I pushed off the couch and headed for the door. But Nolan's next words made me pause. "For whatever it's worth, she still loves you, Mason."

I turned back to him as the other guys silently filed out of the room, giving us a second. "She told Hailey that?" Because the last time I'd talked to Zack, he had avoided the topic of his sister and her feelings about me. Which came as no surprise, given that we had man cards, not ovaries.

"Hailey guessed it, but Nicole confirmed it's true. The question is," he said as we stepped into the hallway, "what are you going to do about it?"

Good question. Too bad I didn't have an answer.

We strode down the hallway to the stage entrance, energy flowing through my veins, eager to feed off the fans' excitement. This was what it was all about. The fans. The music.

So why did it feel like that was no longer enough?

37

NICOLE

Six weeks after Hailey's visit, I was busy helping a bride-to-be and her mother choose the flower arrangements for her upcoming wedding. I was alone in the shop—Heidi was home sick, and Cindy had had to leave a little early to pick her daughter up from school for a medical appointment.

Even though Heidi was the one who usually dealt with the weddings, the meeting had been put on the calendar a few weeks ago, and the clients weren't able to reschedule. I knew enough to help them, though, and if anything came up that I wasn't so sure about, Heidi was only a speed-dial away.

"I'm not a fan of roses," Julia explained. "They're pretty, but I'd rather have something else."

I flipped through the pages of an album containing photos of bouquets and table floral arrangements Heidi had created, as well as pictures she had printed from the Internet. I stopped at the photo I was looking for and showed it to Julia and her mother.

"Freesias make beautiful bridal bouquets," I told them. "They're available in so many different colors, and because they're in season for your wedding, we can definitely make them work with your budget."

The bell above the store door tinkled. Out of habit, I glanced over at it.

Mason stood in the doorway.

My heart screeched to an abrupt standstill. He was wearing checkered gray and orange board shorts, sandals, and a plain navy T-shirt that hugged his chest, shoulders, and abs perfectly. Not a single part of my body was immune to seeing him there —all ached for different reasons.

Julia gasped. Without even looking at her, I could tell the sound had nothing to do with the floral arrangements she'd been studying. "Wow, wonder what he's doing here," she said, her voice hushed.

He smiled at me, and my insides combusted. Then he winked at me, and I was a goner. I sighed longingly, the sound echoed by Julia's own wistful sigh. If her mother thought we had gone crazy, she chose to keep it to herself.

Mason strolled to the giftware display against the wall, and my heart pounded so loud, I wouldn't have been surprised if everyone felt the vibrations through the floor.

"Excuse me for a moment," I told the two women. I didn't know if Julia had heard me. She was still too busy gaping at Mason. Her mother said something about a photo in the binder, her words lost on both of us.

I walked hesitantly over to Mason. He looked much better than he had the last time I'd seen him—healthier and happier.

He was inspecting the glass etchings, T-shirts, postcards, and magnets, all with the various butterfly and musical designs I had drawn. "You made these?" he asked.

I nodded, stunned into silence. I longed to ask him what he was doing here, but my brain and my mouth weren't cooperating. Only my heart was talking, but who knew if Mason could hear what it was saying.

He reached up and slowly traced his thumb along my bottom lip. Then he lowered his head, his mouth replacing his thumb with a tender kiss. "I love you," he said, quietly enough so only I could hear him.

"I love you too," I whispered back, positive I was dreaming. Any second now my alarm clock would rudely awaken me—and there would definitely be some cursing involved on my part.

The bell above the door tinkled again, and four women and a little girl entered the store.

Mason smiled at me, then walked out of the store, leaving me to stare after him in bewilderment. Had he seriously just driven all the way from L.A. to tell me he still loved me, only to walk away?

I blinked. Then, with my heart cheering me on, I pulled open the door and ran outside into the heat of the day. The glare from the sun temporarily blinded me, so I shielded my eyes with my hand and scanned the parking lot. But it was too late.

Mason had already driven away.

38

NICOLE

"Did you hear about the hot new music store owner?" Heidi asked me two days after Mason had breezed into the store, told me he loved me, and left. He'd sent me a text a few hours later, saying he was thinking about me. I'd responded that I missed him and was thinking about him. And that was that. I hadn't heard from him since. Heidi had told me to give him time. Everything would work out the way it was supposed to.

"Since when do you pay attention to anything that has to do with that store?" I asked. I couldn't remember a time when Heidi had ever needed to go there.

"Since Cindy told me about it yesterday. Her kids take piano lessons there."

"I didn't realize the business was for sale." The last time I'd been there was with Mason. Since returning to Desert Springs, I'd purposely avoided the music store because of the memories associated with it.

"Apparently so," she said, plucking a dead flower off a potted plant. "The owner and his wife decided to move to Alabama, where their grandkids live." She removed another wilted blossom. "I thought maybe you could take a few things over there that you've made, see if he'd be interested in selling them in the store." At what was no doubt an uncertain expression on my face, she added, "What would it hurt to try? The worst he can do is say no."

"True. Okay, I'll do it after work."

"Why don't you go now? I can handle things till you get back."

"Are you sure?" At her nod, I selected a set of glass coasters and prints to take with me. Heidi grinned the entire time, leaving me to wonder what she was up to.

I arrived at the store at the same time as several mothers with their young kids, and I followed them inside. They walked to the back of the store and disappeared through another set of doors. A guy my age was standing behind the counter, writing something down on a piece of paper. His messy black hair had purple streaks in it, and his eyebrow held several hoops.

At my approach, he glanced up. "Hi. Can I help you with anything?"

I flashed him an uncertain smile, feeling out of my element here. I was used to selling things in Blooming Love, but this was nowhere near the same thing. "I came to talk to the new owner."

"He's not here right now. Is it something I can help you with? Or you can leave a message and he'll get back to you."

I handed him my business card. "I'm Nicole McCormick, part owner of Blooming Love, the floral boutique." I quickly added the last part, so he didn't think I meant an online dating website. "I've created a line of music-themed items I thought your boss might be interested in including in his inventory." My mouth was dry; my palms, not so much.

I set the coasters on the counter, along with the selection of prints. "I can leave these with you and he can get back to me one way or another."

The guy inspected them. "These are really good. I think I've heard about them. Aren't you donating a portion of the proceeds to charity?"

"That's right," I said, smiling. At least word of what I was doing was getting out. I'd already landed a few orders because people who knew someone who'd battled an addiction were excited that I was helping the charity.

"I'll be sure to tell him as soon as he returns. There's a chance he might be interested. You never know."

I thanked him and returned to Blooming Love, on the way back grabbing a couple of sandwiches from the deli as lunch for Heidi and me. The store was busy when I arrived, and I didn't have a chance to talk to her until near the end of our workday. At one point her cellphone rang, and she disappeared into the back. She returned five minutes later, grinning like a cat who'd singlehandedly caught five canaries.

"Change of plans for tonight," she said.

"We're not seeing a movie?"

"Nope, we're going to Mike's Bar."

My eyebrows shot up in puzzlement. "You want to go to a sports bar?" Since when did she like sports, other than watching her boyfriend play touch football?

"Turns out they have live music on Thursday nights. Well, more like it's open mike night."

This was even more baffling. "Since when do you like singing in front of a crowd? Or have you been taking music lessons on the sly?" The Heidi I knew and loved wasn't a good singer. Not even close.

"No, but a friend of mine is singing tonight, and I want to be supportive. And I want you to meet him."

I groaned. "You're not trying to set me up again, are you? You promised me you wouldn't do that anymore, because you and Cindy suck when it comes to finding me Mr. Right."

She gave me the puppy dog eyes that always did me in.

"Please? You won't regret it. It'll be fun. And if it isn't, then we'll leave."

I let out a deep sigh. "Fine." Given that I'd been hiding away in my house for so long, working hard on my designs, I figured it was time I returned to real life.

"I'll pick you up at seven," she said, and walked away smiling.

It turned out that Mike's on Thursday nights was super busy. Heidi and I squeezed through the crowd to the front of the room. On the stage, a twenty-year-old girl was belting out the lyrics to a Kelly Clarkson song. As I listened, I realized Kelly had been right when she'd pointed out that whatever didn't kill you would only make you stronger. Loving Mason and walking away from him hadn't killed me. It had made me stronger. It had been the inspiration behind my line of gifts, which had become popular. It had inspired me to donate a portion of the proceeds to a charity that helped individuals and families dealing with addiction. It had made me a better, stronger person . . . even though I missed him.

The final notes of the song faded away, and everyone applauded as she left the stage. Then the emcee strolled up to the mike, wearing a navy T-shirt with MIKE'S BAR on the front in white. "Okay, next up we have someone many of you may recognize, though he won't be playing the instrument you expect. And he'll be singing a song he wrote." Instead of introducing the singer, the man stepped away from the mike, and Mason emerged from the shadows and walked onstage.

The girls next to me started screaming, and I could've sworn one of them was about to faint. I glanced around, searching for the rest of the band. If they were here, they were well hidden.

Mason sat at the keyboard and adjusted the mike to his height. Then he began playing and singing a ballad, and I instantly melted. I'd never heard him sing before, other than when he sang backup vocals in the band. His voice was rich and deep and soulful, and filled every part of me with hope and longing.

I gripped Heidi's arm. Was I dreaming? This wouldn't be the first time I'd dreamed about him since walking away from him all those months ago. Although this would have been the first of my dreams where not only was he singing, but he was singing a song I'd never heard before. A song about loving someone and letting them walk away. A song about regretting it every day of his life.

"Did you know he was going be here?" I whispered to her.

She winked at me and went back to watching him as he sang, "I need you tonight."

The song finished and the crowd erupted into applause, with some of his fans surging forward to get closer to him. I could only continue staring at him, my head spinning with all kinds of questions.

Mason didn't seem to notice the applause. He was watching me with the same love in his eyes I had seen so often. He stood up from the piano bench, his gaze still locked on mine.

Heidi nudged my arm. "Go talk to him," she said. When I didn't move, she nudged a little harder.

That was all the prompting my legs required. Before my brain knew what I was doing, I stumbled toward him.

As I grew closer, I caught some of the questions being tossed at him: "What are you doing here?" "We've heard rumors the band's splitting up—are you?" "Is it true that you're the new owner of the music store here in Desert Springs?"

The last one got my attention, and my step faltered for a second.

But Mason ignored the questions, his focus solely on me as

he pushed through the last of the crowd separating us. From the heated look in his eyes, I half expected him to kiss me in front of everyone.

But instead of turning it into a moment worthy of a Hollywood movie, Mason leaned in, his warm breath brushing my cheek. "Let's get out of here so we can talk."

"I'm here with Heidi." I turned around, but she was no longer where I'd left her. I scanned the area, searching for signs of her. Then I realized what had happened: apparently my best friend had set me up, bringing me to the bar where Mason would be playing, and then she'd bailed. Which meant that if he really was the new owner of the music store, she already knew that.

I looked back at Mason, who was grinning. Yup, those two had definitely been talking since he kissed me two days ago—maybe even before that.

"Heidi knew you were performing tonight, didn't she?"

"Yes. And she might have helped me out with a few other things." He winked.

Mason rested his hand on my lower back, and I'd be lying if I said my body didn't respond to his touch. He led me through the crowded bar, thanking his fans but making it clear that we were leaving and not stopping to socialize.

His car sat in the parking lot, but that wasn't where we were headed. The sky was cloud free, with stars twinkling down on us. The warm summer night hugged us, though the temperature was comfortable after the heat inside the bar.

Mason threaded his fingers with mine, but he still didn't kiss me. Part of me wanted to kiss him right there. But I held back, sensing he really did wish to talk to me first.

Or maybe that was all he wanted to do.

My chest tightened, squeezing my insides like a python crushing life from its prey. Maybe he had come to his senses and had finally moved on—even if only two days ago he'd declared he still loved me.

Still holding hands, we walked to a nearby park and sat on a wooden bench overlooking the water fountain. White spotlights around the circumference shone up through the water, making it glimmer.

"So is it true?" I asked. "Are you the new owner of the music store?" His home and the band were in L.A., which was why I had a hard time believing it.

He nodded. "The papers were finalized the other day."

"What? Why would you want to invest in a business so far away from where you live? Won't that be tough to manage, especially since you're on the road so much?"

"Nope. I've officially moved here. I needed to get away from L.A., and this town has grown on me."

My heart came to a complete standstill. Holy shit. Mason was living in my town? "It does seem to have that effect," I said numbly. This had to be a dream. And like with the rest of the ones I'd had about him, I would wake up and he'd be gone. "So you mean you'll be commuting back and forth between here and L.A. when the band records the next album?" I laughed. "Because that's gonna be one hell of a commute."

"I sold my loft, and there won't be any more albums for me. I've left the band."

I blinked, positive I'd misheard him. His music meant everything to him. His bandmates meant everything to him. They were his family. "But why would you do that? You guys were on the verge of making it big! That's always been your dream."

"It was," he said, not a hint of regret lining his face. "But as much as I loved playing and touring with the guys, it wasn't healthy for me. I'm a recovering addict. I'm facing enough challenges as it is without making things more difficult for myself." He stroked his thumb against my cheek, a sweet reminder of what we'd once had between us. "But more important, you weren't there with me. Once you left, it wasn't the same anymore. Everywhere I went, I saw you. I missed you, Nicole . . . but I also missed who I was while I was staying here with you."

"So you've really left the band?" I whispered, still unable to believe it was true.

"It hasn't been made public yet. I broke the news to the band last week. I wanted to tell you first."

Oh God. They must be freaking out. How could they go on without him?

"What's going to happen with the band? Are they splitting up?" It would be a damn shame if they did. They'd all worked hard to get where they were.

"No. They're replacing me. A friend of ours, Tomas York, is going to step in. He's a brilliant drummer."

I nodded like a bobblehead figurine, the shock from his news still confounding me. "You're really living here?"

With a small nod, he smiled.

A longing surged through me to kiss him, to make sure he wasn't a mirage.

"I'm so sorry for how much I hurt you, Nicole," he said, voice low and intimate. "I'm hoping you'll give me a chance to make it up to you. But I want to do things differently this time."

"Differently?" That didn't sound good. "What do you want to do differently?"

"Us."

"Us?"

"We've never been on a date. Not a real one, at least. Our relationship moved fast from the time I first showed up on your doorstep. We made out, we had sex, we fell in love—but we've never dated. We've never been a real couple." He leaned down and ran his lips along my jaw. "I want to be a real couple with you. I want to date you and prove to you that I'm worth taking a chance on."

I didn't have the opportunity to answer before his mouth found mine. The kiss was unassuming and brief and sweet. "Will you go out with me, Nicole?"

As great as the kiss had been, it wasn't enough. My lips crashed against his—and it was like we had never been apart. A tiny whimper escaped me as my tongue slid against his. His fingers knotted in my hair, keeping me close, the other hand pressed against my back. My body ached for him, but I didn't want to rush this moment. Everything about it was perfect.

I don't know how long we had been kissing—it wasn't long enough, if you asked me—but eventually I pulled away and fought to regain my breath.

My answering smile to his question was as bright as the full moon. "Yes, Mason. I'd love to go out with you."

MASON

Following my first stint in rehab, I had rocked the music scene. Back then, being a rock star had been my ultimate dream, and I'd foolishly believed that only then would my life be complete.

But the joke had been on me. Now that I was no longer part of that scene, my life felt more complete than it had ever been.

Five weeks after leaving Pushing Limits to begin my life anew and to start a life with Nicole, I still felt sure I had done the right thing. Yes, I missed the guys and performing with them live, but there wasn't a single moment when I regretted my decision to walk away from the band, from the media, from the pressures of being on the road.

The waiter placed a slice of chocolate cake on the table between us. Nicole and I were celebrating our one-month anniversary. For the past four weeks, we had been dating like a regular couple—including the part where I had gotten Zack's permission to date his little sister. Not that it would have made a difference, but it was nice to have his approval. We had also taken Bernie on a few walks for old times' sake. Nicole and I had done lots of things together since that night at Mike's Bar, but the one thing we hadn't done yet was make love.

I was waiting for the right time.

That didn't mean we hadn't done some serious making out in the meantime. We had. And Christ knew I deserved a medal for the level of restraint I'd shown when it came to not touching her the way I wanted to.

Nicole dug her fork into the rich dessert and slipped it between her parted lips. She closed her mouth, and the erotic moan vibrating at the back of her throat had my dick wanting me to say screw it and make love to her again.

"Good, huh?" I asked, laughing. It was her favorite dessert. We got it every time we came here. Which meant I had a hard-on every time we came here. Let's just say this wasn't the first time she had moaned that way while eating a slice of the cake—nor would it be the last.

"Absolutely." She winked at me and took another bite . . . and moaned yet again.

I groaned roughly. "Nicole, you can't keep making those noises. You're gonna kill me."

A devilish smile curved onto her face. The tip of her tongue slowly traced her lower lip, and my dick jerked in my jeans.

"Maybe I'm after something else." Her gaze fell to my mouth. "Maybe I'm tired of taking things slow." Her voice was low and heated. It required every ounce of willpower I had—and then some—not to take her right here on the table, dessert be damned.

I indicated to the waiter we needed the check, stat. "And we'll take the dessert to go," I added. Nicole laughed.

We returned to her house. I was currently renting an apartment near the music store, not that I spent much time at my place. It was just somewhere to sleep, nothing more. Plus I was still busy with renovations around her house. We had already discussed updating the kitchen. It needed it, even after we had torn down the tacky 1970s wallpaper last fall and repainted the walls.

I opened her front door, entered, and flipped on the hallway light. I set the dessert box on the side table, then my mouth found Nicole's and I kissed her until we were both breathless.

"Oh God, Mason," she murmured against my ear. "I want you so badly."

She didn't have to say it twice. I hoisted her up, and she wrapped her legs around my waist. I carried her upstairs to her bedroom, turned on the light, and laid her on the bed. Then I stepped away and just watched her for a heartbeat. With her hair messy from my fingers roaming through it and her kiss-swollen lips, she looked goddamn sexy. "So beautiful," I said huskily, climbing onto the bed with her. I kissed her again while my fingers crept under her tank top.

My thumb found her nipple, hidden under her lacy bra, and I brushed it against the tight bud. Nicole groaned into my mouth, which made me harder. My cock pressed against my zipper, begging to finally feel Nicole's soft heat around it once more.

I continued to tease her. She arched her body, pressing her stomach against my junk. The desire to sink inside her grew in intensity. It had been almost nine months since I'd last made love to her. Nine months of jacking off to memories of her on the bed. In the shower. On the kitchen counter.

I shifted away from her and helped her remove her tank top. That and the bra ended up somewhere on the floor, along with her skirt. I bent down and kissed the tattoo above the elastic waistband of her panties. It was one of Nicole's designs, but it wasn't on anything she had created to be sold. She had gotten it months ago, shortly before Hailey had visited her.

"Christ, I love this." I kissed the tattoo again.

"I love yours too." She stroked the one on my right shoulder. Like the tattoos I'd gotten after my first time in rehab, this one was also in Sanskrit. All the new tattoos were. And like my previous ones, all were messages of affirmation: "One life, one chance," "Strength comes from an indomitable will," and "Action defines us."

All of my tattoos were a reminder of what I had gone through, a reminder that with hard work and determination I would never sink back to my previous life. The life in which I'd almost destroyed everything I had and the people I loved.

The words from one of the earlier tattoos, "Without music life shall be a mistake," were also stenciled on a wall in the music store, thanks to Nicole. She'd created the design to represent the shift in my career. A career that now included teaching and writing music and occasionally performing—but not touring.

I gently tugged on Nicole's panties and slid them down her legs. "Do you know how long I've waited to taste you again?"

She didn't answer, but her heated gaze told me everything I needed to know. I wasn't the only one who had felt the same way. I spread her legs open and planted small kisses up the inside of her thigh . . . until I found the spot wet dreams and morning wood were made from. I tasted her, my tongue running along one side of her sex and then the other. She wiggled under my worshipping touch.

I grabbed hold of her hips, keeping her steady while I ate her out. My tongue stroked her clit and she let out a moan, telling me she was getting close. And a moment later, with the help of my thumb and my tongue, she cried out her release, leaving me smiling at the power I had over her—the same power she had over me.

While she recovered from the aftershocks, I ripped open the foil package and rolled the condom down my length. I positioned the head of my cock at her entrance and slowly pushed my way in. Her heat hugged every inch of me, turning my brain numb with desire. My balls tightened and I groaned. Right here, with the woman I loved, was the only place I wanted to be.

Nicole wrapped her legs around my hips, my cock seated deeper inside her. I pulled back so just my tip remained inside, then I plunged deep into her once more. I kept repeating the motion until Nicole called out my name, her warmth clutching me tightly. At the sound of her erotic cries and the feel of her grasping my length, I came hard with another groan.

With sweat covering our bodies, our breath ragged, I collapsed onto the bed. Once my brain was able to function again, I got up and disposed of the condom in the trash.

I returned to the bed and pulled Nicole against me. She rested her head on my chest, listening to my heart tell her how much I loved her.

"Are you still planning to have two-point-four kids, a dog, and a cat one day?" I asked her, caressing her lower back and grinning down at her.

She pushed herself up on her elbow. "I would like to have all of that." Her gaze dropped to my lips. "But it depends."

"On what?"

"On if the man of my dreams wants them too." Her gaze flicked up, her light brown eyes meeting mine.

I kissed her forehead, the tip of her nose, then her lips. "I want it too. All of it. The kids. The dog. The cat. You as my wife." I kissed her again. "But how about we get a dog who's not quite as big as Bernie?"

Nicole laughed. "Deal."

EPILOGUE
MASON

Five Years Later

"Daddy. Up," Chelsea said, standing in front of my chair and holding her arms up to me. The two-year-old's black hair was pulled into two semi-tidy pigtails. That was the best Nicole had been able to manage, since Chelsea wasn't a huge fan of sitting still for long.

Unless she was sitting on my lap.

On the seat next to mine, my gorgeous wife of three years was cradling our three-month-old son. Kevin was sleeping peacefully, having no interest in the outdoor wedding about to commence.

"Daddy. Up," Chelsea repeated. This time she banged her palms against my thighs—much as she enjoyed doing to my drum set.

I hoisted her onto my lap and she peered over at her brother.

"Baby sleep," she said rather loudly.

I placed my finger against my lips. "Shhh. That's right, Kevin's sleeping." My voice was several decibels quieter than

Chelsea's had been. "Which means we need to use our indoor voices."

By the way, telling a two-year-old to use her indoor voice was like expecting a mermaid not to swim. It just didn't happen.

Craving to taste Nicole again, I leaned over and lightly kissed her. I wanted to do a lot more than that to her, but this was neither the time nor the place for what I had in mind. Fortunately, Chelsea wasn't at the age where she found kissing gross. Yet. Which was just as well, since I hadn't grown tired of stealing kisses from Nicole whenever I could.

"Ewww, Uncle Mason," ten-year-old Logan said as Jared and Callie sat down next to me, Jared holding their two-year-old daughter. "Kissing is gross."

Nolan laughed, his arm around his pregnant wife's waist. Hailey had recently graduated from her physical therapy program and become pregnant shortly afterward—with twins. Nolan had laughed when he told us, claiming it was because they had to quickly catch up with Jared and me in the family department.

"Don't worry," I told Logan. "One day you won't think kissing is gross." He gave me a disbelieving look that said it would be a hot day in Antarctica before that happened.

"How are you doing?" Nicole asked Hailey after her friend took the seat next to her. Nolan sat next to his wife and placed his hand possessively on her protruding stomach. Even though I'd left Pushing Limits five years ago and Nicole and I still lived in Desert Springs, Nicole, Hailey, and Callie had become close friends. And thanks to the newest twist in my career, we visited them in L.A. every couple of months.

"Not bad so far," Hailey said. "More tired than anything."

Nicole smiled sweetly at her, although there was no missing the humor in her eyes. Hailey was just four months pregnant.

The exhaustion would only get worse . . . especially after the babies were born.

But Hailey didn't need to know that yet.

"Well, if your husband is as sweet and amazing as mine," Nicole told her, "he'll give you back and foot massages several times a day."

"She's right about that," Callie chimed in.

"Good idea," Nolan said, beaming at his wife.

"Izzy," Callie said to her daughter, who was already squirming on Jared's lap, ready to cause mischief, "can you give this to Chelsea?" She handed the precocious two-year-old a small gift bag, and Jared lowered her to the grass.

Izzy toddled over to Chelsea and then gazed up at her mother, confused about what she was supposed to do next.

Callie tapped the bag. "Give this to Chelsea."

Izzy lifted the bag up and I helped Chelsea take it from her.

"It's my latest book," Callie explained. "It's not out for two more weeks, but my publisher sent me a few copies ahead of time."

At Jared's encouragement, Callie had pursued a career in illustrating kids' books. And then she started writing stories and landed a publishing contract. The third volume in her picture book series about a group of zoo animal friends had even hit the *New York Times* bestseller list.

Nicole let out an excited squeal, somehow managing not to wake up Kevin. "Let me see it."

I helped Chelsea open the bag and remove the book. "Give this to Mommy," I said, pointing to the book in Chelsea's hands. "I don't think Mommy can wait any longer before reading it." They both loved the series, which came as no surprise. Callie's colorful computer-generated illustrations were both cute and breathtaking.

"Hey, guys," Kirk said as he and Aaron approached us, both

in tuxes. Aaron was one of the groomsmen. "Glad you could make it."

We all stood, and the guys and I gave Kirk one-arm hugs. "We wouldn't have missed it for anything, puck boy," I said. "Especially given how long it took before Beckie finally agreed to marry your sorry a—I mean, backside."

He laughed at that. It hadn't taken long at all . . . once he got around to proposing to her. But even though it had taken more than four years from the time those two first hooked up, he and Beckie had been dating exclusively the entire time. And because Kirk was as loyal as they came, Beckie never had to worry about him straying while touring. Like Nolan and Jared, he was completely committed to the woman he loved. I didn't have to be touring with the band to know that.

I one-arm hugged Aaron too. Unlike the others, I hadn't seen him in several months, but I owed him big-time for the unexpected twist my musical career had taken. Two years ago, he'd introduced me to a movie producer at a charity event the band had been involved in. The casual conversation eventually led to me writing songs for a project the producer was working on. The movie went on to land several Academy Award nominations and wins—including for best original song. My original song.

That's right—in addition to managing the music store and teaching, I was writing songs for movies and for recording artists who weren't songwriters. In addition to my Academy Award, I had also gained a Grammy nod.

I wasn't the only one who had scored with the music awards. Pushing Limits now held several from the Grammys and the American Music Awards. I couldn't have been prouder of the guys. They deserved each and every one they won.

At the tug on my pant leg, I glanced down.

"Daddy. Up," Chelsea said, her arms reaching up.

I picked her up, and she waved at Kirk. "Puck boy," she said

—except from her it sounded more like "fuck boy." Logan snickered, and I half expected him to tell Chelsea to cough up a dollar for his swear-word jar.

Speaking of swear-word jars, Chelsea also owned one. She'd had it since the day Nicole found out she was pregnant. But with Chelsea's jar, the amount I had to pay skyrocketed compared to what Jared had charged me. Now the going rate was five dollars a swear. By the time she was born . . . well, let's just say her bank account was very happy. Luckily, I finally learned to curtail my cussing around her, and the amount wasn't growing as fast as before.

Since the wedding ceremony was starting soon, Kirk and Aaron returned to the altar. The music began, and Aaron's fiancée—one of Beckie's cousins—exited through the patio door of the large estate house. Her blonde hair was pulled back in an elaborate bun. Like the bridesmaids after her, Lisa was wearing a light peach sleeveless gown.

We stood as Beckie stepped out of the house. When Nicole and I had gotten married, we'd invited a few of our closest friends to join us in Hawaii, where we got married on the beach. Nicole had worn a simple white gown that looked both gorgeous and sexy on her. With those memories of our wedding day in my mind, I looked over at her now and smiled.

Our wedding had been small and simple. Not so for Kirk and Beckie's wedding. Theirs was an elaborate and elegant affair.

"She looks like a fairy princess," Nicole whispered in awe. And I guess Beckie did—from what little I knew of these things. Although I wouldn't be surprised if that changed soon, once Chelsea discovered the Disney princesses.

As Beckie walked down the aisle toward the man she planned to spend the rest of her life with, I leaned in and murmured in Nicole's ear. "She does. But she's nowhere near as beautiful as the woman I love. The woman I want to get naked with as soon as I can make that happen."

Nicole giggled softly. She replied in a low voice, so that Chelsea couldn't hear her, "I think it can be arranged. Because I definitely want to get all sweaty and naked with the hottest man here. The only man I want to spend the rest of my life with."

She grinned at me, and—just as what happened every time she looked at me that way—I fell in love with her all over again.

READ ON FOR AN EXCERPT FROM ONE MORE CHANCE

SIMONE

The main door to the café opens. Lucas walks in wearing worn-in jeans and a faded navy T-shirt that skims his Marine-cultivated chest and shoulders. And it's as if all the oxygen in the room has been sucked out, taking what little is in my lungs with it.

A craving stirs inside me to reach out and touch him, to have him hold me like he used to when I was afraid.

But that...none of that is possible.

Not anymore.

The last time I saw Lucas was at dinner over ten years ago with his parents, Grams, Aiden, and me. A series of memories from that night march through my head.

The stolen kiss between Lucas and me in the hallway outside the restroom. Making love to him that night—the last time we were together. The way he smelled like mountains and sunshine and hope.

He's not the same boy who was once my close friend. Nor is he the same man I sent letters to while he was in the Marines.

Sent letters to until everything crumbled into a pile of bent and twisted metal.

I draw in a long breath, reminding my body, my heart, my lungs, that I no longer feel anything for him. My eyes, though, take a moment to feast on the man he has become.

He's still tall and dark-haired with warm brown eyes, but there's a hardness to him that wasn't there the last time I saw him. A hardness I'd witnessed in my brother after he returned from Afghanistan, the playful boy I'd once loved long since dead and buried.

Why couldn't Lucas have waited another five minutes before entering the café?

I would've been gone by then. Seeing him, after all these years, hurts too much. Hurts because I lost Aiden. Hurts because I lost my baby—Lucas's and my baby.

Lucas is one more reminder, the biggest reminder, of all of that.

Fortunately, Troy is with him, and I relax a little. Troy is one more buffer between me and his brother.

Lucas sees me, and his eyes widen imperceptibly. "Simone. I didn't know you were here. I'm sorry about your grandmother. I just heard." Sadness seems to pull his lips into a smile.

And that smile, filled with sorrow and regret, squeezes the air from my lungs in a *whoosh*.

An image of what our daughter might have looked like sneaks in. Her warm brown hair and eyes and her love for everything to do with the mountains.

Like her father.

I shake the image from my thoughts. I can't go there. Not here.

Not now.

Two of Grams's friends approach, their smiles wide. Delores hugs me. "Rose will be thrilled to see you, Simone." She steps back, and her eyes give me an appraising once-over. "You look amazing. How's big city life treating you? I bet you have a special someone in your life?"

Samantha hugs me next. Her scent of lavender and eucalyptus and ginger reminds me of Grams, and I sink into her hug a little more, wishing she were Grams.

"If she did," Samantha says, "you can guarantee Rose would've already told us about him."

Delores lifts her chin, the familiar impish gleam in her eyes. "Maybe Simone has a secret boyfriend Rose doesn't know about."

Samantha chuckles, the sound of old paper softened with time. "If that's the case, do you really think she would tell us? You'd spill the beans faster than I can cable-knit a row in a sweater."

"I'm too busy with my career to worry about finding someone." I avoid looking at Lucas.

In reality, there's no point being in a relationship when no man wants to be with a car wreck like me—as my ex-boyfriend so kindly pointed out.

"How long are you in Maple Ridge for?" Lucas asks, and I don't have a choice but to look at him. He's smiling at me as if he can't believe I'm standing in front of him. Like I'm some sort of mirage.

And I can't help but smile back. "For as long as it takes Grams to recover. I quit my job."

"You did?" The only way I could have surprised Zara more would be if I'd told her I was moving to Iceland.

ONE MORE CHANCE is now available.

ABOUT THE AUTHOR

Born in Brighton England, Stina Lindenblatt has lived in a number of countries, including England, the US, Finland, and Canada. This would explain her mixed up accent. She has a kinesiology degree and a MSc in sports biological sciences.

In addition to writing fiction, she loves photography, and currently lives in Calgary, Canada, with her husband and three kids.

For news about her books, social media sites, and to sign up for her newsletter, check out her website at stinalindenblattau thor.com. Newsletter subscribers will receive a bonus short story.